Praise for *Dept*

Depth of Field in essence is portraiture taken at the young edges of society. Iltners' protagonists grapple with social isolation, new parenthood, poverty, and dependence. Skilfully stitched together, this is a novel that exposes the truth as grainy and low-res; as unreliable as a photograph. A compelling debut from a striking new literary talent.

Sarah Sasson, author of *Tidelines*

Depth of Field is like a cosy rogue's gallery scattered up a staircase wall. But what lies just beyond the camera's focus? The framed moments? Kirsty Iltner's dazzling debut peers beyond the composed filtered shots we curate for public viewing. What happens if we adjust the lighting, fiddle with the focus, or expand the view? What do we choose to remember and what can we never forget? Memory is a slippery tale and this one delivers.

Sharlene Allsopp, author of *The Great Undoing*

An incredible debut full of love, grief, regret – how trauma can collapse the lives it affects – and the possibility of redemption.

Graham Akhurst, author of *Borderland*

Affecting, innovative and original. Such an impressive debut novel.

Brendan Ritchie, author of *Carousel, Beyond Carousel* **and** *Eta Draconis*

Depth of Field

About the Author

Kirsty Iltners is a writer and photographer living on Jagera and Turrbal Country in Brisbane with her two daughters, her border collie, and three axolotls. *Depth of Field* is her first novel and won the 2023 Dorothy Hewett Award.

Depth of Field

Kirsty Iltners

UWA PUBLISHING

First published in 2024 by
UWA Publishing
Crawley, Western Australia 6009
www.uwap.uwa.edu.au

UWAP is an imprint of UWA Publishing
a division of The University of Western Australia

THE UNIVERSITY OF
WESTERN
AUSTRALIA

ISBN: 978-1-76080-275-2

A catalogue record for this
book is available from the
National Library of Australia

Cover image: Shadow on Wall by Kara Riley
Cover design by Mika Tabata
Typeset in 12 point Dante by Lasertype
Printed by McPherson's Printing Group

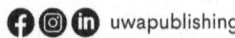 uwapublishing

MIX
Paper | Supporting
responsible forestry
FSC® C001695

For

Caitlin and Larissa

Photography is a balancing act.

I didn't realise when I first started—all I cared about was what I could see through the viewfinder. Eventually, I realised the camera doesn't care about what you can see. All it cares about is light: how much light is let in, and for how long. With every shot, you make adjustments. This concept is called the exposure triangle, a way to explain the relationship between aperture, shutter speed and ISO.

If you want to freeze something fast, you increase the shutter speed—but it makes the image darker.

If you want a shallow depth of field, you prioritise the aperture—but it reduces what's in focus.

If it's dark, you bump up the ISO—but it adds grain.

In photography, you don't get to have it all. You are always making choices, always making sacrifices.

To capture the light.

In the end, it doesn't matter how perfect your settings are, how well you balance them, how carefully you follow the rules of composition.

People will always find something wrong.

Always think they could've done it better.

Admit it. You do too.

I. Shutter Speed

Tom

0"3

As a child, I couldn't understand time. I was good at maths—addition and subtraction, multiplication and division—but the concept of time, I couldn't wrap my head around.

If Mark catches the train to work at 8:47 am and gets to his destination at 9:11 am, how long was the trip?

The answer seemed obvious to everyone else. *Twenty-four minutes.* But no matter how carefully I considered it, I always got it wrong.

My teachers couldn't understand it. I could do the calculations, so why couldn't I work it out? But it seemed to me there were so many factors that hadn't been accounted for. What if Mark had an important meeting that day that he was dreading? Then the trip would surely go faster. Or if he were running late that morning, it would take longer.

Had none of my classmates ever experienced waking up early on their birthdays and waiting desperately to be allowed to open their presents? Had my teachers never stared at the clock, waiting for the bell to ring? How could you calculate time when it warped and shifted depending on the circumstances? How could everyone else pin down something so fluid?

A particularly astute teacher finally kept me back after class one day to try to make sense of the discrepancies in my grades. When she realised my error, she covered her mouth with her hand, suppressing a laugh.

'Oh Tom, time doesn't change speed. It always moves forward at the same pace.'

I argued at first, explained my observations, but she simply shook her head, kindly at first, then with increasing impatience.

'It's not up for debate, it's just a fact.'

So time was fixed, not flexible, and eventually I learnt to accept this in the same way I'd accepted that just because you couldn't always see the stars didn't mean they weren't there and even though it didn't feel like it the Earth was a sphere. And that my experience was just my perception.

Not reality.

It was Adeline who introduced me to photography, and perhaps the ability to manipulate time is what first entranced me. Freezing split-second moments that otherwise would be missed, too fast for the naked eye. Slowing down the shutter to give a photo movement. Immortalising time itself.

I'd never picked up a camera before I met her, but before Adeline there had never been anything I wanted to capture. I wasn't the sentimental type, or so I thought; I just didn't have anything worth holding onto.

Until her.

She had a passion and energy that I wanted to keep to myself. Hide it away in a box, like a precious jewel.

Adeline was drawn to anything artistic.

Piano.

Poetry.

Pottery.

Painting.

Photography.

She had an old Leica and dreams to turn photography into a career. She loved those heart-stopping, unforgettable moments—the ones that people frame and hang on their walls, tuck into wallets or whip out for grandchildren to see in years to come. A groom's expression as he sees his bride, the glow of ninety-nine candles on weathered skin, the nervous smile of a child on their first day of school.

The big moments.

It was never about the big moments for me. I wasn't interested in the memorable or perfect. I wanted the everyday, the imperfect. Not only her mane of red curls but also her crooked toenail that had a habit of falling off. The scar above her eyebrow, as well as her emerald eyes.

All of her.

Click. Adeline sitting cross-legged on the kitchen bench with a bowl of corn flakes. *Click.* Adeline glaring at me over the top of a book she would never finish. *Click.* Adeline sleeping, a tangle of white sheets, red hair and pale limbs. Adeline brushing her teeth, hair piled messily on top of her head. Adeline hypnotised in front of the TV, eyes glazed. Adeline shaving her legs in the shower, brow furrowed and tongue out.

Click. Click. Click.

Glimpses in time that would have simply passed unnoticed and forgotten but which now belonged to me—immortalised on glossy paper and glued into heavy albums.

But that was a long time ago.

It's just a job now.

Golden hour.

The slip of perfect light right before sunset, when photographers climb out of their dens and migrate towards bodies of water, grassy hills and dilapidated buildings. For me, it's the last job of the day.

The homeowner, Helen—or maybe it was Heather?—has followed me all around the house. She's like a fly buzzing around the room as she fluffs up pillows and wipes invisible dust from shelves: harmless but annoying. I've heard all about their big move. How they are selling the family home to be closer to their grandchildren, for babysitting duty. She's told me all about her husband's recent knee surgery, and how her daughter-in-law is struggling with post-natal depression after baby number two.

She has tidied up, but not enough. The house smells strongly of citrus and there is an undercurrent of bleach, but there is still too much personality here. Someone is a fan of musicals: a *Wicked* poster hangs in the study, in the lounge room a *Phantom of the Opera* mask lies on the coffee table. Lining the walls are family photos of their four children over the years. Full circle: from cute kids in matching outfits to gangly pre-teens with bad hair, to awkward teenagers trying to look sullen, and ending as adults, back in matching colours. When Heather leaves the room to answer the phone, I temporarily put the *Phantom* mask behind the lounge. The family photos, I'll replace with neutral landscapes in Photoshop.

Photographing homes is not hard. Convincing homeowners that their precious possessions, all handpicked and meaningful to them, detract from the photos, is. Real estate agents will say that people want to be able to imagine themselves in the house, but that's not entirely true. They want to imagine their ideal selves in the house—better, cleaner, more organised. Early January versions, when New Year's resolutions have been set and they still believe *this* year will be the one when they start drinking more water and making their bed each morning. And *this* house is the fresh start they need.

They can't do that looking at *Phantom of the Opera* memorabilia.

Helen comes back out, and stands beside me, gazing at the camera with interest. 'You know, I always wanted to be a photographer. My uncle had a Voigtländer and I would sometimes borrow it. He used to tell me I had an *eye*. How long have you been doing photography?'

I pretend to think, but I don't have to.

'Too long,' I answer, with a dry laugh.

Long enough to suck any last drop of passion from it.

She beams at me. 'Your family must be so lucky, to get so many photos. I bet they love having a photographer around.'

'Yeah, they do.'

I don't bother correcting her and am relieved when she changes the subject.

'See that mark there?' She points to a dark stain on the rug, the size of a palm.

Wine, perhaps. Or blood, but looking at Helen it seems unlikely.

'I know it looks like wine, but it's red cordial. My grandson found the bottle.' It seems important to her, to specify this detail. 'Will you be able to photoshop that out?'

It's simple, two seconds with the clone stamp, but I pretend to consider it for a minute before saying yes.

She clutches her chest. 'Oh, thank God. I've tried everything but it just won't budge.

Whenever I get asked about Photoshop, I always leave that fraction of uncertainty. I like to make it sound like those additional requests are a lot of work and it's not just a magic wand.

Even though it kind of is.

On the way home, I make a quick detour to the bottle shop, and then the Indian restaurant down the road. They are usually efficient, but tonight they appear understaffed and my order takes longer than usual. They apologise when they finally call my name and I reassure them it's okay, but I'm feeling tired and just want to get home.

When I finally turn into my street there are cars parked everywhere. They line both sides of the road, slotting into the spaces between driveways, and I have to drive slowly, occasionally pulling to the side to let a car pass in the opposite direction. Someone must be having some kind of party.

The culprit is number twenty-two, directly across the road. It is as though they have let a toddler loose with the decorating. There are festoon lights dangling precariously from tree branches and strings of fairy lights dripped unevenly along the fence and twirling up the front steps. Over the doorway is a lopsided Happy Birthday banner. Out in the front yard, people are milling about in groups or sitting on foldout beach chairs. Even with my car windows up, I can hear the bass of a song, robotic and unfamiliar.

A green Mazda with personalised plates is sitting smugly in my usual spot. There's not much room, but I manoeuvre in behind them, blocking my own driveway. It only goes to the detached garage at the side of the house that hasn't been used in well over a decade, nearly two. These days it's more of an ancient relic than a usable space, and overrun with vines.

The night air is cooler than I expected and vibrates with music. I loop the plastic bag of food over my arm and have to squeeze between my car and the one behind to get to my boot to fish out my camera bag and tripod. Behind me there's movement in the dark; it's a couple from up the street. I've never officially met them, but they own a red kelpie that they go jogging with at least twice a day. She is holding a gift bag, and he is holding onto her as she wobbles along on impossibly high heels. They are less than two metres away but don't notice me. Or pretend not to.

I sling my camera bag over my shoulder and make my way to the front gate. It drags along the gravel, shrieking like something otherworldly being woken. I remind myself I really need to oil the hinges. Over time, my to-do list has become more of a daily chant, a meditation of sorts. Oil the hinges, wash the car, weed the garden...

The lights across the street make this side seem darker in contrast, but I know the distance from the gate to the base of the stairs by feel and how many steps up until I reach the front door. Expertly, I dodge the bougainvillea stretching across the path, blindly feel for the familiar edges of the key, and slide it into the lock at just the right angle with a well-timed jiggle and a shove.

Mayfield creaks loudly as I walk inside. Whenever it starts to cool down, she carries on, protesting about the coming winter.

She is a battered old Queenslander, raised off the ground on timber stumps to encourage airflow in the Australian summers. There are ornate breezeways above all the doors and a large veranda out the front. Cool in summer, a fridge during winter.

I know what you're thinking, but I didn't name her. When we bought her, the name was written on a wooden plaque hung near the front door.

'Mayfield,' Adeline read on the day we moved in. 'How cute! It sounds like she's a doting old lady who collects cats and spoons.' And just like that, the house had a pronoun and a personality.

There are three bedrooms: the first two come off the lounge and the last, down a small hall opposite the kitchen. My room is at the front, and I've turned the middle one into an office, complete with a desk, two computer monitors and cubed shelves for my camera equipment. I had good intentions, but I never use it; I don't know how people can work facing a blank wall. Instead, I put all my bags in a pile in a corner of the lounge room, kick off my shoes and toggle my laptop awake. While the photos import, I pour myself a glass of red.

Mayfield sighs softly as the wind whips around her and races through the open windows. I never shut them completely. I prefer the cold to the stuffiness of a closed-up house.

Across the road, karaoke has started. I turn up the volume on the TV to try to drown it out. It doesn't take long to edit the jobs from the day. When I first started, I'd pour over each photo for far too long, tweaking the settings ever so slightly. Contrast up. Exposure down. Shadows lifted. No. Shadows back down. Exposure up, just a little more. I whittled away time overanalysing and over-editing, never managing to get them looking just the way I wanted. No matter how long I worked on them, something was always missing, and I always fell short.

It was only after everything imploded that I took it up as a job. Prior to that, it had been Adeline's thing and something I just dabbled in for fun. But after, it became my lifeline. I didn't mind clients' difficult last-minute requests or the time wasted on barely perceptible adjustments; it all served as a distraction to the gaping nothingness my life had become, and it felt like a link—albeit a tenuous one—to everything I'd lost.

Over time, I've become efficient. Now, I have my favourite settings saved and it's simply a matter of selecting the right one and syncing it across all the final images. Any individual tweaks are made in Photoshop: the family photo on the wall becomes an unobtrusive contemporary painting, the cordial stain never happened. Voila!

I click 'export', sit back and pour myself another glass of shiraz. It's Friday, after all.

You know when a song you don't like gets stuck in your head? The same few lines over and over. As the lights in the nearby houses flicker off, and the music from the party across the road fades, Helen's voice slips back into my head.

Your family must be so lucky.

A presumptuous comment perhaps, but well-intended. Unknowingly barbed.

Your family must be so lucky.
Your family must be so lucky.
Your family must be so lucky.

If only she knew.

When I finish the first—or was it the second?—bottle of red, I go to the kitchen in search of another. The wine has dulled the voice from a loud hammering against my skull to a soft murmur somewhere in the distance, barely audible. So quiet it could be the breeze blowing through Mayfield's open windows.

What was that now, Helen? I can't hear you.

It takes me a while before I find the bottle, down in the bottom drawer among rolls of baking paper and dirty oven mitts. An odd place to put wine. A thought flickers in my head: the *Phantom of the Opera* mask behind the lounge, hidden from view. I forgot to put it back and I wonder if Helen has found it yet. Did she even

notice it was missing? Or will she only find it when they are packing their house to move?

I think of all the things I would need to sort through to move
house. All my stuff is scattered around in sporadic piles, like weeds
that pop up in unexpected places. Not to mention the sunroom.
The vine-covered carport.

Things that haven't been disturbed in years.

A year or two ago, I had to replace my fridge. Underneath, I
found an old shopping list, clearly meant for me; Adeline's curly
handwriting was still visible under the layers of dust.

Bread (the multigrain one)

Garlic (fresh!)

Big block of tasty cheese

Paprika

Dog food

I loved her handwriting. Always had. I couldn't throw the list
out, so I slipped it into a box to keep.

In limbo.

I can't look at it again. But can't get rid of it either. Imagine
what shifting a whole house of furniture would reveal.

I couldn't.

My glass is empty again.

I pour more shiraz, watching it lick the edge of the glass. Adeline used to run her finger around the rim to make the glass sing.
Mournful, drunken melodies. It seemed only natural she could
conjure up such beauty from an ordinary object.

Like Snow White.

I dip my finger in the wine and trace it along the edge.

Nothing.

Even the piano complains when I play it. Adeline said it was the
easiest instrument to get right. But not for me.

I try again. Not even a squeak.

I'm clearly not Snow White.

Maybe I'm the hag.

With the poison apple.

My finger is stained red now.
A high-pitched wail rings out through the kitchen.
Like someone screaming.
Nearby, the sound of glass.
Smashing.

MY MORNING COFFEE is the only routine I follow religiously. I used to buy disposable pods, but Lena bought me a 'Coffee Lovers Kit' for Christmas one year, which included a hessian bag of beans, a cylindrical handheld grinder and stainless-steel pods. I have to admit, I prefer doing it myself. It's surprisingly satisfying, feeling the crunch of the beans as they're crushed into a powder, scooping the fluffy grounds into the silver pods and compacting them with the tamper, leaving you with a little silver ball of magic.

My parents never drank coffee. Tea only. Earl Grey in the morning, chamomile after midday.

She never said it explicitly, but Mum thought coffee was *worldly*; something that looked innocent enough but was really a tool of the Devil to lure you to his side. Coffee, she believed, was the precursor to alcohol, which was the gateway to smoking, which was only a short stop away from weed, which would lead to ice or whatever the most prominent fear-inducing drug was at the time, and undoubtedly end with dying in an alleyway, a needle hanging out of your arm and either surrounded by prostitutes or working as one, depending on your gender.

'They're called sex workers,' Lena told her once. 'And guys can be sex workers too. Why aren't you ever worried about Tom selling himself?'

I can't remember what Mum said back, but I can imagine. Her response was always similar wherever Lena was concerned. She was the one Mum blamed for her grey hair and for her frustrations that fizzled over into full-blown anger. Rebekah and I had come first: two quiet, obedient children—a perfect pigeon pair—and lulled her into a false sense of security. Then she'd had Lena. Chaotic, spirited, stubborn. God was testing her, she often said, testing her patience and faith, but this statement only served to accentuate Mum's problems. Rebekah, sensing a shot at being uplifted to favourite, seemed to go out of her way to be more helpful, using Lena's difficult behaviour to paint her own in a more positive light. And Lena seemed to believe it was her sole purpose in life—her destiny, if you will—to challenge our mother. Meanwhile, I filled the role of the peace-keeping middle child, trying to patch up the relationships, keep everyone happy, not rock the boat. Interestingly, Lena drinks and smokes—both tobacco and weed—and had a few years of experimenting with anything else she could get her hands on, but she doesn't drink coffee or anything else with caffeine. Not Coke, not Pepsi. Not even Earl Grey.

Mum would be shocked to learn that my first experience with coffee was with her. I remember it so clearly because I rarely saw her outside our little bubble. To me, she had always appeared confident and self-assured. She could have dinner cooking in the oven and sheets drying on the line while sorting out fights between us kids, checking our homework and serving customers in the shop at the same time.

But outside of her usual domain, she suddenly appeared uncertain. Smaller, somehow. A wall of extravagant glass bottles towered before her. We were in a department store, and it must've been just before Christmas because I remember silver decorations dripping from the high ceilings. A woman in a white coat with bright red lips sprayed different perfumes onto strips of thick cardboard for

14

Mum to smell. Some she described as having a floral scent, others fun and fruity.

Until then, I hadn't known that fun had a smell.

Mum frowned, shook her head, no. She wasn't fun and fruity, nor florally.

I quietly agreed. She was fresh linen and rosemary. Vicks VapoRub and eucalyptus. Hot Milo and roast chicken.

'Maybe this one? It's a bit more sensual.'

Another shake of the head. Firmer this time.

Among all the beautiful bottles, I noticed a little paper cup of brown beans. They seemed out of place surrounded by so much elegance. Surely they had been put there by mistake? The woman saw me frowning at them. She picked up the cup and waved it under my nose. Out of all the scents, it was my favourite.

'Coffee beans,' she said with a wink. 'They clear the palate.'

When I looked confused, she explained. 'After a while, your nose gets overwhelmed by all the different scents. Smelling coffee beans is like beginning again with a blank slate.'

As the machine hums away, I throw a piece of frozen bread in the toaster and crack an egg into a frypan before turning my attention to the carnage from the night before. Empty wine bottles. A shattered glass. Shiraz pooled on the floor. A half-eaten container of takeaway.

The flashbacks come creeping back slowly. Sheepishly.

Heather's words.

Adeline's shopping list.

A Disney princess?

Deftly, I sweep the glass into a dustpan and dampen a tea towel to blot the wine stain. I know from experience it's a pointless exercise; with timber floors, the damage is well and truly done. But it's not too bad. The size of a palm, if that, and discreetly hidden behind the island bench. Not that it's something to be ashamed of. Accidents happen. And wear and tear like that is just part of owning an older house. It adds character, doesn't it? Something

Mayfield already has a bit too much of, but which I would prefer any day over those newer houses lined up in symmetrical estates. Bare gardens and identical layouts.

I throw the empty bottles into the bin just as the toaster pops. The bread is a bit too burnt.

The settings on the toaster, I've decided, are purely symbolic. It's like a sultry teenager doing whatever the hell it wants. I scrape on some butter and tip the egg on top just as the coffee machine chirps. The scent of burnt sugar and caramelised nuts settles around the kitchen, overriding the stale, acidic smell from last night.

Just like it never happened.

I eat outside, on the front veranda, overlooking the street. During the week, it's quiet by nine, everyone already at work or school, but on the weekends it comes alive. Next door two boys are playing handball in their driveway, the court marked with yellow chalk. A few houses down a young girl is washing her car, a P-plate sticker displayed proudly on the windscreen. Somewhere nearby, I can hear a mower starting.

Bright orange yolk explodes across my plate as I cut into my egg.

Ever since Lena got chickens, I always have too many eggs. Not as many as her, I suppose. These days, she seems to always travel with a dozen or so, desperately handing them out to whoever crosses her path. A protein pusher.

An inquisitive magpie flies over, landing heavily on the branch of the jacaranda. When we first moved in, that tree was barely taller than me, with sparse leaves. It made for an ugly centrepiece, and I suggested pulling it out, but Adeline convinced me otherwise. Now, it's as tall as Mayfield, and every October it blankets the front yard in delicate purple flowers, somehow a more poignant marker of time than any calendar.

The magpie hops closer to inspect my breakfast. They're intimidating-looking birds. Glossy black feathers contrasted with stark white. A sharp beak, the end dipped in midnight. Those piercing amber eyes, always glaring.

'Off you go.' I wave my arms in his direction, but he doesn't move, doesn't flinch. 'Shoo.'

His expression is that of someone who has grown tired of the dramatics. He stares directly back at me, head held high, eyes sharp. Clearly unimpressed.

I'm not sure which scent Mum ended up choosing in the end, but it was a small, rectangular bottle, much simpler than the others on display.

That Christmas morning, we all sat crowded around the tree. Rebekah, Lena and I cross-legged and as close to the tree as we could get, as though our gifts might run away without our bodies fencing them in. Dad sat back in his recliner while Mum crouched on the ground with the camera, handing out presents and taking photos simultaneously.

When it was Mum's turn, she picked up a small box from under the tree and put the camera to the side while she opened it. She looked excited. It was wrapped in the same paper ours had been—silver, with a crimson ribbon tied around it.

It was a rectangular bottle of perfume.

The rectangular bottle.

The same perfume I'd seen her buy.

Still, she seemed surprised by it. With a smile, she sprayed it on her wrist and gushed about how wonderful it smelt, went over to Dad and kissed him on the cheek, thanked him for her present. He sat back, nodding. Accepted the thanks without question.

It was the first time I realised the appearance of something could be more important than the truth.

I still can't work out who she was trying to fool.

WE ALWAYS MEET at her place. She insists mine is too far out, although of course it's the same distance for me to drive to her as it would be for her to come to me. Just quietly, I prefer it this way. It means I don't need to rush around tidying up, scrubbing the shower and washing the sheets. And seeing her at Mayfield would be too jarring. She is too smooth, too polished, would look out of place amid the wild garden and mismatched furniture.

And it would only remind me that she isn't Adeline.

Freya opens the door wide, and I step inside. She's wearing yoga pants and a crop top, with her hair piled into a messy bun. She gives the impression of being casually beautiful, like she's just rushed home after a workout, but she smells of coconut body wash. I've seen how attentive she is to her appearance, and I know she's put effort into her look. Faux dishevelled. Her apartment is the same. Spotless, but with blankets thrown nonchalantly over the corner of the couch and a pile of books heaped on the coffee table, as though she just hadn't had time to put them away yet. She doesn't read though. When I asked how they were going, she laughed and told me they were just for decoration. Like a vase or pot plant. I wonder how Margaret Attwood would feel about her work being reduced to an ornament.

I was Freya's rebound. A rebound that has been going on for three years now.

She had been scared off relationships—a point she pressed regularly—but she was looking for something, I suppose much the same as I was. More than a friendship but without the rules and expectations and disappointments that automatically seem to attach to relationships, no matter how hard people try to fight them. We promise ourselves we won't change for a partner, but we always do. We spin on a dime, and most people don't even realise until years down the track when everything's fallen apart and they find they actually don't care about soccer at all, and, fuck it, cereal for dinner is a completely viable (and great) option.

I'd changed when I met Adeline.

Unfortunately for me, I was a better person with her.

For Freya, she had given up too much. Sliced away little pieces of her life to patch up the holes in his. She met him online and moved for love. Away from Adelaide, where she'd grown up among vineyards and posh accents, where you could 'get any-where' by driving ten minutes in any direction—a claim I found dubious, but she insisted was the case. Away from her family and her nephew, who no longer recognises her when she visits. Away from the friends she'd grown up with.

She'd spent years trying to save a house deposit, but gave half to him to help him get his new mowing business off the ground because he was (and I quote) *so unhappy* in his job as a labourer. He'd be able to turn his life around, he'd implored, if only he had the funds to follow his passion.

I'd stopped her at that point in the story and spluttered, 'Wait. His passion was mowing?' But she insisted it was more about feeling free and having the ability to make money without the constraints of answering to a boss.

Five years later, she was alone, a two-hour-and-forty-minute flight away from her family and friends, lumped with a credit card debt in her name but for things she no longer possessed. He'd run off with the neighbour, their French bulldog and the Toyota Hilux.

We fuck with the lights out. Always with the lights out. Freya doesn't like her tits, her arse, her stomach, her thighs, herself. She is always counting calories, going to the gym and focusing on self-improvement. When I met her, I thought her passion for fitness would mean she was confident and self-assured. I've realised it's the exact opposite. Like her house, she is immaculate, but only because she focuses so intently on the negatives—the dust and the mould, the cellulite and the bumps. Her bathroom cabinet is crammed with lotions and potions, and she obsessively works cream into the ends of her hair and rubs oil into her cuticles.

The sex is good—when is it not?—but there's no passion. Not real passion anyway. Sometimes we can act in the moment, tearing at each other's clothes, scratching and biting, her moaning in my ear, but when it's over, lying there in the dark, an uncomfortable silence descends. It's almost like a script, but at least I know my lines.

'Want a smoke?'

The bed shifts and I hear Freya moving around the room, the rustle of fabric, the rifling through a drawer. When she flicks the lamp on, she is wrapped tightly in her satin bathrobe, her hair smooth and lips plump with gloss.

'Sure.'

Freya doesn't smoke. Only after sex.

I don't smoke either. Only with her.

We sit on the balcony, the tips of our cigarettes glowing brightly. Her apartment is low, only two storeys up, and overlooks a row of shops that are always closed by the time I arrive, their doors locked and shutters pulled down. It's not much of an outlook, but I imagine the apartments above would have an amazing view of the glittering city skyline.

From inside, I hear my phone vibrating, but I make no move to get it. Freya glances at me, one eyebrow raised.

'It'll be Lena. I'll call her back tomorrow.'

'Lena...' I can almost see her brain ticking over, trying to place the name. 'Your older sister?'

'Younger.'

'Close.'

I know she has a brother, older I think, but I can't remember his name either, and I'm relieved she doesn't ask me.

Freya pulls hard on her cigarette, the glowing ember reflecting on her face. A familiar feeling of melancholy settles over us, a kind of sadness that the best parts of our week are spent with someone closer to being a stranger than a friend.

I NEVER SPEND the night with Freya. It blurs the boundary too much, bleeding into relationship territory. A casual dinner below her apartment is one thing, but waking up next to each other, with bed hair and stale breath, is another altogether. There's a vulnerability to seeing someone as they wake up, having not yet placed themselves back in reality. Before they have set the mask they wear for the world.

My sheets drape onto the wooden floorboards, and the fan keeps a methodical rhythm above me. The clock on the wall is long dead, but I can tell it is late in the morning by the position of the sun outside the window. When you've stayed in one place long enough, everything becomes as familiar as your own hands. I can tell the time by the shadows on the floorboards, the seasons by the smells wafting through the windows, and the weather by how often Mayfield creaks.

It's been almost twenty years since I signed that dotted line, and the memories I have here are a mixed bag.

I love it here.

But I hate it.

Countless times I've considered selling and moving somewhere completely new. Shedding Mayfield like a skin that's become too tight, too suffocating. But something always stops me. Laziness probably—sorting and cleaning this place would require the kind of effort and organisation skills I don't possess.

But something else too.

I get out of bed, leaving the sheets strewn about where they are. My mum once bought me a book about making the bed and the changes it will inspire in your life. Success! Determination! Orderliness! I could drive an Audi, be a CEO, change the world! If only I could neatly tuck in my sheets, smooth out my quilt cover and replace my pillows each morning. 'Or maybe,' I countered, 'by not making my bed, I'll have more time in my day to accomplish other things.'

'Aha!' She said gleefully, her point proven. 'But *do* you?'

'Of course not. And maybe correlation does not imply causation.'

'Meaning?'

'Meaning, maybe making the bed doesn't cause you to be successful at all. Maybe successful people are naturally more organised and therefore more likely to make the bed.'

She threw her hands up. 'I give up.'

I couldn't blame her. I'd given up on myself long ago.

I pop one of my silver pods into the coffee machine and wait for it to work its wonder.

My childhood was structured and predictable. My parents owned a corner store, creatively called The Corner Store, with our house behind it. As kids, work and play were interchangeable to us. We played games in the shop and folded brochures in the house. Toys were hidden behind the register, and boxes of excess stock were piled in the kitchen.

Our parents knew everyone in the town and everything about them. The shop gave them prime position for hearing all the gossip from multiple angles, and Mum, in particular, took great pleasure in relaying it all in excited whispers. It gave her a great deal of currency, knowing things about people and being able to build them up or break them down with nothing but words. If someone new arrived in town, all it took was for her to share an unfavourable opinion with a few regulars—*that new bloke came into the shop this morning I get a weird vibe about him*—and that person, no matter how genuine, would find it very difficult to be welcomed by the locals.

Hers was the face most people looked forward to seeing when they came in to pick up their morning paper, but it was Dad's shop. His domain.

Although the community was part of our lives, Dad never really trusted outsiders. We had a pile of résumés behind the counter, thicker than the White Pages. Dad didn't like letting others into his space, which meant we were expected to help out most afternoons until dinner, and on Saturdays—serving behind the register, pumping fuel, sweeping floors or stocking shelves. Most of it fell to Rebekah and I; Lena often seemed to be able to weasel out of it, but she was the youngest, so we let her.

Sunday—the day of rest—the shop was closed, but only because the Bible said so. It was the only thing that stopped him.

The shop closed down fifteen years ago. Like most small businesses, it was surpassed by the construction of a brand-new shopping centre. People promised they would keep coming, but convenience is just too tempting.

Mum and Dad have stayed in the same house. The boarded-up shop is still there too, blocking their view of the mountains. At first, they planned to knock it down, but there was always some reason not to. Money, time, having the flu, preserving history. Mum still talks about it sometimes, but without any conviction.

I guess it's a family trait, not being able to let things go.

WHEN I ARRIVE, the real estate agent is already there, leaning against a little black car plastered in advertising. She's new to the job, only in her early twenties, and already far too serious. We've met a few times now, but I can't remember her name—some kind of precious stone.

'Tom,' Ruby-or-whatever says, shaking my hand firmly. 'Nice to see you again.'

Her nails are like talons, painted red.

'Busy day?'

'Yeah, crazy,' I say. It's a standard response, no matter how slowly my day has plodded along. You can't really admit to having a sleep-in followed by a leisurely breakfast with the local magpie and lying in front of the news instead of doing laundry. Downtime is scandalous in this overworked, underpaid economy, where your success is judged on how little free time you have. Is your life even worthwhile if you haven't scheduled every spare minute?

'Yours?'

'Oh, absolutely hectic,' she says. 'I didn't even have time for lunch today.'

Her expression and words don't align. Her voice is suitably frustrated, but her eyes have a satisfied glint.

A group of kids on brightly coloured bikes come peddling madly down the hill towards us. Blue, pink and green flash past.

'It's such a beautiful neighbourhood, this one,' Pearl says. 'Nice, wide footpaths, heaps of parks, a BMX track close by. It's great for kids. The kind of place where neighbours really look out for each other.'

Her real estate spiel is always on, like a child who has just learnt how to add numbers and walks around reciting them to whoever crosses their path. *Two plus two is four. Six and three equal nine.*

The house is lavish in a generic way. You can tell every piece of furniture, every item from the dining table down to the candle in the toilet, is of the highest quality, but there is no common thread to it. Dark leather couches clash with marble side tables and white-washed bookshelves. A grand piano sits in the corner, covered in a fine layer of dust, and I wonder if anyone can play.

It's a four-bedroom house. They have one child, a boy, if the amount of blue in the bedroom is anything to go by: the walls are periwinkle, and the bedding is cobalt and covered in cars. In the corner are cubed shelves and sitting neatly in the middle of each cube is a single toy. A plastic Tonka truck, a stuffed giraffe, a wooden helicopter. The toys look almost ornamental, and I think of Freya's pile of books.

They have a dog. A great big golden one with curled fur. He stares at me longingly through the windows from outside, his nose leaving smudge marks against the glass. I'll have to edit them out later but I don't mind. Dogs get special allowances.

As I move through the rooms, I try to get a sense of what the people who live here are like. What the structure of their family is. What they do for work. Their ages. Their hobbies. Their lives. It's like going to a shopping centre and people-watching, but without the crowds and without the people.

This was one of Adeline's favourite things to do. At the beach, in a waiting room, at a restaurant, she would pick out people and tell me stories about them.

'They're on a first date. His name is Brad and he picked this restaurant because he knows the owners and it will make him look important. His sister set them up because she is sick of him complaining about being single. He's having a great time, but Arabella's not interested.'

'You think her name is Arabella?'

'Why not?'

'How many Arabellas do you know?'

'Fine. Bethany. Known as Beth. She's not impressed but she's too polite to make it obvious. Brad won't stop talking about his promotion.'

'Or he keeps talking about his ex—'

'No, promotion. That part's true, I've heard him mention it at least three times now. He's insecure because his job isn't that impressive, so he has to talk up his pay cheque. He wanted to become a lawyer but didn't get the marks for uni, so became a police officer instead.'

'I don't think he would be insecure about that.'

'True. Police officers love themselves sick.'

'He's the manager of a printing company.'

'Yes! What about her? I'm thinking she's a social worker, newly graduated who is recently back in the dating scene but already wishing she wasn't. But she'll still go back to his place and have pity sex.'

Facts and fiction melding together.

I didn't understand it at first because how can you know if you've guessed correctly? But that was the point of it, Adeline told me. There are unknowns in everything; you may as well have fun with it.

These days, I play it in my head.

He's a financial adviser. She does injectables. They both grew up poor but are embarrassed about it, so they buy everything based on the price tag with no thought to how it fits together. But it makes them feel worthy to look around at all their things, knowing how much they cost.

'Hey, Boy.'

When I step outside, the dog goes ballistic, jumping up repeatedly and running in frantic circles. I crouch down and he rolls onto his back, tongue lolled to the side, tail thumping furiously against the outdoor chairs.

He is some kind of poodle cross—a labradoodle? Groodle? Spoodle? Cavoodle?—his thick wiry fur matted into knots. I look around for a brush but can't find one. Not a brush, not a toy, not a bed, not even a crappy tennis ball. The only dog-related thing out here is a ceramic water dish that is completely dry.

Amber appears at the door. 'Oh, sorry! I forgot they had a dog.'

I wonder if, perhaps, they also forgot. If I led him through the side gate, out to my car, how long would it be before they noticed?

'All good, I love dogs.' I grab the bowl and take it to the nearby tap. In an instant he is beside me, almost inhaling the running water.

'Me too,' says Emerald, but she stays behind the glass door.

For the rest of the shoot, he follows me closely, his head butting up against my legs, as I pace the perimeter of the yard. As I set up each shot, he sits on my feet and nuzzles his head into my hands, grateful for whatever attention I give. A big, happy shadow.

But I don't feel happy.

And I really wish I could find a brush.

I drive away with the dog's mournful howls echoing in my ears and Adeline in my head.

She always is. But in these moments, I can see her face clearly. Pleading with me to *do something*. Take action, the way she always did.

Impulsively.

But I see this dog, in different houses, in different yards, every other week. Golden retrievers with sad eyes. Labradors fat from not enough exercise. Staffies that roll onto their backs, submissive and anxious. Chihuahuas that slink and tremble at heavy footsteps. Ridgebacks crossed with huskies, and maybe a bit of mastiff somewhere down the line, that chew table legs from boredom. All adopted with good intentions but neglected by families too busy with work and after-school activities to pay them attention.

What can I do, really? It's never bad enough to report. The animal welfare agency has bigger situations to deal with than dogs that aren't being walked. They aren't going to remove an animal due to a lack of toys or a coat in need of a brush.

I can't save them all, I want to say to her. I'm not you.

T HE DAY I met her, it was the peak of summer. The stifling week between Christmas and New Year, when everyone is on holiday and uncertain of the day or what they should be doing, the busyness of Christmas finally over, but still too early for New Year's resolutions.

The heat had driven everyone towards the water. The beach, for those close enough or who didn't mind the drive, backyard pools for the lucky ones, hoses or baths filled with cold water for those who were desperate, and rivers and dams for everyone else. There was a river five minutes from my place. It was a beautiful spot, always busy with people picnicking, fishing or kayaking. I drove past every day and always intended to go there, but something would inevitably come up—university lectures, work, assignments to get started on, mowing, cleaning the shower, groceries, lightbulbs to change.

Basically, life.

But I was on holiday from university, not rostered on at work, and my rental was a hot box, so I decided to go to the river.

And that was when I first saw her.

It's strange, isn't it? How many life-changing moments seem to happen on the days when people do something out of the ordinary. A man who has never bought lotto before buys a ticket on a whim. A woman impulsively takes a different route home from work on the day of a bridge collapse. They break their normal routines and he becomes a millionaire, she dodges death.

I broke mine that day.

As kids, we were never allowed to buy soft serves from the van that drove around the streets lulling children out of their houses with traditional folk music. It made no sense, our parents told us, to spend all that money when we had a fridge full of cost-price ice creams in the shop.

That day there was a pink Mr. Whippy in the car park, 'Greensleeves' tinkling from the speaker. To most people this was the soundtrack of summer, coconut tanning lotion and ice cream, but to me it signified an indulgence.

The queue was ridiculous, with people flocking from all directions. Some had books tucked under their arms, others were wrapped in striped towels, dripping puddles onto the bitumen that dried almost as quickly as they formed. Adeline and I both reached the back of the line at the same time. We each hesitated as to who should go first.

Only I didn't know her name yet.

At that time, she was just another passer-by: a background character in my life, as I was in hers.

'You go first,' she said, taking a step back. 'I saw you power-walking up the hill. A man on a mission.'

'No, you go.' Dad's voice was in my head. Chivalrous, but only in words. 'Ladies first.'

She didn't smile sweetly at that, the way I thought she might. For a moment, I saw a flash of Lena.

'I'm not a lady.'

She was wearing a faded denim skirt, a white string bikini, and was severely sunburnt. Her collarbone was a bright fuchsia, her shoulders an angry red. A white line cut across her back, stark against the burn, from where the bikini string had shifted.

'People suffering from heat stroke first,' I corrected, clumsily. 'You look like you need ice cream more than I do.'

She laughed at that and stepped in front of me. 'That's true. Although lathering myself in it might be the best course of action at this point. I think my shoulders are actually on fire.'

Enjoying the banter, I decided to take a risk. 'Or perhaps using sunscreen next time?'

I held my breath, but she turned and laughed. 'I gather you don't know many redheads. This *is* with sunscreen on.'

'How quickly do you think this line will move?'

There was one man inside the pink van. From where I stood, he looked around Dad's age. I hoped he would work with the same vigour.

'Not quick enough. "Greensleeves" has clearly worked its charm. Pair a neutral stimulus with ice cream and we're all like Pavlov's dogs, salivating at the bell.'

Pavlov.

'Let me guess,' I said confidently. 'Psych major?'

'Incorrect. I'm not studying, but you clearly are. Only people going to university are arrogant enough to presume it's the only way to learn. Fun fact: you can go to the library and borrow the same books they read at university for free.'

I didn't know how to respond.

'Relax. I'm right though, aren't I? You're studying?'

'You're right.'

She let out a squeal. 'I knew it! Maybe I should be a psychology major after all.'

'That was a lucky guess.' But I was impressed, and she knew it.

In front of us, a little boy bounced up and down impatiently as his mum searched through her bag for loose coins.

'You'll just have to get one without a flake,' she said. 'I'm twenty cents short.'

He looked around, crestfallen. As he glanced in my direction I gave him a half smile. Too bad, it said. But in front of me, Adeline had already pulled twenty cents out of her pocket and passed it to him.

The mother looked around, shocked. 'Oh no, you don't have to,' she said. 'He can just go without.'

'It's just twenty cents.'

I wondered why I hadn't thought to do the same. She was right. It was only twenty cents. Nothing to us, but a chocolate flake was the best part of the day for a little kid.

We shuffled forward.

'Okay then,' she spun to face me. 'I'll guess your degree.'

'That was eating away at you all that time?'

She narrowed her eyes and searched my face, looking for clues. I wondered what was written there, and looked away awkwardly. I became acutely aware of my posture. My breathing. The sweat beaded on my forehead. I wiped it away hastily. Her eyes travelled down to the polo shirt I'd been given for Christmas, my hands stuffed in my pockets, rubber thongs.

'Well, it's nothing creative, that much is clear,' she said, with an air of assertion. 'I'm tossing up something to do with business. Maybe law.' Her eyes slipped back to my outfit. 'No, not law. Business.'

We shuffled forward.

Close. So close. 'Wrong.'

'Damn, okay, tell me then.'

'Accounting.'

Her eyes widened. 'Accounting?' She tilted her head back and laughed. 'That's pretty much the same as business. I deserve a point for that.'

'Fine, but I get to guess what you do.' Obviously something that didn't require a degree. Something outside the box.

'You already had a guess, remember?' She arched her eyebrows playfully. 'You said psych major, so you lose.'

A man came stalking up the footpath, dragging a German shepherd puppy angrily behind him. The puppy was wet, with big ears, too large for its head. It stopped to sniff at interesting smells on the ground, but the man didn't slow. A few people smiled uncertainly. They were used to smiling at puppies, but this one was attached to an angry man. Their smiles faltered.

A pool of spilt ice cream caught its attention, and it jerked on the lead, tail wagging, trying to reach it.

'Don't you fucking dare.'

His foot connected with the puppy's nose. It yelped. Loudly.

'Fucking dog,' he mumbled. He pushed through the line, which broke apart and re-formed almost immediately. The line for Mr. Whippy is not easy to disrupt.

Most people glanced at him uneasily or looked away as he got to his ute and threw the puppy into the back with so much force it slid across the slippery tray like a bowling ball. When it sat up, dazed, its head was low and its tail between its legs. After a moment of sharing concerned looks, the people around us turned their attention back to the line and to the important decision. So many options: freckles, choc top, sherbet, nuts, choc nut, choc sprinkles, single cone, double, waffle cone, an optional chocolate flake.

But Adeline didn't take her eyes off him.

He tied the lead tightly to the ladder rack, flicking the puppy on the nose as he did. It cowered. Adeline flinched.

'Some people shouldn't own dogs,' I said to her with a frown and a shrug of my shoulders. I meant for it to lighten the situation or make it more palatable somehow, like when people watch horrific stories on the news and shake their heads sadly. *The world is so unfair.* No one does anything and nothing changes, but everyone feels a little better that they aren't alone in their feelings.

Emptiness masquerading as compassion.

But something crossed her face. Something I couldn't quite decipher.

'No,' she said, her voice hard. Firm. 'Some people shouldn't.'

I turned back towards the van, squinting at the menu of faded photos stuck on the window. I still hadn't decided. Sprinkles or sherbet? A single or double cone?

'We have to do something,' she said.

'Maybe report him?'

'No one is going to do anything without evidence. That puppy will be completely traumatised by the time they step in. No. We have to do something now,' she repeated more forcefully.

It was a joke, surely.

'What?' I laughed nervously, my eyes travelling to the guy. He was leaning against his LandCruiser, smoking, his eyes trailing after all the girls walking by in bikinis. What could we possibly do?

'I'll distract him, you grab the puppy. I'll meet you down at the bend in the river.'

'Wait, what?'

I realised it wasn't a joke.

Time began doing something abnormal. Struggling to keep moving forward at a regular pace. It was whirring, turning back on itself.

My mother's voice was in my head.

I was twelve, serving behind the counter when a woman entered the store. Her clothes were skimpy, her feet bare. She picked up a box of tampons and I watched as she counted loose coins into her palm. Calculate that it wasn't enough. I watched as she dropped the box down her top. I didn't say anything, didn't stop her.

She must've needed it.

My mother was watching me watching her. 'Did that woman put something down her shirt?'

I nodded and Mum approached the woman with an aggression I'd rarely seen. Pointed to me. Threatened her with the police.

'There's no excuse for stealing,' she told me angrily once the woman had thrown the tampons onto the counter and scampered out. 'It's one of the seven deadly sins.'

I tried to reason. 'She seemed desperate.'

But Mum held her finger up to silence me. 'There are other ways. Honest ways. She could've gone to the church. They have provisions to give to people in need. We are giving people. We donate. But the way she did it was dishonest.'

35

Mum thanked me for my honesty and let me pick a lolly from the counter as a reward. 'You did the right thing, Thomas.'

But I often thought of that woman and wished I had lied.

My heart racing, I turned to Adeline. 'You want us to steal it?'

'No.'

I relaxed for a moment.

'Save it.'

Save. As though it changed the meaning somehow. As though it turned something illegal into something justifiable. Compassionate even.

I looked at the man across the road. He was around my age, maybe a year or two older. Tanned. Muscular. Someone who spent his time outdoors. Working out, lifting weights, not pouring over numbers. I imagined his fist colliding with my jaw, my head getting smashed into the hot bitumen. I'd managed to avoid conflict all my life. Dodged schoolyard fights. Made sure I didn't get involved in things that weren't my business.

And she was a total stranger. I'd known her for less than five minutes. We'd had some light-hearted banter in line for ice cream, and now she was asking me to steal a puppy with her. It was wild, she was wild. Wild in a fearless, impulsive way.

I didn't even know her name.

But already, I knew I would.

Just as no one had paid attention to the man kicking the puppy, no one looked twice as Adeline and I slipped out of the line.

I worried she wouldn't be his type. There are other girls, more beautiful. Tanned bodies, smooth hair, and breasts that spill from the flimsy bikini tops. She was pale and sunburnt all at once. Arms and legs too long and skinny. I worried she wouldn't hold his attention while I slipped behind the ute. But I was wrong: there was something about her that drew him in.

Just like she had drawn me in.

She used the puppy as an excuse to approach him, while I looped around the car park, watching from a distance. He puffed out his chest and reached out to pat the bewildered dog. It cowered under his touch, licking his hand tentatively, uncertain about this sudden shift in his demeanour.

Rage replaced with charm. The dog had a purpose for him now.

Somehow she managed to entice him to the front of the Land-Cruiser, and that was when I snuck over. I could hear his voice less than two metres away. His booming laughter. She'd gotten him talking about himself, and I could tell he was lapping up every bit of space she gave him to impress her.

But the puppy's lead was tied to the bar of the ute. How the hell had he managed such a tight knot?

Time was too fast and too slow, all at once. My shaking fingers worked at a snail's pace, but I could hear the conversation charging ahead.

But he had somewhere to be.

I ducked down as he moved towards the driver's door.

It opened.

Slammed.

I could see his elbow hanging out the already-open window. The kind of guy who never worried about closing it, confident no one would ever mess with him. Steal from him. Confident if someone did, he could take them on.

His laughter.

Hers.

The ute roared to life, the exhaust pipe near my face spluttering a burst of warm air, and he revved the engine a few times; some kind of last-ditch attempt to impress her.

He was about to drive off. And I hadn't got the puppy.

I jumped up and lunged at the collar. I'd have to forget the lead—probably should've left it from the beginning, but I had limited experience with dogs. Limited experience in high-stress situations.

The collar fell away just as the ute lurched forward. I grabbed the puppy.

And I ran.

I ran like my life depended on it.

Because maybe it did.

I didn't stop running until I got to the bend in the river, where the reeds were thick and the trees messy and untamed. Only kayakers or bushwalkers would venture this far away from the barbecues and toilet blocks. I felt shattered, zapped of all energy, but when Adeline caught up a few minutes later, she looked like she was buzzing, high on adrenaline.

'Put him down and let him have a bit of a play,' she said to me, and I did so, robotically. In the grass, she found a stick and the two of them began playing a game of tug-of-war while I collapsed heavily beside her in shocked silence.

'Are you okay?'

I inhaled deeply, allowing my lungs to expand. My brain was still catching up. 'We stole a dog.'

'Saved.'

Saved. As though it were nothing. Something noble, even.

'You don't think what we did was wrong?' I asked. 'Even a little bit?'

'Wrong how?' There was no remorse on her face. Not a glimmer of it.

'Legally,' I said. Then, more weakly, 'Morally.'

The puppy climbed onto her lap and curled into a fuzzy ball of black and tan. She smiled down at him, running her fingers over his ears.

'I get it's against the law,' she said, 'but sometimes laws don't protect us and we need to look out for each other. If that's what he's like to a puppy, at a park, in front of a huge group of people, imagine what he's like when no one's watching?' As she spoke she seemed to deflate, her shoulders slouching forward, her body crumpling into itself. 'People are always worse behind closed doors.'

I looked away, heat creeping up the back of my neck. She was right and my arguments disintegrated on my tongue like popping candy, leaving nothing but a faint fizz.

'You didn't have to help.'

'No,' I said. 'You're right. I would do it again.'

She smiled at me. Cautiously.

'I just haven't stolen anything before.'

'Seriously?' Her laugh skipped along the water and bounced between the trees. 'Never? Not even, like, a chocolate bar? A packet of gum?'

The woman was back in my head. Her bare feet and threadbare clothes.

'Definitely not.'

'You'll make a good accountant. I mean, people might not be impressed with the size of their tax returns, but the books will certainly balance.'

It didn't feel like a compliment.

A family of black swans glided past us, the parents at the front and two fluffy cygnets behind. We both turned to watch them.

'So, what now?'

'Well, Stu gave me his number, so what's an appropriate amount of time before I can call to organise a date?' She laughed.

'Stu?'

'Stu. He was very specific about that. He *hates* being called Stuart. I guess it doesn't really align with his whole aesthetic.' She paused, frowning at me. 'Actually, I still don't know your name. Hopefully it's not Stu; that would be embarrassing.'

'No, it's Tom.'

'Tom,' she repeated.

I liked hearing my name in her voice. It sounded different somehow. Better.

'I'm Adeline.'

Adeline. I had never heard the name before, but it was clear she could never have been called anything else. She wouldn't have suited something common like Anna, Sarah, Nicole. Amanda.

The puppy had gone to sleep, cocooned in her arms, and she was looking down at him, crestfallen.

'I can't take him.' Her voice was quiet. 'I didn't think that far ahead. My boyfriend's allergic to dogs.'

Boyfriend.

Time danced around the word.

'I don't know what to do,' she continued. 'I could drop him to a rescue where he could find a new family. But what if Stuart tracks him down?'

'Do you really think he'd bother? He didn't seem to like him that much.'

Adeline gave me a look I couldn't quite read. 'The dog is his possession. Fondness has nothing to do with it.'

I wasn't so sure. It seemed unlikely a guy like him would bother going to all that effort, but she looked convinced.

She buried her face in his fur. 'I think I'm in love already.'

I couldn't have agreed more.

'I'll take him.'

Adeline looked up at me, her eyes wide, excited. 'Really? Are you sure?'

'Yeah, I've always wanted a dog. And I was the one who stole him after all, so he is really my responsibility.'

A smile broke across her face, and my heart skipped a beat.

The sun was getting lower in the sky, the shadows stretching out across the grass. Adeline looked at the horizon. 'I better go. Gerard will be frantic, wondering where I am.'

She leaned over and placed the puppy into my arms, planting a kiss on his nose. 'I'll miss you,' she whispered to him. 'But hey,' she straightened up and looked at me. 'Maybe I might even bump into you guys again? Like if you were to ever come back here for a morning walk or something?'

'Maybe. I'm sure he'll be needing plenty of walks.'

One hour.

That's all it had taken.

Instead of a soft serve in a waffle cone, I was leaving with a stolen German shepherd.

It's INTERESTING WHICH memories stay with you over time and which ones fade away.

I remember, so clearly, the day I first spoke to Adeline in the ice-cream line. I can still see the string of her bikini cutting across her sunburnt back, but the colour of the string changes. In some memories it's white, in others pale pink, but it was just as likely blue.

I don't know the exact details of the conversation when I agreed to help steal Floyd, but I remember being reluctantly swept along and the fear coursing through me as my fingers fumbled to untie his lead.

I can't recall agreeing to keep him, but I know I wanted Adeline's approval and being excited when I got it.

The feelings are what stand out the most—bright and bold, while the surrounding details are constructed from our imaginations or pieced together with the aid of photographs. Then there are the memories that have slipped away unnoticed or become disfigured with time; the truth painted over with our wants, dreams, hopes, prejudices and biases.

You'll have to bear with me. My memories of Adeline are part of me, running through my blood and buried under my skin, but some of the specifics have become fragile and crumble at my touch. From scraps, I've had to build them into something solid. Fill in the blanks.

I named him Floyd, after the park where I found him. Met her.

It's been seven years without him, but tonight, as I wrestle with Mayfield's lock, I miss the sound of his claws scratching on the door, desperate for me to walk through it, and his excited greeting when I did. He would spin in dizzying circles, bounding up to lick my face. Lena, whose dogs were impeccably trained, told me it was bad manners and that I should discourage it. She suggested turning my back if he jumped, and only paying him attention when he was sitting.

'Reward the behaviour you want,' she said.

But I never managed it.

After, when it was just me and Floyd, his overly enthusiastic greetings were the only thing that kept me going.

I would take all his bad habits—his digging, barking at motorbikes, chewing on table legs, jumping up—just for a minute more with him.

Mayfield is quieter than usual, and I hum to myself as I extract the memory card from the camera and slot it into the side of the computer. Once the progress bar begins filling, I find the TV remote stuffed down the side of the lounge and start scrolling through the options. There aren't a lot of things I enjoy watching these days. Comedy is too light-hearted. Horror, too dark. The news is too real, and fantasy not real enough. And the last thing I want to do is watch someone else's drama. It leaves me with travel, documentaries, cooking or sport.

I settle on travel.

Many times, I've considered getting another dog. Once, I even drove to the pound with the intention of adopting, but when I pulled into the car park I couldn't get out of the car. Another dog would be beautiful but it would never be Floyd, and I guess on some level I knew that I'd always compare them. Always be disappointed.

Floyd had brought me to her.

And saved me after.

Once the photos have been imported, I sort through them, marking the ones to edit. The dog features in some, and I drag those images into Photoshop, erasing his presence with a click of the mouse. The desperate streaks from his tongue across the windows become lush grass. His curious head peering inside turns into neat hedging. I zoom in, blending the edges until it looks seamless.

Pfft.

Just like he was never there.

It doesn't feel that far away from his reality. A messy, energetic, muddy puppy, bought by people who don't like mess or mud and have no energy for him. His howl as I drove away comes back to me: the loneliness in it. He isn't a dog in the pound, but I wonder if it makes much difference.

He is just another object to be owned. A marker of success.

My wine glass is empty, and I go to the kitchen to top it up. Next door, my neighbour is yelling at her son. The words are muffled; I can't make them out, but the disappointment mingled with anger is clear.

A partner. A ring. A dog. A house. A baby or two. Everyone is sprinting to tick off an invisible checklist so they can compare it with everyone else's invisible checklist, rushing from one point to the next until somewhere along the line the image becomes more important than the truth.

I'm not judging. I did it too. Fell into the trap of focusing all my attention on the next milestone and forgot what I had right in front of me. You think it will get better and that you'll stop and smell the roses after the next deadline, the next promotion. Next week. Next month. Next year.

But here's a secret: the checklist never stops.

It is only in the early hours of the morning, when the sky is a bruised purple and only the birds and the cyclists are waking up, that I finally stumble into bed.

And I see her. As though she is right there in front of me.

So real I could almost reach out and touch her.

Sometimes I like to float in this dream state for a moment or two. It's like being underwater in some alternate universe. Nothing but muffled noises and blurred shapes above you, shadows moving in and out of your peripheral vision.

Underwater is quiet. Calm. But like being underwater, you can only stay for so long.

I need to breathe.

I look at her once again, her face happy. Smiling. Serene. But then I blink and I see her lying there, the smile gone. Asleep.

Only not.

I gasp for air but there is none. Only emptiness.

1/15

THE NEXT MORNING the magpie is back, perched on the handrail, inspecting my breakfast with his maroon eyes. This time, I don't bother trying to scare him off—it's clear he won't be fazed—but I watch him out of the corner of my eye as he eats. He is like an avian judge, black robe, white wig and a perpetual scowl. Judge, the magpie.

There's a loud rumbling noise as my neighbours turn into their driveway. They drive a giant Prado, complete with a shiny bull bar and roof racks. It looks immaculate—I've never seen them use it for anything other than taxiing their young son to various activities. They've lived next door for years. I've never spoken to them, and they've never acknowledged me.

In all the time I've lived here, the people on the street have come and gone so many times I've lost track. There is no one left from back then—no one to remember—but still, my neighbours seem to avoid me. A group of them go for early morning walks together. There's a street Christmas party every year that I've never been invited to. And last Halloween none of the kids knocked on my door, even though I'd accidentally left the outside light on. It doesn't bother me, really. I wouldn't go to a street Christmas party anyway, and I never have any chocolate bars for trick-or-treaters. But I do wonder if what happened is stuck to me forever. If the story gets passed on and on and on, small details changing each time, warping me, warping the events with each retelling.

A game of Telephone, played over decades.

The kid climbs out of the car, wearing a crisp white martial arts uniform that is a couple of sizes too big. He opens the gate and stands impatiently as the car crawls through, barely able to squeeze past the fence posts. The car is only just out of the way when he jumps onto the gate, kicking off to swing it shut. A deep, long line is carved into the gravel.

He isn't even school-aged yet but already seems to be a bit of a troublemaker. I only know because I often wake up to the sound of his mother yelling. There are weekly threats to throw the Xbox away unless he cleans his room or stops talking back. Empty threats clearly. Just yesterday she was screaming about the Xbox again. I'm half tempted to go over there and toss it myself.

'Josh!' His mum storms down the driveway. 'Get off the gate. For the millionth time, you'll break it!'

Josh jumps down and skulks towards the house, scuffing his shoes in the dirt, pebbles exploding at his feet. His mum walks over to the gate to check it's closed properly. They have a puppy—a little fluffy white thing—that had a habit of escaping until they got one of those shock collars. Now it spends its days lying desolately near the front door, too scared to go within several metres of the fence line. But she rattles the gate anyway.

Judge hops along the handrails to watch her, and as she turns, her eyes catch sight of him. With a small scream, she raises her hands above her head protectively and sprints towards the door, her eyes darting wildly around the sky, alert for black-and-white missiles raining down.

But they never come.

'Tom.'

We are lying side by side in the dark. Naked. Freya's voice is light, but she only ever brings up things of depth under the blur of alcohol or cover of night. Or both.

'Why have you never taken any photos of me?' she asks.

'Oh.'

Her question is unexpected, but I should've seen it coming. Wherever I go, people seem to assume I want to photograph them. And Freya's phone is full of selfies.

'I can take some photos of you. I'll bring my camera one day.' I try to sound interested, inflect my voice like it's a good suggestion, but I'm glad of the darkness hiding my frown.

'Oh, no, you don't have to.' Her voice has changed. Silly. Playful. 'I don't think I would be very good in front of a camera anyway.'

'You would too.'

'Really?'

'Of course. You're beautiful.'

I'm not lying; Freya is beautiful. Perhaps one of the most beautiful women I know. But even so, my voice is full of a confidence I don't feel. Being beautiful doesn't equate to being photogenic.

Freya cares too much. Her self-worth is attached to numbers: kilograms on the bathroom scales, reps written on a whiteboard at the gym, calories printed on food packaging, figures on her payslip each fortnight. And the best photos are the real ones, no matter how imperfect.

'I bet she was pretty.'

A pause. 'Who?' Even though I know who she's talking about. 'Your ex.'

I let out the breath I don't even realise I've been holding in.

Adeline.

Very. I want to say. But not in the way Freya means.

The things that drew me to Adeline—her real beauty—weren't things you could see.

I feel Freya shift beside me, rolling over onto her back. 'I just remember you saying that an ex got you into it. You'd been doing accounting or something and had never picked up a camera before you met her.'

I remember our conversation.

She had been asking about photography and I'd mentioned Adeline in passing. I'm always careful not to talk about her too much, but Freya had latched onto the small details I'd unwittingly thrown out. Maybe she had sensed they weren't as insignificant as I'd tried to make them appear.

'It sounds like she was kind of your muse.'

Early the next morning, I stop at the florist near my house. It's part of a strip of shops—along with a hairdresser, cafe, fish and chip store and bottle shop—with parking out the front and a post box on the corner.

I choose some orange flowers and take them up to the counter, where a young girl is serving. She's new. It's not the fumbling that gives her away or the nervousness in her voice, but the fact I come here every Sunday and haven't seen her before.

'Such happy flowers,' she says, wrapping them in paper.

I nod, wondering if there's such a thing as an unhappy flower. A Venus flytrap perhaps. Or one of those hideously depressing rainbow roses—white roses with their stems split open and forced to suck up coloured water, as though a rose—a rose!—isn't beautiful enough.

I hate the cemetery.

I hate the drive there, along country roads where dust-covered utes with bull bars and stickers of half-naked girls fly past, the drivers giving the finger even when you're already pushing the speed limit. The rules still apply to you even when no one else is around, dickhead.

I hate the fact it deceives you; that at first glance you might think it's just a bit of parkland. People think this is nicer than towering headstones and wrought-iron gates, and while it's true a lawn cemetery would be a poor setting for a horror film, the pain of watching a coffin getting lowered into the ground is the same, regardless of where you're standing.

I hate that they have pretty names for different sections. The Rose Garden. Lorikeet Lane. As though they think they can trick you into forgetting it's a fucking depressing place.

I hate she is down there, nothing but a corpse. Her beautiful skin wasted away. Those green eyes hollowed out. If I could have a do-over, I wouldn't agree to put her down there in the dirt. I would've chosen a cremation and taken her somewhere beautiful—nearly as beautiful as her—and let her fly out into the horizon, mixing with the sunrise, the tall grasses, the salty air, the swirling water. Although, of course, if I had a do-over, she wouldn't be there at all.

But mostly, I hate it's my fault.

Lottie

1/25

MY FLAT SMELLS of fish.

It intensifies in the heat and in the middle of the day when the sun is at its strongest, but even on autumn nights like this one, when the weather starts cooling down, it still lingers. It settles into the mottled grey carpet and buries into my clothes. Sometimes I detect it clinging to my hair like a bad shampoo.

It's just one of the joys of living above a fish and chip shop. There's no yard, but there's a small landing out the back with some narrow, rickety stairs that lead down to the rear of the shop and a large car park beyond.

Early every morning, they bring the fish in white Styrofoam boxes to be scaled and filleted. If I stand at my kitchen window, I can see them below, wearing heavy gumboots and vinyl aprons, fish guts splattering onto the concrete. Once finished, they hose the area clean, and the smell of blood and innards is replaced with bleach mingled with cigarette smoke, as it becomes an unofficial break room.

I wasn't exactly in a position to be picky.

It's a private rental. My budget was impossibly tight, and it turns out not many landlords are willing to rent their investment property to a pregnant teenager. When I stumbled across the listing, miraculously within my price range, I was convinced it would be snapped up before I even made the call, but luckily a pokey one-bedroom flat directly above a fish and chip shop isn't that highly sought-after.

That, or not many people are searching for rentals on community noticeboards.

The owner was a waddling elderly woman who had been left in charge of her late husband's property portfolio and didn't have the knowledge or the skills to maintain it to regulation standards.

She barely glanced at my growing belly that I'd tried (and failed) to hide. 'I don't care about your story,' she said sternly, 'but I want to be clear: it's being rented as is.' My eyes travelled to the yellow water stains on the ceiling, the carpet rippled and lifting in the corners, the bathroom door missing a doorknob. 'I don't want any dramas. Understood?'

I understood.

Really, it's not so bad.

I've always dreamed of living at the beach, and although the smell is different—too much fish, not enough salty air—if I close my eyes, I can almost trick myself and pretend I'm there.

Though sometimes I worry the fish odour lingers on me. In the shower, I scrub myself furiously, obsessively, but the minute I step out it hits me again. Attaching itself to me, weaving into my hair and threading through my clothes.

Can everyone smell it on me when I walk past?

It's bittersweet when Frank shuts up the shop at nine p.m. and goes home. The hum of machines and the constant activity below evaporates. The customers that mill downstairs and the office workers from the nearby buildings go back to their houses in the surrounding suburbs. The traffic goes from a heavy flow to a light trickle to nothing.

It becomes a ghost town.

All the busyness from the day only serves to accentuate the stillness at night. The absolute loneliness of it makes me jittery, and the distant wail of sirens coming from the police station up on the hill does nothing to ease my paranoia.

Before bed each night, I walk around the flat and check everything. First, I flick off all the switches. I'm scared of fires, and I heard it saves on electricity. There are heavy iron bars across the front door and on the windows, so next I pull at them all in turn, testing their strength. They don't budge. I rattle the front door to make sure it's locked. I know it is—I checked as soon as the sun went down—but you can never be too sure. The last thing I do is turn off the lights.

In the dark, I go to the kitchen sink and get myself a glass of water.

The kitchen overlooks the small landing and the deserted car park. Dark bitumen stretches out like a smooth, black ocean on a windless night. The smell of fish adds to the illusion, and I close my eyes for a moment, pretending I live somewhere else. My mind conjures an image of a charming beach shack high on a hill and overlooking the sea instead of asphalt, rickety stairs leading to an alcove of powdery sand instead of concrete. I'm surprised by how realistic it feels.

I open my eyes and see two shadows gliding along the water— no, through the car park—moving quickly towards my flat. When I first moved in, Frank had come upstairs with a box of crispy scallops, crab sticks and chips as a welcome gift. 'Just make sure you lock your door at night,' he'd said, almost as an afterthought. 'There's a lot of break-ins around here.'

Panic surges through me and I become a statue, frozen with my glass halfway to my lips, blood pounding in my ears. It's so loud I feel certain they will hear it, or that it will wake Coral and they'll come to investigate. But the shadows don't turn towards my stairs. Instead, they continue on towards the little alleyway between the fish and chip shop and the hairdresser next door.

It takes a moment before I'm released from whatever Narni-an-witch magic hit me and can move again. With shaking hands, I lower the glass to the sink. I'm not thirsty anymore, the adrenaline has pushed the need for everything else from my mind.

I can hear them. Sniggering. Grunting. Moving about below. My phone is on the counter beside me, and I grab for it, gripping it tightly like a tiny cricket bat, as I creep towards the window that overlooks the alleyway. Cautiously, I peer out into the darkness below.

It takes my eyes a minute to adjust. A figure is pressed against the bricks and a taller, bulkier figure is thrusting behind. The grunts turn into groans, and I feel heat wash over me as I realise they are not breaking in, not spraying graffiti. It's just two people fucking.

Sheepishly, I back away from the window, the panic draining from my body as quickly as it came, leaving me exhausted. The feeling of being hyperalert, like a deer or rabbit, isn't a new one to me, but I thought it was a childhood demon. I'd hoped moving out on my own—being independent—would make it dissipate, but fear is a shapeshifter. Instead of mythical monsters lurking in dark corners of the room, it has contorted into something worse.

Someone breaking in.

My phone out of reach or dead.

No one nearby to hear my scream.

No one to help.

Real life, I've realised, is far more terrifying than anything my younger self conjured.

I recheck the front door again. Just to be sure.

In the bedroom, I move slowly so as not to wake Coral.

It doesn't have much in it. No wardrobe, only a cheap portable clothes rack, which sits beside the window. In the corner of the room is a mattress I got off Gumtree. Just the mattress—no frame. The ad said it was barely used and had only been in the spare room, but there's a slight tang that lingers no matter how many times I douse it in baking soda. Mum had said I could take my old single bed—the one with white metal tubing I'd been sleeping in my whole childhood—but in a moment of optimism or stupidity, or both, I declined. I had plans to buy a new bedroom suite—a timber-framed queen bed and matching furniture in the hope of tricking myself into feeling more like a competent adult. I'd managed to save a decent amount from my part-time job. Enough to buy a cheap car or take a skiing holiday. Definitely enough to give me a false sense of security. I had grossly underestimated the cost of just surviving.

I'd thought furnishing the flat would be a montage-worthy shopping spree, but it turns out it takes a long time to get all the things you need to make a home. The bond alone took most of my savings. The fridge took the rest. It's a slow process, collecting things like a bowerbird: a spatula added to the grocery shop one week, a picture book picked up at the second-hand store another. Then there are the things you forget are important—like a can opener—until you're trying to break into a tin of tuna with a paring knife. When I'm really good with my money and save for a while, I'm able to get something more substantial, like a toaster or frypan.

Coral is a small blob in the middle of the mattress. Her hands are balled into fists, and a dummy presses against her cheek. I slip in under the covers, careful to move slowly.

She doesn't have a cot, but she wouldn't like it anyway. The only time she sleeps for a decent amount of time is when she's in my arms or lying on my chest. A cot's an unnecessary expense.

People talk about money stretching, money growing, money working for you. It's as though their money heads off each morning, joining the peak hour rush with a suitcase in its hand and a bounce in its step. But to me, money seems to dart and scurry. Elusive and slippery like a prey animal. Hard to catch and harder to hold onto. Just when you think you have it, it dashes past, out of reach, and is gone.

I didn't know how to write a budget when I first moved out—it isn't something they teach you in school—but I've learnt quickly.

Now, I record everything in a blue-lined book, with the pages folded into neat margins that would've made my maths teachers proud. I write down every expense—rent, electricity, water, groceries, phone bill, bus and train fares, doctors' visits—and calculate the fortnightly amount to be set aside for each category. For fixed expenses it's easy, but for variables, I set myself a strict limit. This ensures I don't overspend on groceries, leaving me without enough to pay rent. On another page, I track all my purchases right down to the 50¢ book from Vinnies and the impromptu bottle of soft drink and subtract it from the total in my account. Of course, I could just log in and check the banking app, but I find writing it out keeps me accountable. Plus, it's handy to have a record when I run out of phone data. Right now, I have $25.42. But knowing doesn't help much. No matter how long I stare at the numbers, I can't make more money appear.

It's been nearly eight months, but the flat still has a hollow feel to it, like the robotic fish I got for my birthday instead of the puppy I'd begged my parents for. I try to be optimistic and focus on the things I do have, but it's hard sometimes when the empty spaces seem to command attention just as loudly. Photo frames or candles would make a difference. Those unnecessary extras that people buy to fill a space, to make it feel more homely. Maybe some nice indoor plants.

I add them to the list.

Can opener.
Photo frames.
Candles.
Plants.

I TIP OATS into a measuring cup for our breakfast. Coral has been eyeing my food for months now, but I've only recently been game enough to start her on solids. Before I gave them to her the first time, I borrowed some books from the library. I read about how much food to offer and what kind of foods to start with. There was a list of things you should wait to introduce in case of allergies: nuts, eggs, seafood, honey. And they said you need to keep calm about gagging. You're meant to give them space to sort it out first and only intervene if they start turning blue.

I put it off for as long as I could, but it turns out Coral loves solids. The taste of everything, the independence of it, the mess.

Especially the mess.

The last time I took her to the baby clinic to be weighed, the nurse had seemed impressed with everything she was eating.

'And you prepare all her meals yourself?' She was new, just filling in while the regular woman was overseas, and had a thoroughness the other lacked.

When I'd told her that yes, I enjoy cooking, she'd seemed surprised. 'I have a son close to your age,' she'd said, 'and he can't even fry an egg. Your parents must've taught you well.'

I couldn't help but bristle at that.

Carefully, I tip the oats into a saucepan with water and a scoop of powdered milk while Coral lies at my feet, chewing on a spatula. She can sit up, but not for long before she topples sideways. Wherever we go in the flat, a pillow goes too.

The porridge begins bubbling, big thick bubbles. Witches soup—or wombat stew—depending on whether you grew up with Roald Dahl or Marcia Vaughan. As I'm stirring, I notice my phone on the kitchen counter light up with an incoming call. Out of habit, I check who it is, even though there's really only one person who ever rings me.

I pretend to myself that I don't hear it.

I have to be in the right kind of mood to deal with my mother.

Once the porridge has become suitably gluggy, I pull it from the stovetop and tip it into the bowls on the counter. It drips out tentatively at first, then all at once. I sprinkle a teaspoon of sugar on mine and crush a couple of raspberries into Coral's. Berries are too expensive to justify for myself, but I don't want Coral to miss out.

Her porridge turns pastel pink.

It takes me a while to get organised and out of the house. Not in the practical way you're probably imagining—packing spare clothes, nappies, a change mat, folding up the pram and lugging it down the stairs —although you're right, that does make it hard too. But just in building up the courage to be around people, with their endless opinions and judgements. I feel their eyes on me constantly, weighing me down with their stares. It's crushing. I often have the feeling of the air being slowly squeezed from my lungs. Before Coral was born, it was foreign to me, feeling that way: watched.

I'd always been a chameleon.

At school, I blended in. I played sport, but only when it was mandatory and usually in the B or C team. I wasn't in the band or any kind of club. I wasn't a trendsetter that other kids watched to work out which shoes to wear. I wasn't the class clown or the troubled kid who spoke back to teachers. Nor uncool enough that people would go out of their way to avoid me. I got good grades—great grades really, but never quite good enough to be top of the class and receive the academic award at the end of the year.

No one dreams of being mediocre, but there's a safety to it.

I used to wonder what it would take for them to notice me. I fantasised about being famous, having people gossip about me or turn to watch as I walked down the street. Who knew all it took was having a baby a decade earlier than expected?

I don't have a lot of clothes to choose from, but I put them all on before I finally decide on light jeans and a white t-shirt. I try out three different styles for my hair, before twisting it into an unobtrusive bun.

Since having Coral, I've changed how I dress. I got rid of anything pink, anything with bold logos or cartoons, anything too short or low-cut. Less teenage girl. More competent adult.

Now, all my clothes are plain. Simple. Sensible. Neutral colours.

Just blending in.

Outside, it's colder than I expected.

I leave Coral upstairs on her play mat and lug the pram down the stairs. There are a couple of middle-aged guys sitting out the back of the fish shop on plastic milk crates, smoking and laughing. I don't think they work for Frank; a lot of workers from nearby shops congregate here for their breaks.

The balding one is showing the fat one something on his phone but stops as he sees me. They both turn and watch me struggle, the pram bumping loudly against each step.

'Need a hand?' one calls out.

The other sniggers.

I push my shoulders back. 'I'm fine, thanks.' My voice is confident, assertive.

Not at all how I feel.

I hear Coral begin to cry and run back upstairs. That minute I was out of her sight was a minute too long. When I pick her up her fist latches firmly to the neck of my shirt as though she's worried I'll disappear if she isn't tethered to me.

Back downstairs, the men are still watching as I bend over the pram to strap her in. I try to hurry, but the plastic clip gets caught in the wool of her jacket. I force myself to slow down. Breathe. Do it properly.

'How old are you, love?'

I put my head down and turn the pram towards the alleyway, pretending I don't hear him. A used condom lies discarded in the middle of the path, and I push the pram around it and out onto the street.

Traffic noise and chilled wind assaults me, and I reach into the pram and pull Coral's blanket up around her. Snug as a bug in a rug. I wish I'd worn a jacket, but the only one I own is still damp—I should've thought of that before I washed it.

I may not have many jackets, but Coral is not lacking in blankets. When she was born, there wasn't any help or support or even many visits, but among the gifts were seven blankets in various shades of pink and five rattles—four of which were identical and three that are now lost. Coral loves tossing things out of her pram. In protest, I imagine, at not being carried.

By the time I reach the bus stop, my hair is falling out of the bun and my lips and hands feel dry. I wish I had some hand lotion.

Coral starts crying. I lift her out of the pram and she immediately quietens.

Before I've had time to catch my breath, the bus rounds the corner, pulling up alarmingly fast and a fraction too far from the kerb. The doors whoosh open.

Balancing Coral on my hip, I step into the bus and try to pull the pram after me with my spare hand.

'Need some help?' The bus driver swivels in his chair, frowning at me.

'Fine, thanks!'

I lift the handle again, but the back wheel hits the door frame and the pram crashes onto the ground. Coral starts wailing.

'Out the way, I've got it.' The bus driver is not an athletic-looking guy, but he lifts it easily, as though it isn't twelve kilos and cumbersome. Somehow, this makes me feel worse.

'Thank you,' I mutter. 'Sorry.'

He squeezes back into his seat with a nod.

A middle-aged man sitting up front looks at me darkly and checks his watch. I've put the bus back by forty seconds and he's not impressed. His feet tap the floor.

It feels hot and suddenly I'm glad I don't have a jacket. 'Sorry,' I repeat to no one in particular as I bustle into the aisle, trying to keep the pram as out of the way as possible. It lightly bumps a woman's shoe. 'Sorry.'

I can't help apologising. For making the glowering man a minute late. For being unable to lift the pram onto the bus. For not having a licence and needing to rely on public transport in the first place instead of being able to drive Coral around in a cushy, air-conditioned car.

For existing.

The woman across the desk from me has an angular face, black hair cut into a short bob, and a blunt fringe sliced across her forehead. Everything about her is sharp with hard edges, and she studies me from over the top of her computer monitor with an expression of distaste, even though it's her who was running fifty-five minutes behind schedule.

Fifty-five minutes, on top of a twelve-minute walk and a forty-two-minute bus journey.

'I'll just bring up your file.'

I nod and smile at her. She doesn't smile back.

'So, you dropped out of school at sixteen when you fell pregnant?'

Before I can say anything, she powers on.

'And you're now seventeen, a single mother with no high-school certificate, no qualifications. Do you have any career plans?'

I sit up a little straighter, blinking at her.

The letter I received a couple of weeks back had sounded supportive. It had the appointment details listed and a bit about the program, which was for single parents with babies six months and older, to help with planning for the future. It's mandated, of course, as so many government programs are, but the positive stories of mothers now working in their dream jobs sounded promising. I'd been looking forward to the appointment. I'd thought it would be like going to see a career counsellor, someone who would help me sort out all the puzzle pieces of my life and arrange them so they were easier to put together—corner pieces over here, edges over there, blues together, greens piled here. I didn't want someone to do it for me, but I thought they might be able to help me make sense of it all. Tell me what the end picture is supposed to look like, at least.

I'm beginning to think I may have been mistaken.

Impatiently, she strums her long, manicured nails on the table, waiting for an answer. Still, something in me wants to impress this woman in her polka-dot blouse and patent-leather ballet flats, a photo of a curly-haired dog on her desk. I know what she's thinking—that I'm useless, a drain on society.

I want to prove her wrong, be more than a bunch of red crosses on paper.

'I've been applying for jobs—'

'Unsuccessfully, I gather.'

It's not a question.

'It's just there's not a lot that fits…Coral's only six months old. She's still being breastfed, so I can't really do long shifts and—'

She holds up her hand to silence me. 'Breastfeeding doesn't mean you can't work. You can pump during breaks or supplement with formula. It's important not to limit yourself. Have you got any work experience?'

'I worked in hospitality for a couple of years before she was born. At a cafe.'

Coral is bored of the few toys I brought along and is done with the rusk she's been sucking on. I jiggle her on my knee as she begins whining and pawing at my shirt.

'Have you tried applying for hospitality jobs again?'

I had.

In fact, recently I'd been offered a job interview and I'd hired a babysitter from the internet to watch Coral while I went. The girl who turned up was around my age, but I'd barely made it to the bus stop before I had a call to come back. Coral was hysterical and so was the girl. She'd ignored my request for more babysitting the following week, the day care centres I enquired at were all full, and the next babysitter I booked didn't even turn up.

'I have, but I have no one to watch Coral and—'

The woman holds up her long fingers, counting. 'There are day care centres, family, friends, babysitters. Dear me, you're going to need to work on your problem-solving skills if you want to turn your life around and make something of yourself. Have you considered studying? Having a qualification would really open up your options, so it'd be a good idea to get started as soon as you can.'

'I'm not really sure what—'

She looks bored. 'Yes, that's really for you to sort out. We're here to help you get a job, not decide your direction in life. There are plenty of tests online to help you work out what careers would suit. But do be realistic. There's no sense in following your passion if there are no jobs available at the end. A short course with good job prospects would be best.'

I feel my eyes prickling but continue to nod, to smile. The appointment is going too fast, rushing ahead of me, and I can't catch up, can't seem to glean anything worthwhile from it.

At the same time, not fast enough.

'I encourage you to think about something to study, and we can discuss it at our next appointment in a fortnight.'

She ticks something off in the notepad beside her with a satisfied grin and turns back to the computer, typing rapidly. Her acrylics are impossibly long, ending in a sharp point and painted a glittery gold. I look down at my own hands, nail-bitten and childlike.

'Socialising can be another good way to get contacts, which can lead to jobs. Are you taking your baby to any activities?'

'Not at the moment.'

She purses her lips as though she is not surprised at all. It bothers me that she presumes I wouldn't have Coral in activities.

It bothers me even more that she's right.

'We go out most days,' I add desperately. 'To parks or the library. And I do activities with her at home too—'

But it's as though I haven't spoken.

'Committing to getting out once a week and attending an activity would be a start. Something structured.'

Her watch buzzes and she glances at it, scrolling to read a message on her wrist. I think of all my trips to the library just for an hour of free internet, and I'm hit by the realisation that this woman will never truly see me. I want to tell her I could cook dinner before I knew my times tables. That before having Coral, I worked most afternoons and all weekend while averaging A's. That I'm trying my absolute best.

But it doesn't matter what I say. Her opinion of me is set.

It was set before I walked through the sliding glass doors.

She gets out a piece of paper and begins crossing things off it with a thin black pen. 'Because your baby is only six months old, you won't be able to do some of these, but there's still plenty of options. You could do swimming lessons, playgroup or baby sensory classes. What do you think?'

I hesitate, wary of the costs. I don't have room in my budget for swimming lessons or sensory classes, but I don't want to tell her that. Her satisfaction would crush me.

Coral starts crying, loud and frustrated. I reach down into the pram and grab her another rusk from the packet, willing her to be patient for just a bit longer. Just five minutes until I can get out of here. But Coral is done. With a wail she throws the rusk and it bounces off the woman's shiny shoe.

'I'm sorry,' I begin, but her face is closed off and unamused.

'You'll have to pick something for us to sign off on your plan.' She's impatient now, and she taps at the piece of paper in front of her. 'To demonstrate compliance.'

Outside, I feed Coral while leaning against a tall garden bed. Across from me is a middle-aged woman wearing a tight, low-cut dress and smoking. Coral pulls back suddenly, exposing my nipple and the woman gives me a disgusted look, but I'm too drained to care.

I'd signed something, an agreement of some type, hurriedly and without paying much attention. I'd been shown an app I'd need to update weekly to demonstrate compliance. There was something about demerit points. Something about privacy. Something about payment suspensions. The information was repeated on loose papers, now stuffed down the bottom of the pram between spare jumpsuits and nappies. Another appointment had been booked for two weeks' time.

I don't know what I'd expected, but not that. Instead of helping me make sense of the puzzle, she'd lifted each piece up one by one, inspected them critically, and put them back exactly where they were. My version of reality was simply too far removed from hers.

I feel like crying but blink it away rapidly, instead focusing on the clouds, low and dark in the sky. If I rush to the bus stop, I might just beat the downpour of rain.

Can opener.
Photo frames.
Candles.
Plants.
A jacket.
Hand lotion.
A driver's licence.
A car.

THERE'S NO LAUNDRY. Instead, the bathroom has a long vanity, with space underneath for a front-loader washing machine, or maybe even one of those combination types that wash and dry in one go. A few months back, I found someone online selling theirs—not the fancy dual type—for fifty dollars, and they offered to drop it off for an extra ten. It looked almost brand new, not a mark on it, but the first time I turned it on water leaked all over the floor and I had to use every towel I owned to mop it up.

The second time was the same.

And just to be sure, the third.

I had to go back to washing our clothes in the bathtub, and now it sits in the corner mocking me. I can't carry it back down the stairs. I can't use it. So instead, I repurposed it as an expensive medicine cabinet, since Coral can't get into it, and there isn't much storage in the flat.

When you don't own much, everything you have has to work extra hard. A candle isn't just a pretty trinket that people gift you when they run out of present ideas. It's also a perfume for the house, a door holder if it's big enough, a paperweight. You can use the wax on squeaky door hinges, to fix frayed shoelaces or help make sticky zippers glide.

If things are dire enough, a candle is your light.

The bathtub moonlights as a washing machine or a pool on hot days.

Pots and pans double as toys.

A saucepan as a kettle.

An oven as a toaster. Or a microwave.

Used teabags become eye patches or a body scrub for the bath.

Shoes wear out quicker when you can't alternate between as many pairs. Clothes fade faster. I've become an expert at removing stains from Coral's jumpsuits and mending small holes. I've learnt to tighten the screws on the frypan handle when it gets loose and how to glue the soles back onto shoes when they start coming apart.

All our things still look nice, but it's a constant battle.

Washing clothes bent over the bathtub is time-consuming and laborious, but I try to make it into a calming activity. Watching the bubbles form, clumping together and popping. The clothes swirling and tangling, a kaleidoscope of colour. My hands running back and forth through the water, making gentle waves.

I tell myself that some people do daily yoga or morning meditation, and that hand-washing our clothes in the bath is somehow equivalent.

My own—somewhat inferior—version of mindfulness.

Out on the landing, right where the morning sun hits, I take the pile of wet clothes and begin pegging them up on the clothes horse. There was a washing line in the corner of the balcony when I first moved in, but when I tried to use it, it turned to dust in my fingers, so I bought the clothes horse from the cheap shop down the road. It's small, flimsy and prone to toppling over if I don't balance it perfectly, but it does the job.

Coral sits beside me, playing with pegs, a pillow behind her just in case. She reaches towards a nearby terracotta pot, pressing her fingers into the hard dirt. The pots were here when we moved in, the plants all long dead. One day, I'd love to buy something to plant in them. Some flowers maybe, or vegetable seeds. Something to make the balcony a bit more appealing.

Below, there is noise and movement as Frank gets back from the fish markets. His truck beeps as it reverses into the small space behind the shop, and he and another man begin to unload the boxes. I haven't had breakfast yet, and the smell of fish is overpowering on an empty stomach.

I do up the last bib, in the very corner, and pick up Coral before she can put her dirt-covered fingers into her mouth. The clothes hanging from the frame look like a colourful cubby house, and I imagine Coral in a year's time, trying to play in it.

How much can Coral's imagination grow, I wonder, stuck in this small flat like a goldfish in a tiny bowl. The walls are too close. There's no yard to run around in. No dirt for making mud pies or grass to tickle her feet. No room for a swing set, trampoline, or pet to keep her company.

When she's older, I'll buy her a guinea pig or a budgie. Whatever we can sneak into our rental.

Maybe even a dog? Something small, like a Maltese or a chihuahua.

Whatever she wants.

At least once a day, I try to get out of the flat. It doesn't matter where I go. Down the hill to have a drink at the cafe, even just downstairs to Frank's shop to watch the people coming and going. Crawling just beneath my skin is this irrational—or perhaps not so irrational—fear that if I don't push myself out there into the world as often as I can, I might just settle down within these walls where it's familiar and safe and stay here forever.

Just like Mum.

There's a park down the hill, within walking distance. I've gone past it on the bus and made a mental note to go, but always end up making excuses not to. It's too windy, too hot, too cold, too cloudy, too close to Coral's nap time, too close to dinner. But really, there is only one reason I avoid it —it's too busy.

Is that how it all started for her?

It's late afternoon by the time Coral and I arrive at the park, and although there are still a lot of families scattered around, there's a sense of calm in the air. The type of sleepy contentedness that people get when they've finished eating and the kids are finally slowing down. That beautiful lull before the next burst of activity hits.

Coral sits in the sandpit, scooping up handfuls of sand and letting it rain down in front of her eyes. She's mesmerised.

Everyone here, I begin to realise, is part of a couple or a group. I suppose, because it is a Saturday afternoon and that's the kind of thing normal families do on weekends—spend time together. I try not to focus on it, but it's like walking past a bakery window when you haven't eaten all day. They all seem like they are having a great time watching the kids play, taking photos, talking with animated hands, laughing.

I smile at Coral. 'How fun is the sand?'

She reaches towards some brightly coloured beach toys that have been temporarily discarded by a group of kids, but I hand her a little stick instead, as a makeshift shovel. It gets tossed aside. Instead, she watches with fascination as the kids return, carrying buckets of water, and begin work on a sandcastle. They sit together in a circle helping each other dig out a moat and decorating the turrets with leaves and gum nuts—a little construction team at work.

Coral doesn't take her eyes off them. When one of the girls notices and waves in her direction, she twists away, desperately grabbing at my shirt, trying to get to safety.

Maybe the government woman was right—socialising will be good for both of us. Coral needs a chance to be around other babies, and it will give me the opportunity to meet some other parents. We're meant to start playgroup next week. The thought of it makes my heart start beating faster, but I try to trick myself into thinking it's from excitement.

Can opener.
Photo frames.
Candles.
Plants.
A jacket.
Hand lotion.
A driver's licence.
A car.
Flowers or vegetable seeds.
A pet.
Beach toys.

THE WALK TO the library isn't too bad. It's a few blocks away, but it's mainly flat. An easy walk.

I've packed the books to return in the bottom of the pram, and Coral is happily sucking on a pouch of vanilla yoghurt. There's a pedestrian crossing at the top of the hill, but it's still about fifty metres away, so instead I stand in front of the fish and chip shop and wait for a break in the traffic.

Across the road, there's a park. No playground. Just a large statue dedicated to the Anzacs and a homeless man who sleeps on a bench, a plastic bag of belongings at his feet. I've watched from my bedroom window as the police approach him and move him on, but he always seems to return.

It's here the footpath splits into two: one running alongside the road, the other winding through the gardens. I scan around me but the only sign of him is his bag of possessions, so I decide to take the scenic route.

It's a nice park, really. Shady trees and bright flowers in neat garden beds. I imagine when Coral gets more mobile she'll like running around out here. And it's just across the road, almost like an extended yard.

As I pass by the seat, I glance at his things bundled underneath. It's a big space. Perhaps I could avoid him.

As soon as the glass doors of the library swish open and I step inside, a sense of calm washes over me. I don't know if it's the soft silence after the walk along busy streets, the computers lined up with free wi-fi, the chilled water station in the corner, or the books themselves on anything you could dream of. Everyone at the library is lost in their own thoughts and their own projects. No one looks up as I stop the pram by the chute in the wall and feed books into it, one at a time. No one pays attention as I walk past the front desk and head towards the kids' corner at the back.

The kids' section is decorated like a forest. There are round cushions made to look like toadstools scattered on the floor, a canopy of painted leaves suspended in a fishing net hung from the ceiling, and stuffed animals hidden throughout the bookshelves: bears, rabbits, deer.

I set up Coral beside a spare computer in a little nest of stuffed toys and thick cardboard books. The internet here is slow and limited to an hour, but it's free. When I first moved out of home, I ran out of data within days. On my next top-up, it lasted a week. Now, I can get it to stretch until the end of the month. Just. If I use it sparingly.

I type in my library card number, and a timer starts in the corner of the screen. 59 minutes and 59 seconds.

58 seconds.

57.

Watching the numbers tick down always stirs an irrational panic inside me—some kind of Pavlovian reaction learnt from school exams. But as much as Coral loves it here, she will only lie happily beside me for fifteen minutes max, and then maybe a further fifteen minutes on my lap if I'm lucky.

I never use the whole hour.

Using the chunky mouse, I navigate to the search engine and double-click to open. The cursor blinks in the search bar, endless possibilities awaiting. But my fingers hesitate on the keyboard.

71

Finally, I search for 'personality test'. Then 'personality test + career'.

The results are endless, so I choose one at random.

You have a free afternoon. Would you rather, a) have a picnic, b) read a book, c) catch up on some housework, d) party with friends, e) watch a movie.

It's quite a lengthy test, and I struggle not to overanalyse what they're looking for in each question. Will my answer to the sleep habits question mean they suggest a job that involves shift work? If I tick *yes* to 'prefer hanging out with children' (Coral) does that mean it'll automatically suggest being a teacher? Is that how simple it is?

It's not that I'm completely without interests, but I wasn't allowed to try dozens of different extracurricular activities to see what stuck, like my friends were. And Mum seemed to see very little value in anything I enjoyed. I remember bringing home a painting from school once and telling her I wanted to be an artist.

'Oh, please don't,' she'd said with a venom I'd not expected. 'You don't want to spend years slaving away for nothing.'

In the end, it doesn't matter. I'm down to the last few questions when the mouse freezes.

I wait patiently.

Impatiently.

I click the mouse.

Press random keys on the keyboard. A combination of keys.

Nothing.

Eventually, one of the librarians sees me and restarts the whole computer. 'Sorry about that,' she says as it jolts back to life. 'That computer can be a bit unreliable. I hope you weren't in the middle of anything important?'

'No,' I say. 'Nothing important.'

I try not to think of it as a sign.

Soon after my sixteenth birthday, I went to see a psychic. It wasn't planned or anything. I was at some markets with Lionel and Aisha, and we just so happened to walk past his tent.

It was Lionel's idea. His parents were going through a divorce, and everything was up in the air—if they were going to keep or sell the house, which one would move out, who he'd live with. Lionel's easygoing nature had turned anxious and edgy seemingly overnight. 'I want to know what's going to happen,' he said. 'Even just a hint.'

Aisha had refused. She had her future mapped out and didn't want to risk anything that might create uncertainty, so I'd agreed to join him.

The guy sitting behind the table was younger and more typical-looking than I'd expected. I guess it was narrow-minded of me, but I'd anticipated unruly hair, linen clothes and an amber necklace, maybe even a beard, but he was plain and unadorned.

He looked like someone who would sell life insurance.

'He doesn't look like a psychic,' I muttered.

Lionel didn't share my doubts. 'That's proof he must be good. He doesn't feel the need to appear a certain way. If you were a fraud, wouldn't you go out of your way to look the part?'

'I guess?'

'What's the worst that could happen?'

Even the table was bare. A purple tie-dye tablecloth would've helped, or a collection of crystals.

His name was Marcus. Marcus the Psychic. But despite my scepticism Marcus had known things.

Immediately, he saw the upheaval and confusion in Lionel's life and how he was going through a time of major change. He told Lionel the house would be sold. Not immediately—it would take at least a year. He could tell Lionel was an Aquarius and described him as creative, open-minded and sensitive. Lionel cried when he told him things would eventually settle down and he would find his place in the world.

When it was my turn, he described me as being lonely and disconnected from my parents; an outsider in my own house. 'You're determined and will achieve anything you set your mind to,' he said, staring deep into my eyes.

Most excitingly though, I would fall in love within the year.

I blurted it out to Mum as soon as I got home. The elation—
that overwhelming feeling of being understood—was bubbling
away inside me, and I needed to share it.

'You can't be serious, Lottie?'

I was filled with indignation. *This* was the disconnect he had
seen. 'He knew things,' I said desperately. 'Lionel's parents are
getting divorced and he knew about it. He talked about all the
confusion in Lionel's life.'

Mum snorted. 'He's a sixteen-year-old kid. Everyone's confused at sixteen.'

'He described him as artistic and sensitive.'

'That's obvious to anyone.'

'He knew he was an Aquarius.'

'And what star sign did he say you were?'

'He didn't.'

But she was right. He'd guessed I was a Taurus when I was
really a Gemini. He said I had a sister when I really had a brother
and mentioned a family dog. When I told him we'd never owned a
dog, he said it must have meant I'd have a dog in the future.

'The thing with psychics,' Mum said, 'is it doesn't matter what
they say. People who go to them are looking for direction, any
direction. They only need to guess a handful of things and people
will make them fit. No one pays attention to all the things they
get wrong.'

Once Coral is down for the night, I spend a few hours cleaning.

I always start with the dishes from the day. I wash them in
water so hot it turns my hands red, then dry them carefully and put
them away. Next, I wipe down the bench with a spray that is meant
to smell like crisp apple but doesn't. Then I sweep the kitchen floor
and mop it. Vacuuming the carpet needs to wait for morning, as
does washing the clothes, towels and sheets. Everything else gets
done as needed: cleaning out the fridge, dusting, wiping down the
pantry shelves, emptying the bin, boiling vinegar in the kettle to

get rid of calcium build-up, scrubbing grout and cleaning the bath, bleaching the toilet, washing the windows.

Most people understand feeling a sense of satisfaction from a clean house, but it's more than that for me.

It's a feeling of safety.

A sense of control.

Before I turn out the light, I cast my eyes around, looking for anything out of place. Coral's plastic blocks could do with a wash, I decide. I don't check the time as I refill the sink. It makes no difference; I won't be able to sleep until everything is perfect.

The results from the career test—or the lack of—are niggling at me. I try to be rational, but the truth is, I was looking so forward to getting an answer that it feels like I've lost something important.

I'll have to go back to the library and try again.

My life was not going the way I had imagined and I felt alone, without a compass. Just like with Marcus the Psychic and the woman with the gold fingernails, I was hoping for guidance. The quiz could have told me anything and I would have adjusted my worldview to make it fit. I just wanted something to follow.

Can opener.
Photo frames.
Candles.
Plants.
A jacket.
Hand lotion.
A driver's licence.
A car.
Flowers or vegetable seeds.
A pet.
Beach toys.
A sense of direction.

SHE CALLED AGAIN this morning while I was vacuuming. Even though I could hear the trilling of my phone clearly, I pretended I couldn't. I already knew what she would say. There would be some small talk, followed by a complaint about how long it'd been since I'd visited. How Coral would barely remember her.

You might think I'm being unfair, not going out of my way to facilitate the relationship between Coral and her grandmother, but stop for a moment and ask yourself: if it's so important to her, why hasn't she visited me?

I couldn't tell you exactly how long it's been since I've seen Mum out of the house, but there was a time when we used to go out.

I remember a park that Mum would sometimes take us to. It was beautiful, with a playground big enough to keep Edward and me entertained for hours but small enough to be able to see its entirety from one location. There was a lake nearby, with a bike track around it, and groups of ducks that would harass people for food. Families would bring bags of bread and throw pieces into the water for the ducks to fight over, but Mum never let us, no matter how much I begged.

'Bread isn't good for ducks,' she'd say with finality. 'It pollutes their water.'

I understand now, but it's hard to care about pollution at seven.

At the time, Edward would've only been a toddler. I liked to pretend he was a wolf or some other scary creature, and I'd spend the whole time running away from him whenever he came near. Edward was too young to realise he was part of a game, but his endless energy meant he played the part perfectly.

Mum never joined in. She'd collapse under a nearby tree, physically present but completely checked out. Her eyes were always on us, but sometimes when I'd talk to her she wouldn't realise until I repeated myself loudly a second time.

I don't remember when we stopped going. No doubt our last trip to the park would've been just like any other.

Only significant in hindsight.

I'M THE FIRST to arrive. The hall where the playgroup is held is long and rectangular, set back from the road and nestled behind the little church, which sits proudly out the front. Off to the side is a two-storey house, presumably belonging to the priest? Pastor? Minister? All the buildings are painted in a matching butter-cream yellow.

Out on the road, there's a sign that reads 'TRY PRAYING INSTEAD OF TEXTING'. Only a few weeks ago, a P-plater crashed their car into the traffic lights on the corner and died instantly. The news reports said they were on their phone.

I wonder if it's in response to that.

I wonder how their family would feel seeing the billboard.

Despite it being a cold morning, the long walk from the bus stop has made me sweaty, and my shoes have rubbed blisters onto the sides of my feet. If only I'd thought to put deodorant or Band-Aids into the nappy bag, but of course everything I have is for Coral.

There is a bench seat under a tree, and I push the pram up onto the grass and walk over to it, unclipping Coral and letting her sit at my feet.

My eyes feel heavy, and I allow myself to close them for a minute. I didn't sleep well. My dreams were an endless loop of chaos—searching for things just out of reach, unable to focus my eyes or walk properly, losing my clothes, my teeth, my mind. I woke early feeling stressed and anxious.

Coral starts whining, and I lift her onto my lap for a quick feed before everyone arrives. I know the other parents would be understanding, but I'm still anxious about feeding her in front of other people. Breastfeeding tops are expensive, so I've had to make do with normal clothes, lifting them up over her head or pulling them down. It makes me feel like I'm exposing more than I should be, drawing unwanted attention in my direction.

I will her to hurry up.

Straight away, I start off on the wrong foot. The coordinator, Georgina, tells me everyone is expected to bring a five-dollar note each week. She goes on to explain that the money is used to cover the morning tea, and if enough people don't contribute she is forced to dip into her own pocket to cover the shortfall.

'I'll let it slide this once,' she says, touching me on the shoulder. But she seems annoyed.

Seven parents turn up. Eight if you include Georgina, who has two kids with her but is too busy organising and setting up toys to socialise. They are all older than me and glance my way with curiosity, but no one talks to me. It feels a lot like school.

There's a lot of comparing. One toddler is eating olives and sun-dried tomatoes.

'Such a sophisticated palate,' someone exclaims.

Another slept through the night from a few weeks old. A nine-month-old has just started walking. One of the toddlers can write their name already.

There's one dad there, a guy named Ivan, who has full custody of his daughter, and it's clear they all worship him. When he pulls out a container of grapes, sliced down the middle, there's a collective orgasm.

'My husband wouldn't even *realise* you're supposed to cut grapes,' one says.

'My husband wouldn't know what kind of food to pack!'

'Mine wouldn't even think to *bring* food.'

Ivan sits back, bathing in compliments and admiration. His mediocrity is a beacon, dazzling and shining. He's had the forethought not to let his baby starve or choke. What a guy. When he catches me watching him, he flashes a smile, mistaking me for another admirer.

'Looks like you're not the youngest anymore, Hayley,' one particularly loud woman exclaims when the conversation about milestones dies out.

Hayley doesn't look that young but still looks relieved to be passing on that particular badge.

'I feel old,' another woman chortles. She speaks in my direction but doesn't make eye contact. 'You look like you could still be at school.'

A statement, not a question.

She's wrong. Just. My class graduated last year.

I'd been invited.

Aisha offered to bring me as her date, but I couldn't imagine trying to squeeze my swollen belly into an overpriced dress and tottering around in heels. When I saw the photos online I knew I'd made the right choice. The boys who had once seemed boyish and immature were suddenly handsome in their suits, and the girls completely unrecognisable beneath hair extensions, false eyelashes and layers of makeup. They wore sparkly dresses that dipped low around their cleavage and clung tightly to their bodies before spooling around their feet.

They all looked breathtaking. I would've looked awkward and out of place among them. A talking point for all the wrong reasons.

Once the hour and a half is up, everyone walks out to the car park talking about their plans for the rest of the day. I stay back in the long shadow of the hall, crouching down and rifling aimlessly through the nappy bag. I pretend to be looking for something but I'm really just buying time until they leave. I don't want them to see me walking up the long driveway and realise I've walked here from the bus stop.

One by one, the cars begin filing out of the car park, glinting in the sun as they accelerate towards the road, their indicators flickering in the direction of their homes. I don't relax until it's just Coral and I left.

It's clear I'll never fit in here.

I'm too old and too young all at once.

When I see photos of my friends relaxing on the beach or pouting into the camera, I feel too tired and worn out to be seventeen. But these other parents will never accept me either—they don't think of me as one of them. I'm just a kid to them, playing pretend, cooking plastic vegetables over a wooden stove, wearing my mother's shoes and bouncing a rubber doll.

I don't drive.

I don't even own a car.

I don't own a house.

Or have a backyard.

Even a pet.

I don't have a partner.

Hell, I don't even have a bed frame.

That night in bed, I allow my mind to run over the events of the day.

I blink at the ceiling, Coral lying in the crook of my arm, her soft breath against my collarbone, her hand clutching the edge of my shirt. The playgroup was meant to be a way to connect with other parents and make new friends, but I feel even more lonely than before.

It wasn't meant to be this way.

I wasn't meant to be doing this alone.

Underneath my shirt, I can feel my necklace, the stone of it lying in the curve of my neck. It's only small, but expensive stones often are—the big, flashy diamonds so many girls wear are usually imitations. It hangs from a gold chain, even though I have nothing else gold. Gold seems like something for people who have their lives together.

Sometimes, it feels wrong wearing it. I've considered dramatically tossing it into a river, like in the movies or taking it to Cash Converters to see what I can get. But I just can't.

It is the prettiest thing I own.

And despite everything, part of me still misses him.

Stupidly.

I shake my head and try to block him from my thoughts. Imagine him getting squeezed to the corners of my mind, pushed outwards, towards the precipice where conscious thought ends.

I don't want to think about him—can't allow myself to— because the truth is, I don't know what to think.

What *should* I feel? What *do* I feel? How can you feel so many conflicting things at once?

Desire and admiration. *Flip.* Shame and disappointment.

Longing, so desperate it hurts. Disgust, so intense it makes you numb.

Love.

Flip.

Hate.

It's a cocktail of emotions so strong it makes me feel drunk. Fuzzy.

Suddenly, I feel so desperately alone.

Only I'm not.

I hug Coral tightly to my chest, feeling her small body against mine, grounding me.

The night is still, and the silence covers me like a blanket. No cars on the road. No one close by. Even the police station up on the hill is quieter than usual; I haven't heard any sirens tonight. Or maybe I just don't notice them anymore.

I'm not alone. I'm not.

I have her. I have her, and she's everything. As long as we're together, we'll be okay.

Flip.

Nothing will ever be okay.

I cough into the darkness just to hear the noise bounce back to me.

Can opener.
Photo frames.
Candles.
Plants.
A jacket.
Hand lotion.
A driver's licence.
A car.
Flowers or vegetable seeds.
A pet.
Beach toys.
A sense of direction.
A five-dollar note.

DO YOU REMEMBER the first time you fell in love?

Was it even love? Or was it lust? It can be so interchangeable in the beginning—impossible to tease apart.

Mum once told me it becomes clearer over time, as you add to your list of deal-breakers and separate what you want, from what you are inexplicably drawn to. That clarity comes with hindsight, and you can't always tell when you're in the middle of it.

'Don't go jumping all in with the first person you meet,' Mum said. 'Give it space. It takes time to get to know someone and even longer to know what you really want.'

She had been hoodwinked by lust. She never told me that, but she didn't need to. Her and Dad must have been happy once—surely something had driven them to marriage and two kids—but that hadn't been the case for as long as I could remember. When I cast my mind back, I can't think of a single instance when they were happy. Or even a time when they didn't seem to actively dislike one another. Most kids dread the idea of their parents getting divorced, but I often wished for it.

Mum's misery was palpable. It leaked out of her and lingered around the house, swirling and settling on everyone nearby.

I guess that's why she felt like her opinion was worth something. I guess that's why I felt like it wasn't.

Maybe that's why I didn't tell her about Heath. Her own life had made her cynical about love and happiness, and I was giddy with oxytocin. I didn't want her regret to touch us. Just because she'd been blinded when she met Dad didn't mean the same would happen to me.

That's the thing about miserable people: they can't help but shove their own feelings onto everyone around them and I knew she'd find something negative to latch onto. The age gap between us—which wasn't even that extreme, really—or the fact he was my boss.

But Heath was different.

No one had ever looked at me the way he did: as though I were something precious and rare. When I talked, he stopped whatever he was doing and listened, no matter how irrelevant or minor the subject was.

Heath saw me.

And more than that, he cared.

Right from the beginning, even before we were anything more, Heath was generous towards me. It was small, innocuous things at first. A hot chocolate in the morning. A blueberry muffin. A bottle of lemonade taken from the fridge. Since it came from his cafe, it barely seemed like anything at all. But when he realised my journey home from work involved not only catching a bus but also walking along quiet country roads on the cusp of darkness, he offered to drive me home. It made sense—he lived in my direction anyway.

Before long, all my shifts were on the close.

It was during those drives, as the sky slipped from blue, to pink, to orange, to black, that we evolved into something more. There's something about that time—the delicate transition between day and night—that suspends reality.

I thought my friends would be more accepting.

'What the hell?'

Aisha's reaction when I told her what was happening, blushing and dazed the next day before the morning bell, was not what I'd expected. I'd spent all night walking around in a drunk-like state, tripping over my feet and forgetting what I was doing.

It had started the same way as most other drives, with us talking, his eyes on the road and his hand resting casually on my knee. As though there was nothing odd about it. Only this time, he'd let it slip up my leg, ever so slightly. At first I thought I'd imagined it.

Keep talking.

As we spoke about our plans for the weekend, his hand drifted up my thigh. He was going up the coast to visit a friend. I had an English essay to write.

Act normal.

Conversation stopped altogether as his hand slid under my skirt. The sun ducked behind the trees, averting its eyes. On the radio, there was an ad for health insurance.

Breathe.

He pulled the car off to the side of the road.

'I think about you a lot.' His voice was smooth, but his eyes were intense.

The truth was, I'd thought about him too. At night, in my single bed down the far end of the house, I would slide my hand between my legs and imagine him inside me. Imagine how it must feel to have someone love you so much they just had to have all of you.

I looked away, at the bright dials on the dashboard, the time in square lights: 5:43.

'Don't be embarrassed.' Heath put one hand under my chin and turned my face towards him, while his fingers slipped into my underwear.

'You're beautiful, Lottie. Inside and out.'

I'd felt seen.

'Shouldn't you report him or something?' Aisha was sitting cross-legged beside me, picking her nails—what was left of them, at least.

'For what?'

'I don't know …' Her voice faded away. 'It just seems creepy.'

But she didn't understand. He wasn't a creep. He was Heath.

'We have a connection.'

Aisha shook her head. 'He's your boss and, like, a billion years old.'

'He's only thirty.'

For the rest of the day, I was angry with her. She was supposed to be my best friend. She'd taught me how to use a tampon when I got my first period at school. We'd googled how to give blowjobs during a sleepy history lesson. But she didn't understand this. And if she didn't, no one would.

Was it really that hard to believe he might just like me for me?

THE PHONE NEARLY rings out before it is answered. There's the sound of something scratching across the speaker, music in the background.

'Hello?'

'Hey—'

'Hello, Lottie? Sorry, hold on a minute. I'll try and connect you to the car.'

Aisha's voice is breathless, distracted. I try not to take it personally, but ever since Coral things haven't felt quite the same. I tell myself she's just busy with her life in the same way I'm busy with mine, but even though she's never said anything unsupportive I can't help but feel paranoid that she's judging me. Stacking up her choices against mine. Comparing their value.

'Okay. I should have you now.'

But still, I miss her.

'I haven't spoken to you in a while,' I say, unable to keep the edge of excitement from my voice. 'And just wanted to see how you are?'

A rapid ticking noise floods the phone.

'Oh yeah. Yeah, I'm good. Busy though. Have an assignment on the influence of Greek culture on the Romans that's due in a few days, so I've been madly working on that. Trying to get it submitted early so I'm not stressing at the last second, you know?'

'Sounds interesting. I thought you were studying art?'

'Yeah, an arts degree, but my major is ancient history.'

'Oh, right.'

'Sorry, I just thought everyone knew that.'

Before Heath, Aisha and I had talked about going to university together. I silently curse myself for the slip-up. It only highlights how little I know about that world of beautiful, old buildings seeped in prestige and expensive pieces of paper that can open doors. How much our lives have diverged.

'What about you?' Aisha says. 'What've you been up to?'

I pause, realising I hadn't planned for this question.

'Well, I've started taking Coral to a playgroup. She seems to like it, but—'

'That's great to hear, Lot, but I've got to go. I'm just meeting some friends. We'll have to catch up soon, though.'

'Yeah, definitely.'

'Okay, see ya!'

The line goes dead.

One minute and nine seconds.

89

It poured last night. I'd planned to go to the library today to return some books and use the computers to find a course that might interest me, but when I woke up it was still drizzling and overcast—the view from the barred window nothing but a wet, steely grey. No colour. No people. Just giant, heavy clouds pressing down on the rooves of nearby buildings.

Weekends are always quiet without the nearby offices open, but today, the streets are completely deserted. A dystopian city. I guess everyone's cosying up at home, playing board games, snuggling up to watch movies.

The flat feels even smaller when it's overcast, and I walk around with Coral on my hip, turning on lights, but it barely makes a difference. It's still too dark, too empty, too cold, too silent.

I plug my phone in and pick a playlist, something upbeat. Usually I avoid eating into my precious data, but I can't spend the whole day stuck inside like this with nothing but my own thoughts. It feels like being in a jail cell, barred windows and all; Coral and I, caged, pacing the perimeters. 'There,' I say to Coral, spinning her around. She laughs. See? We can still make our own fun. I waltz with her through the kitchen, and afterwards we sit on the floor and stack her newly washed blocks. I make the tower as high as I can while she watches on, chewing the corner of a long rectangular piece. When she gets bored of that, we play peek-a-boo with the bed sheets, then I read her a book from the library about a tiger, making my voice deep and raspy.

'Want another book?' I ask, but she squirms impatiently. 'Or maybe it's snack time?'

When I offer her a banana, she bats it away angrily.

'I'm trying Coral. I really am.'

In the end, I sit her in front of the kitchen cupboards and let her play with saucepans and cutlery while I mindlessly scroll on my phone. Lionel's been posting daily photos of his trip to Vanuatu: smiling on the beach, drinking cocktails, finding starfish. Travelling was something I'd dreamed of doing.

I close his profile.

Aisha's last post was over a week ago. Just a photo of a guy biting into a churro. A heart emoji underneath. A new boyfriend?

We used to tell each other everything, and I feel a tinge of jealousy that she hasn't mentioned him to me. I zoom in on his face, but there's too much motion blur.

A text pops up at the top of the screen. *You have used 85% of your data. Want to top up?*

I throw my phone to the side, out of reach.

There were many things I'd expected about having a baby, but the widening divide from my friends wasn't one of them. Aisha and Lionel had seemed supportive at first—not of the relationship, but of me. I guess we just don't have enough in common anymore. Coral lets out a cry, and I pick her up. 'It must nearly be time for your nap,' I tell her, checking my phone. For a moment, I think the screen has frozen, but no. Time is still moving along, I realise, just excruciatingly slow.

Eight forty-five.

Not even nine a.m. yet.

Each minute, each second, ticking deliberately by. Another twelve hours until I can go to bed, and this day can be over.

Tick.

Tick.

Tick.

Eventually the day draws to a close. The sun meanders over the horizon, the streetlights outside my bedroom window flicker on, and I count down the final moments until Coral's bedtime with an equal mix of impatience and guilt.

I'm propped against my pillow breastfeeding when Mum calls for the third time this week. The day has been too long and too lonely. My usual defences are down.

This time I answer.

'Finally.' Her voice sounds relieved. 'I was worried I'd have to send out a search party.'

Send out. Not search herself.

'What are you up to? I haven't caught you at a bad time?' She's in a good mood tonight, but that's not surprising. I rarely hear from her if she's not.

'Just in bed, feeding Coral. She's nearly asleep.'

Only moments before, Coral's eyes were heavy, but my voice has grabbed her attention and she studies my face as she drinks.

Mum sighs wistfully into the phone. 'You always loved your milk.'

I hate it when she does that. Pretends like things were perfect.

Like she was perfect.

She continues with a laugh, 'But my nipples didn't.'

I'm surprised by her comment. Edward had been bottle-fed and I'd always assumed the same had applied to me. 'I didn't know I was breastfed.'

'Yeah, for eighteen months. I would've loved to keep going but…you know how it is.'

I didn't.

'So, what made you stop?'

A brief pause, followed by a casual laugh. 'Oh Lottie, it was so long ago, I don't remember all the intricacies. And I don't see how it even matters now?'

She's right. It doesn't matter. But it's not the specifics I care about, it's the fact that we never seem to have a real discussion, she always deflects. Our conversations have always been surface-level, lacking any substance. When I was younger, I thought it was my age and immaturity that stopped me from truly connecting with her. But now here I was, out on my own, and she was still as evasive as ever.

There's a lull in the conversation.

'You'll need to visit again soon, Lot. It's been so long, Coral won't remember me.'

Her words are a trigger, and they swirl around in my head like a storm brewing. Dark clouds roll in. My brain buzzes with electricity. There are so many things I want to shout into the phone.

Why can't you visit me? I want to ask. *Why can't you be like other mothers?*

But when I open my mouth, they dissolve on my tongue.

Just rainclouds.

'Yeah, Mum. I will.'

Can opener.
Photo frames.
Candles.
Plants.
A jacket.
Hand lotion.
A driver's licence.
A car.
Flowers or vegetable seeds.
A pet.
Beach toys.
A sense of direction.
A five-dollar note.
Mobile data.

I GUESS I should clarify a few things. First, it's not that my mother is a bad person.

She's never *done* anything.

She's *never* done anything.

She's never done *anything*.

Which is her saving grace and her downfall simultaneously.

It's the absence of her that hurts the most.

She tries, I know she does. But not enough. And not when it counts.

II. Aperture

Tom
f/1.8

My muse. That's what Freya called her.

And I suppose she was right.

Adeline. Perched on a fallen log, lazily swatting at stray ants as they crawled up her leg. Floyd was somewhere nearby in the long grass, nothing but triangular ears and a fuzzy tail. Her camera was lying discarded on the grass between us, tossed aside. She'd told me how long she had saved up for that camera, and it surprised me to see her leave it so carelessly on the ground, the lens cap missing, no protective bag in sight. She seemed to treat her possessions with reckless disregard.

With people, she was the opposite.

She could make anyone feel like they were important. Listened to. Valued.

When we were together, in our spot by the river, the rest of the world faded away into the periphery. I could forget about everyone else. About everything.

For a moment, at least.

I picked up the camera and looked through the viewfinder. 'Can I take a photo?'

'Go for it. Good luck capturing him though. He's pretty fast.'

I heard Floyd rustling in the bushes nearby but turned the camera towards Adeline. She wore a white lace top that hung loosely off her shoulders and her hair was wrestled back into a thick ponytail, a tangled mess of red curls. The remnants of blue polish on her nails. Small silver earrings in the shape of a lock. A smattering of dirt across her knee. An ant, halfway up her arm.

At that moment Floyd propelled himself out of the bushes to lick her cheek and she screwed up her face—half disgust, half laughter. I may have taken him in, but it was Adeline he loved.

Click.

All the settings were wrong. It was overexposed by a stop or two. A rogue sun flare flashed across her forehead. Every rule of composition had been broken. The aperture was set too wide, the focus on the wrong place—the lace of her top, instead of the eye, where it should be. Technically it was a disaster, but I pocketed it and kept it in my bedside drawer.

Eventually, I learnt to master the controls: how to set the focus point, how to position the subject in the frame. The aperture was more difficult to master. A narrow aperture meant the whole photo would be sharp and in focus but at the expense of light. A wide aperture was more aesthetically pleasing but trickier to achieve—the focus point only a sliver, the background melting away to nothing. The risk with such a shallow depth of field was too much movement, from either the photographer or subject, and the focus point could land on the wrong spot.

But by playing with the aperture, eventually I was able to capture things exactly how I saw them.

Adeline in focus. Everything around her, nothing but blur.

f/2.0

THE FLOWERS ON the coffin are yellow. Even from where I'm standing in the foyer, I can see them. Bright and cheery.

I wonder who picked them.

No doubt it was because Dad drove a yellow Commodore. Never mind the only reason he bought it was because Rebekah was having trouble selling it, after baby number four came along and she needed to upgrade to a seven-seater. He was helping her out but often complained about the car—how it was too bright, too obnoxious—and regularly spoke about selling it. Buying a ute instead. Something with room in the back.

Yellow doesn't suit him. Didn't. It's too bubbly and optimistic, and he was hard-working and practical. But it's funny, isn't it, how unexpected things can attach themselves to you—even things you despise—and somehow become part of your identity.

Breathe in.

One. Two. Three. Four.

Hold.

One. Two. Three. Four. Five. Six. Seven.

The world feels hazy.

I am standing, somewhat awkwardly, in the front foyer of the church, trying to remind myself that breathing is an automatic process. It doesn't feel like it is. It feels like if I stop paying attention to it—to the act of inhaling and exhaling—I'll just forget, and keel over. The aisle in front of me seems to go on forever and I wonder if it would be inappropriate to slip silently into the back.

People shuffle around me, as though I am not even there, nothing more than a traffic island in the way. To my right is a table with a leather-bound book, where they stop to write their names. They take their time with this, using their best cursive, glancing at the names before them, checking to see if there are any they recognise.

I haven't written in it. I'm not sure of the etiquette, but it feels like something for friends and acquaintances—so Mum can sit down one day and check who came and who didn't. She'd relish that, keeping score of who took the day off work to put on a suit or stiff dress and sit in a church as an arbitrary symbol of support. And more importantly, who let her down in her time of need.

More people have turned up than I expected, most already sitting in the wooden pews, whispering to each other in hushed voices, but many others line up outside waiting to get in. Dad didn't have many—any—friends, but he certainly had a huge number of acquaintances through owning the shop. It feels fake. So many people coming to say their goodbyes when most started shopping at the supermarket the moment it opened.

I wonder briefly how many people would show up to my funeral.

Not as many as this, that's for sure.

Lena finds me rooted to the burgundy carpet. She grabs hold of my arm firmly and walks with me towards the front of the church where the coffin sits on a flimsy-looking silver stand. The photo is one I don't recognise. A rare one of Dad smiling, although it looks forced, the expression unnatural on his face.

Dad had always seemed so large in life, but his coffin looks small and insignificant, dwarfed by the looming pillars and the formidable depths of the high ceiling. I wonder if they build them so tall for that reason—to make sure everyone inside feels inconsequential.

I hate churches, full of moral judgement and false purity, but I particularly hate this church. Usually, I drive the long way through town, contending with five sets of traffic lights and two school zones to avoid passing it. Just seeing the steeple, proudly reaching towards the sky, is enough to make my heart speed up and the fight or flight response kick in.

Run away. Fly.

The front two pews are taken up by family. Mum's grey hair is in a tight bun, and she is wearing a long-sleeved black dress—the picture of a grieving widow. It jars me to see her without Dad. They were so different in personality, but the two of them together had balanced each other so perfectly that I'm not sure I ever quite saw them as whole and complete individuals.

Rebekah is holding Mum's hand, her four boys beside her, all clones of each other in varying sizes. For a moment, I wonder where Lance is, then remember they divorced over a year ago. She smiles at me. Polite, sisterly, but awkward too.

Lena slips into the pew across from them, next to Danielle who reaches for her hand. The estranged side. Beside her is Dad's younger brother. It's been decades since I've seen him, but I recognise him instantly—a more rotund version of Dad. They had a falling out years ago, but no one remembers what it was about now. Something inconsequential no doubt.

They never patched things up.

I go to follow, but Mum grabs at my arm, her long fingers locking around my wrist.

'You're late.'

The truth is I'd arrived at the church early. Almost two hours before the funeral was due to start. I'd beaten the undertakers and watched from my car as the hearse arrived and they lugged the coffin out, chatting about their weekend plans and laughing about some show they had both been bingeing. I'd watched people start to trickle in: the organised ones taking up the leftover spaces in the small parking lot and huddling near the side of the church, out of the chilly wind, chatting in small groups; the people arriving later trudging up the steep church driveway, the women wobbling on heels they weren't accustomed to wearing and the men fiddling with their ties. I'd kept watching as everyone began walking around the front towards the imposing doors as the organ began playing. Unable to get out of my car. My head swimming and legs heavy.

I was late, but I'd made it.

I realise I don't remember what flowers were on her coffin.

White?

Maybe pink?

I don't remember which photo was displayed. One solitary photo. One second in time to capture a life.

I don't remember anything at all from that day. From that summer. The whole year after is a blur. I don't know if anything in my life has ever fully come back into focus since.

The flowers on the coffin swirl, bleeding together like watercolours, and I blink slowly.

Breathe in.

'Welcome, friends,' the priest begins. 'Today, we gather in the house of God, to celebrate the life, and death, of our brother in Christ, Andrew, fondly known to most as Andy. I have personally known Andy for twenty-three years, since I moved here to lead this parish, but him and his wife Carol had been faithful members for far longer.' He finds Mum in the congregation and gives her a sad smile. Mum looks calm, but her hands are shaking. She clasps them together to mask it. Crying in public, even at your husband's funeral, would be unacceptable to her. Emotions are to be kept private and problems stay inside the house.

'Andy,' he continues, 'was a devoted husband, the breadwinner of the family. Many here,' he looks around, gesturing to the sea of black in the pews before him, 'will remember his welcoming smile from The Corner Store, which he owned and worked at for over forty years.'

I frown. Dad was gruff, straight-to-the-point and hated small talk. A nod of acknowledgement or a muttered hello was the most that people could expect from him.

'The number of people who have shown up today is a testament to how many friends he had. How many lives he impacted.'

Acquaintances, I think.

'He was a loving father. His children were his world—'

Mum grabs my hand and squeezes, inclining her head in a nod. Lena and I glance at each other from across the aisle.

I wonder if my funeral will be the same. People who barely knew me coming to pay respects and cry over my coffin. All my mistakes and flaws twisted into their most palatable versions. Messy becomes creative. Reclusive becomes quiet.

But some things can't be turned into a positive.

I travel with Lena and Danielle to the cemetery. It's not the same one. This one is older, more traditional, with large headstones in various states of disarray and graves scattered in no logical order, around trees and up hills. Grey and crumbling. The kind where they do ghost tours under full moons and tacky, horror-themed photoshoots take place.

Dad's gravesite is towards the back, in a newer section, but it has been picked out for a long time, the plots around it already filling up. The hearse has parked as close as it can without knocking over the nearby headstones, but they still have to carry the coffin a fair distance.

The bouquets of yellow flowers from the church have been laid in the spot where the headstone will go, and we stand awkwardly in a semi-circle around a yawning hole in the earth. Mum at the front, with Rebekah and her boys. Lena, Danielle and I slightly behind, on top of Herbert Humphries, a beloved husband taken too soon. I mutter an apology to him, but there is nowhere else to stand.

Lena has linked her arm with mine and squeezes it intermittently in support, but the panic from earlier has subsided. In fact, the minute I stepped out of those double doors and back into the sunlight, I was flooded with relief. I felt like someone who'd spent weeks stranded on a rocky boat and finally touched dry land again, staggering around on sea legs, kissing the ground.

I'm just glad it's a different cemetery.

There are more words spoken, devoid of meaning, before the coffin is lowered inch by inch by inch into the ground. From the corner of my vision, I notice Danielle wipe a tear away. Danielle, whose relationship with Dad was practically non-existent. I should be the one crying. Should be feeling something, anything, but no matter how hard I try, my eyes remain dry.

Afterwards, the three of us hang back, waiting for everyone to drift off towards their cars. It's a moment to breathe, away from obligatory hugs and empty condolences. Or worse, curious glances and whispers behind cupped hands.

Lena pulls out a cigarette and starts rifling through her pockets for a lighter. 'Don't you dare say anything,' she growls to Danielle, who throws up her hands in mock surrender.

'Never.'

She finds a Zippo and flicks the lid open, the noise amplified in such a still, dead place.

'Maybe,' says Danielle, 'we could all share a memory we have? I still remember the first time I met Andy. It's pretty funny now—'

'I'd prefer not to, Dan.' Lena turns and walks off towards the car, picking her way through the graves.

Danielle and I watch her go.

A currawong lands heavily in a nearby tree, his gold eyes fixed on us. He looks similar to Judge, but the lack of white in his feathers means no one pays attention to him. Death has offered him up a smorgasbord: insects buzzing around the flowers and displaced worms in the mound of dirt at our feet. He hops from branch to branch, waiting.

'What was your memory?' I ask. 'Did he throw you out of the house? Give you the cold shoulder?'

'No, he was really pleasant. I met him at Rebekah and Lance's engagement party and he sat next to me. I was studying teaching at the time, and he was so encouraging. Said I had a wonderful disposition and it was clearly my calling to be a teacher. But then—'

'Ah.'

'Yes. Then Lena came over and kissed me on the cheek, and he realised I wasn't just some random friend. I've never seen someone look so uncomfortable in my life. It was as though, he liked me and we both knew it, but suddenly he didn't feel like he could, so he just sat there opening and closing his mouth, his face going red. You could almost see the battle raging in his head.'

'I don't have to ask which side won.'

'No. The twenty-year fractured relationship kind of gives it away.'

Danielle fishes the keys out of her pockets and we begin walking after Lena, who is leaning against the bonnet finishing off her cigarette. Once it's exhausted, she tosses the butt onto the ground and steps on it with her boot.

'When did she start smoking again?'

'The night we got the call...I keep checking in on her to see how she's going, but she's fine, you know.' Her voice is edged with sarcasm.

I nod. 'That's Lena. She always is.'

It's hard to pick out a single memory about someone. One flash of time, from thousands, millions of moments, to best sum up all the facets of that person. All the ebbs and flows of your relationship with them.

But the one that immediately comes to mind, when I think of Dad, is the time he decided to jump on Lena's new bike—training wheels and all—and ride it from the house down to the shop. But he was too big, and the bike too small. He had to lean back for his legs to fit on the peddles, and halfway down the path, he flipped it, landing heavily on his back, still gripping the handlebars, the wheels spinning slowly above him.

Everyone froze.

In that minute, I thought he was dead.

But he sat up, red-faced and laughed. 'Serves me right,' he wheezed. 'I'm not a young bloke anymore.'

The thing is, I only remember that moment so clearly because it was so unlike him. Dad didn't do things impulsively. He wasn't a fun person. He rarely found things funny. I hardly ever heard him laugh.

It stands out from all the other memories because it's different.

An anomaly.

Not really representative of him at all.

f/2.2

THERE'S NO MUSIC.

The wake is being held in the church hall, a long, nondescript rectangular building out the back, painted the colour of whisked eggs. People mill about in small groups, talking in hushed voices. I hear a man nearby telling another about his new car purchase and how he is excited to pick it up next week. He couldn't decide between the steel-grey or the silver but had settled on the silver in the end, figuring it would hide dust better and he could maybe get away with washing it monthly instead of fortnightly. He puffs out his chest proudly as he speaks, but his voice is suitably sombre.

Around the edges of the room are plastic chairs reminiscent of my school days, and in the middle are fold-out tables covered in yellow tablecloths and plates of untouched food. There's an assortment of sandwiches: egg and lettuce, ham and mustard, tuna and mayonnaise, Vegemite (or perhaps it's inferior Promite). Celery sticks and dried-out julienned carrots that have been cut hours too early.

There is no dip.

The allure of food draws people away from the extremities and into the middle of the room. Most people look at the options and retreat empty-handed.

I see some familiar faces of people I haven't seen in ten-, twenty-, thirty-plus years. Old customers from the shop mainly, but also long-lost family—second cousins, aunts and uncles once, twice removed. They don't seem to recognise me, and I don't acknowledge them. Anyone who is only worth seeing at a wake isn't worth seeing at all.

From the small kitchenette in the corner of the room, some of the women from the parish serve tea and instant coffee in flimsy styrofoam cups. Despite the impatient line of people, they move slowly, as though any quicker would somehow be disrespectful.

There is no alcohol.

No doubt it was Mum's idea to have a dry wake. She hates alcohol even more than caffeine, but who wants to be sober at a wake?

'I wasn't sure if you'd hang around.'

I turn to see Rebekah gliding towards me, holding a meatball on a stick. It's been years. Her hair is cropped shorter, hanging just below her shoulders, and her face is showing the subtle signs of ageing—the lines creeping out from the corners of her eyes, the thin cracks around her mouth, the deepening of her pores—but other than that she doesn't look much different. I have a suspicion she wouldn't be able to say the same about me.

We embrace each other in a stiff hug.

'Nice eulogy,' I say finally.

'Thanks. I hate public speaking, but someone had to do it. Mum wasn't in any state to get up there. And you and Lena, well...' She gives a small sigh. 'I thought it was a bit flat.'

It absolutely was. Straight and to the point. No emotion, no fond memories. Just facts.

'He would've liked it that way. You know how he hated gushing.'

There's an uncomfortable pause.

'Actually, Tom.' She hesitates and I know what she is going to say before the words leave her lips.

'It's fine.'

'No, no, it's not. I don't know if you've heard, but Lance and I divorced last year, and it's made me re-evaluate a lot of things, given me a new perspective, and, well, I was too harsh on you.'

'You weren't.'

'I really was. Sorry.'

One of her boys comes over and nuzzles into her. I'm grateful for the interruption. He looks about six or seven, but I don't know many kids so I could easily be out by a couple of years in either direction. Like her, he has big golden eyes, and stares up shyly from behind her dress.

'Do you remember your Uncle Tom?'

He shakes his head, and I don't want to admit that I don't remember him either. My first nephew is Noah, but I lost track after that. I've never really spent any quality time with the others, only heard about them through the fractured grapevine.

'Actually, Noah's eighteenth birthday is coming up. We're just going to have a casual thing at the house. It would mean the world to us if you would come.'

I remember Noah as a baby, as a toddler, cautiously curious and obsessed with animals. He was entranced by Floyd.

'I'll send you an invite,' she says, reaching out and touching my arm.

Eighteen.

Has it really been that long?

Lena finds me sitting on one of the grey chairs, watching a computer monitor that's been set up in the corner. Family photos flash up on a loop, each one with an exciting new entrance. Some fade in and out. Others slide across the top of the old ones. Jarringly, some spin or zigzag, like a PowerPoint presentation designed by an eight-year-old.

She drags another chair over, and we watch together in silence.

'Wow,' she says after a moment. 'I don't know if the person who put this together really understood the funeral vibe. It's pretty energetic.'

'You haven't even seen the star effect yet.'

There are a handful of photos of Dad before we were born. Standing out the front of the shop when he first bought it, arms folded, head held high. Perched on a ladder, painting the outside of our house. Stocking the shop shelves, surrounded by boxes. His head under the bonnet of an EJ Holden.

Always working.

Once we came along, there were fewer photos with him and more of just us kids; he transitioned from the main subject to loitering in the background. Dad looking unimpressed while Lena and I played handball in front of the freezers. Rebekah serving behind the counter under Dad's watchful eye.

'Danielle always accuses me of being a workaholic,' says Lena. 'I just need to show her these.' She cranes her head around, searching the room. 'Ah, she's still in line for the coffee, might be a while.'

The loop starts again, on repeat.

I turn my arm to look at my watch before remembering I didn't wear one. 'How much longer do you think we have to stay?' But I already know I've asked the wrong person. Lena doesn't do anything out of obligation. Some people find her abruptness unsettling, but it's comforting to never have to worry about her motives. If she's doing something, it's because she wants to.

'I'm just here for you,' she says. 'I knew it would be a hard day.'

I don't think she's talking about Dad.

'What about you?' I ask. 'How are you feeling?'

Lena shuffles on her seat, folding her arms. 'Is this coming from Danielle?'

'No, just me, checking in.'

Lena shrugs, her face impassive. 'Well, we didn't really have a relationship, did we? So, it makes no difference, really, whether he's alive or dead.'

It's true.

Kind of.

Almost.

If you want it to be.

f/2.5

THE WORLD FEELS different by the time I escape the church hall and turn in the direction of my car. It's as though the day has been creeping forward in slow motion and only now has reset.

There's a beautiful sunset—the light is soft and chalky, the sky smudged with lavender and pink—but I don't slow down to admire it. I want nothing more than to be back at Mayfield, out of this suit and sitting on the balcony with a glass of red and a box of pizza.

NOW OPEN. NOW OPEN. NOW OPEN.

A flashing sign guides me to the new bottle shop. It's bigger than any I've been to—more like a supermarket—with rows upon rows of shelves, fridges all the way around and trolleys out the front. I grab one, just for the novelty of it, and walk slowly, squinting at the signs as I go. Riesling. Sauvignon blanc. Chardonnay.

My shoulders are tight and there's dull thudding in my head, as though I have overslept or am hungover, except all I've had is a few cups of watered-down cordial.

Pinot noir.

The lights feel too bright and the music too loud. I squeeze my eyes shut against the fluorescent buzz.

Merlot.

Being back at *that* church. Dad's coffin. The fucking yellow flowers. Too many overwhelming moments, all crammed into one shitty day.

Shiraz.

I turn my trolley, looking for my go-to bottles, but there are too many options. Along with the well-known brands, there are labels I've never seen before. A sketch of a frog in a waistcoat. Colourful graffiti. Beige and embossed. A treasure map. Cleanskins. Two for the price of one. A bottle nestled in a wooden box, like a freshly laid egg.

In the end, I pick blindly. A lucky dip.

The boy behind the register looks young, too young to be working here, but then I notice he's covered in tattoos.

I get my excuse ready. When he asks about my day, I'm going to say I've just come from a funeral. But his eyes trail after a group of young girls who've walked in: long hair, short dresses, high shoes, low necklines.

He doesn't care about the purchase of some middle-aged man.

Tom

f/2.8

ON THE DRIVE over, I decide not to tell Freya about Dad.

Not because it is too upsetting to talk about but because it's not upsetting enough.

Freya is close with her parents. Every few days she calls them, and she takes flights back to Adelaide several times a year. I know she would be distraught for me, full of pity, and my neutrality would seem wrong to her. Psychopathic. She would be expecting me to cry, want to reminisce, rage at the unfairness of the world, wring my hands over who could ever replace him in my life. And perhaps, once upon a time, I would've felt all those things, would've struggled appropriately in the way people understand. The type of grief that is approved of.

But, you see, it's too late for that. The worst has already happened.

f/3.2

It's a week later when my phone rings with an unknown number. Half of all the calls I receive are scams but the other half are work enquiries, so I still need to answer. But the voice that comes down the line, soft and uncertain, is the last one I expect.

Amanda.

'Sorry to call out of the blue,' she says, launching into a story about how she had been at Dad's funeral and seen me there but each time she went to say hi someone had come up to speak to either me or her, until in the end she had lost sight of me altogether. I hadn't expected her to be there—forgot that, of course, she would be. Our families were acquaintances, after all, and she had once been like a daughter to my parents. Almost.

'I'm sorry for your loss,' she says now, her voice overflowing with undeserved empathy. 'He really was one of a kind.'

I'm not so sure it's true. Headstrong. Quiet. Stoic. Traditional. Not exactly uncommon traits.

'Yeah, thanks.'

The conversation snags.

'Wow, it's been—' A flashback to the last time I saw her. I cut off midsentence, wishing I hadn't said anything.

'Too long. Twenty years almost?'

Twenty-one years and three months. My memory has an uncanny ability to precisely remember the things I would rather forget. If only it worked that way for everything else, but it's stubbornly selective.

'Yeah, almost.'

'Crazy,' she says, her voice distant as though she is speaking to herself almost as much as to me. 'A different lifetime.'

Yes. A different lifetime.

And yet.

A blink.

'Anyway, you must be wondering why I called, but I got talking to your Mum at the funeral and she was saying you're a real estate photographer these days. She gave me your business card, and, well, it seemed fortuitous. We're about to sell our house and I was wondering if you'd have any time to squeeze us in for a shoot in the next few weeks?'

I hesitate. Truthfully, I'm surprised she would even want to speak to me again, let alone offer me work and invite me into her home. But then, she was always a level-headed person, never one for dramatics of any kind. There's something safe about her.

A *nice* person.

'Tom,' she says, filling the void of uncertainty. 'It was a long time ago. There are no hard feelings.'

'Are you sure?'

'Of course. It'll be good to catch up.'

So, I may have lied. In the story of when I first met Adeline.

Perhaps 'lied' is too strong a word. I just left out some details.

But give me a chance to explain. It was self-preservation. Even though I detest how fake photography can be, I also fall victim to wanting to show off the better side of myself—tell my stories with the gently diffused light of golden hour. Like the magpie, I didn't want our story to be tainted right from the beginning.

I'll endeavour to do better.

I'll tell it again.

f/3.5

It was the peak of summer. The stifling week between Christmas and New Year, when everyone is on holiday and uncertain of the day or what they should be doing, the busyness of Christmas finally over, but still too early for New Year's resolutions.

I'd suggested to Amanda that we go to the river. Something fun before the year clicked over.

You probably recognised the first part of that story. But then it snagged.

I wasn't alone at the river that day.

Amanda was with me.

Every other person, it seemed, had the same idea. All the picnic tables had been taken and every one of the barbecues was in use, the smoky smell of sausages lingered in the air. Along the river's edge, people sat on blankets under trees, huddled under sun tents, or lay sprawled on beach towels.

The water was just as crowded.

We found a spot under a spindly little tree that offered up only patchy shade. 'It's better than nothing,' I said, shrugging.

Amanda had packed a picnic lunch. A wheel of camembert, water crackers, sliced salami and red grapes that she lay on a timber board. A cheese knife was wrapped in a wad of paper towel and a thermos of cordial jingled with ice cubes. She'd thought of everything.

'You're amazing,' I whispered. And she was.

'It's nothing.'

'Are you kidding? You've turned an impromptu picnic into—' I gestured around me, 'this.'

That was the thing about Amanda. She didn't do anything by halves.

Our wedding was booked for late May, and it was shaping up to be incredible. I'd tried helping with the planning, but she'd taken it to a whole different level that I couldn't—or no longer wanted to—reach. The downside to perfection was that it had become all-consuming. There were mood boards, colour-coded spread-sheets and bursting ring binders. Every spare second revolved around the wedding and our conversations about other topics had completely dropped away.

Truthfully, I couldn't wait for it to be over.

'Do you want me to put sunscreen on your back and we can have a swim?'

Amanda was sitting with her legs tucked under her chin. The picnic hadn't gone the way she'd planned. It was too hot for deli meats and dense cheese; the camembert melted into a gluey pool and the flies had swarmed around us. When the ants started coming in search of crumbs and she'd been bitten on the back of the leg, we admitted defeat and threw most of it away.

She gestured to a sign nearby warning of sharks and stonefish. 'It doesn't seem like a smart idea.'

In front of us a group of young kids splashed in the shallows, making mud pies.

'No one else seems too worried about it.'

'That's irrelevant,' she said. 'If someone asked you to jump off a cliff, would you do it?'

I looked to my right at all the kids jumping from the bridge. Some would've only been six or seven. Even the ones who appeared nervous as they stared down at the water below emerged from the river with smiles splitting their faces.

Amanda continued. 'Did you know stonefish can cause muscle paralysis and breathing difficulties and can send you into shock?' A couple floated past us, holding hands. Letting the current take them. 'You can die from heart failure.'

They rolled over and started dog paddling back upstream, laughing at their slow progress.

'I could carry you over the rocks to where it's a bit deeper. You won't even need to put your feet down.'

Amanda looked up at me, alarmed. 'I don't want you getting stung either! And besides, who would watch our stuff?'

'No one will steal our stuff.'

'No one is interested in stealing our wallets? Our keys?'

'It's swim etiquette.' I shrugged. 'What do you think people do at the beach?'

'Go in a group. Or risk their stuff being stolen.'

'We would only be a few metres away.'

She rolled her eyes and went back to watching. 'Just leave it, Tom.'

Instead, we sat on the bank, sweat rolling down our backs, enviously watching all the people—hordes of them—who lived with less fear. On the edge of the fun, looking in.

When I heard the jingling sound of a Mr. Whippy van pulling into the car park, I shot up.

'What do you want?' I asked Amanda excitedly. 'I'll get us an ice cream.'

It was my last-ditch attempt to turn our afternoon into something fun and memorable. A sugar high to erase all the missed opportunities.

Amanda smiled at me, a genuine smile that wrinkled her eyes and creased her nose. 'Surprise me.'

It was her usual noncommittal response. She didn't like surprises but liked spontaneous decision-making even less.

I nodded and turned away from her, heading in the direction of 'Greensleeves'.

I didn't tell Amanda what had happened. Couldn't.

Instead, I told her I found him wandering around in the car park alone and nearly getting hit by cars. She wasn't much of a dog person, but even she couldn't argue against looking after a lost puppy.

Can't you see? I only lied to you because I was already lying to myself.

I told myself it was nothing.

I was with Amanda. Adeline was with Gerard.

But even right from the beginning, I feared I loved her.

And I feared what that meant.

Lottie
ƒ/4.0

I wrote a shopping list while Coral was feeding, only a dozen or so items scrawled onto the back of an old receipt, but when I get to Coles I can't find it anywhere. Instead, I walk up and down the aisles slowly, trying not to look lost.

A plastic shopping basket is hooked over one arm, and I push the pram with the other. Coral has a dummy in her mouth and is sucking on it slowly, staring up at the fluorescent lights tracking along the ceiling.

After Dad took over the grocery shopping, I never got to go. In fact, other than school, I didn't really go anywhere.

School, home. Home, school. School, home.

Until I got my first job, that is.

Edward started playing soccer, and after the game on Saturday he and Dad would go and pick up whatever groceries we needed for the week. When they got home Edward always had a treat with him: Smarties when he was very small, sour worms as he got older. I was so jealous of those treats. He would leave the wrappers around the house, and sometimes I would find them buried between the cushions of the couch or lying near my doorway like a taunt.

I truly hated him in those moments.

Plenty of siblings don't get along, but I wanted to with Edward, I really did. I was ecstatic when I found out Mum was pregnant. I was five and desperate for a playmate, a confidant, a sidekick. *The Parent Trap* was my favourite movie, and although I knew a twin wasn't possible, I hoped for a sister at least.

I had big plans for my sister. I would share my toys with her and we would construct cubby houses under our beds. I'd dress her up and do her hair with all my clips and ribbons, and she would be fearless. I'd train her up to be a super sleuth, so she could steal the tin of Milo at night and we could have a snack while we were meant to be sleeping. She would love peas because I didn't, and I'd sneak them onto her plate at dinner.

I loved her before she was even born. Sometimes I'd snuggle against Mum's belly and whisper my plans so she'd recognise my voice. When she kicked in response, I knew we had an understanding.

I don't remember Mum going into labour; maybe I was asleep. I don't remember who drove me to the hospital—perhaps Dad's sister before she moved away, or our old neighbour—but I still clearly remember walking into the hospital room. I was full of excitement, but passing through the door was like slipping into another dimension.

It was as though I wasn't there at all.

Dad was holding the baby, wrapped in a stripy blanket, with a look on his face I'd never seen before. He brushed at a dark lock of the baby's hair with his thumb in a movement so soft and foreign it seemed as though some alien form had overtaken his body.

He had never looked at me that way. Never brushed my hair with his thumb.

I didn't recognise the man in front of me.

Mum seemed different too. Her eyes were fixed on the window and she looked pale and flat, her belly deflated like an old balloon.

Something was stuck to her arm, a long silvery cord attaching her to a flashing machine. I didn't think she'd noticed my arrival, but I didn't want to approach her. Instead, I shuffled over to Dad, trying to glimpse my new sister. 'Can I see her?'

'It's a boy,' he said. The armchair squeaked loudly as he sank into it. 'Edward. After my dad.'

Tears threatened to betray me, but I tried to think of the positives. There was no reason a brother couldn't steal Milo or eat my peas. I reached out to touch Edward's hair. It was soft. So soft. Even his skin seemed different to mine, the top of his head, almost squishy...

'Lottie!' Dad snapped, pushing my hand away as Edward started crying, a piercing wail that hurt my ears.

At Edward's cry, Mum turned towards the sound. It wasn't just her stomach that was empty, her eyes were too. I wasn't sure how— he looked so small and useless—but it had to be Edward's doing.

A playmate. A confidant. A sidekick. Edward may have only been a few hours old, but I could already tell he was none of those things.

Coral falls asleep in the cereal aisle as I try to decide which muesli I want to buy for breakfast. Cranberry almond or toasted coconut? Then I see the price and decide neither. I choose a bag of home-brand rolled oats instead; porridge is always nice when the weather starts getting colder.

All those years of wanting to go grocery shopping so I could pick whatever snack I wanted.

What an anti-climax.

Last time I went to the library I looked up a few recipes and copied them down in an old notebook. *Cheap!* They bragged. *Four ingredients or less!* There was a recipe I wanted to try—a zucchini bake. I figure Coral would like it too.

In front of the flour, I pause, not sure if the recipe calls for self-raising or plain. I don't really know the difference.

A woman reaches past me and grabs a bag off the shelf. She has a baby strapped in an expensive-looking carrier, around the same age as Coral.

'Excuse me!' Her voice is friendly and light.

I step back, pulling the pram out of the way.

'Thanks.' She glances at me then, and her eyes drift to Coral, now asleep. The smile disappears from her face and she turns on her heel, walking off in the direction of a man pushing a trolley. She nudges him, and he turns, looking me up and down. 'Babies raising babies,' she tuts loudly, not bothering to try to whisper. Not caring that I can hear.

My eyes burn, and I grab two bags of flour, one plain, one self-raising. They are cheap enough, and I will sort out what I need when I get home.

In the express aisle, an elderly woman is rummaging through her bag in search of money, holding up the line. The boy behind the counter folds his arms, annoyed at this inconvenience—cash is more of a drama than a tap of the EFTPOS machine. A packet of Smarties beside the conveyor belt catches my eye, and a memory, long forgotten but crystal clear, comes to me. Edward, popping Smarties into his mouth, one by one, sucking all the coloured coating off until they went white. He never ate the yellow ones, I remember now. He thought they'd taste like lemon, but he threw them away rather than giving them to me.

I reach out to grab a box but suddenly stop myself.

Babies raising babies.

Instead, I select a packet of peppermint Tic Tacs.

I used to believe love was something finite like money or coal, and once you were out of it that was it. It was depleted and there was no more you could give.

It made sense to me because my parents always seemed to withhold it—from me and Edward, and definitely from each other—as though trying to save it for a rainy day.

Mum loved me, I knew that, but her love came in dribs and drabs. Sometimes she would spoil me with affection. We would make cookies, read together outside, snuggle under blankets and watch movies, but this was often followed by a long period of absence when she would only come out of her room to get food or use the bathroom. During these periods, she barely acknowledged me. It seemed as though she had somehow overspent in those beautiful moments and put herself into debt that she now had to pay off.

Dad's love for me was also erratic, but he seemed to be consistently warm towards Edward. He always had time for him, which meant he rarely had reserves for anyone else.

You know, I almost killed him once. Edward. We were in the bath together, and he was only small, maybe a few months older than Coral. I don't know where Mum was. In the house, no doubt, but not around.

I didn't like sharing the bath with him. Before he'd come along, I could spend hours in the bath, putting my head underwater and sliding back and forth until the water began splashing over the edges. I was a mermaid, taken from the ocean and trapped in a bathroom far from my real home.

Sometimes I could forget it was just a game.

On this day, I was trying to be helpful and wash his hair like I'd seen Mum do—lather it up with shampoo and rinse it with cups of water. Edward's hair was different to mine. Darker, thinner. When it was dry, it stood up straight on top of his head as though someone had rubbed it with a balloon. I thought it looked ridiculous, but it looked even sillier when it was wet and stuck down flat. I tousled it a bit, trying to fix it, trying to make him cuter. Some of the soap dripped into his eye. He started screaming.

It wasn't like I wanted to kill him: I just wanted him to stop crying.

So I pushed him.

It probably wouldn't have been more than ten seconds, but it felt longer. Slow motion, like in the movies. Edward falling backwards, the thud of his head hitting the bath and his eyes wide as he slipped under the water. Mum appearing in the doorway, her brow furrowed as she took in the situation.

I panicked. Grabbed at his slippery body. Pulled him up.

His screams even louder. Too loud for the small bathroom.

But I'll never forget how Mum seemed to hesitate by the doorway. As though she, also, just wanted silence.

Can opener.
Photo frames.
Candles.
Plants.
A jacket.
~~Hand lotion.~~
A driver's licence.
A car.
Flowers or vegetable seeds.
A pet.
Beach toys.
A sense of direction.
A five-dollar note.
Mobile data.

f/4.5

THIS TIME I remembered the five-dollar note for playgroup. It was almost more drama than it was worth to find an ATM, then to find something to buy just to break the twenty down—who carries cash these days?—but I wasn't going to turn up again without it, to be seen as a leech. Leeching off the government to live, leeching off the other parents for morning tea.

Georgina seems pleased when I hand it to her.

Today, there is a craft box in the middle of the mat, filled with cellophane, cardboard boxes of various sizes, pastel patty pans, fuzzy pipe cleaners, and tissue paper. Down the other end of the hall, where the older toddlers congregate, desks are set up with tubs of glue. I sit down on the mat with Coral, but I don't want to be here.

'Now, I thought today we could do some craft,' says Georgina, her voice loud and confident, ringing across the hall, and I wonder if she had been a teacher before becoming a mother. 'The older kids can build things or make 3D pictures and the babies can investigate different textures. I've been careful to make sure there is nothing on the baby mat that they could swallow, but there are some smaller materials on the tables, like toothpicks, so if every-one could just be aware.'

Again, the comparing begins almost as soon as we sit down, only I hadn't realised the competition went both ways. Who has it best wins a prize. But so does who has it the hardest. Who's getting the least sleep? Had the most traumatic birth? Whose baby is the most behind on developmental milestones? Whose husband is the least supportive? Who is the ultimate martyr?

Today, a woman named Yolande has won. From what I have picked up, she has three kids, and her husband works away for months at a time. They don't speak to his family and her family is overseas. The eldest child was born prematurely and has a developmental delay, so struggles with school. The middle child is going through the terrible twos and needs his tonsils out. The baby has colic and never sleeps for more than fifteen minutes. On top of that, her husband has a pre-teen son from a previous marriage, who she is solely responsible for while he's away, and despite her efforts their bond is terse at best, but still she persists, begrudgingly driving him to his after-school activities and helping him with his homework. Her days are a balancing act of tutoring and therapies, dealing with tantrums, nursing a screaming baby and providing care for a kid who doesn't even seem to like her, let alone appreciate anything she does.

'You're amazing,' says one of the women after Yolande finishes a story about her weekend. 'I would be rocking on the floor crying.'

'Me too. You're a superwoman.'

Not to be outdone, Ivan decides to share his story of woe. His ex-girlfriend walked out on him, when their daughter was only a few months old, leaving him trying to juggle a fledgeling business and parenthood on his own. 'Out of the blue, she contacted me last week,' he says, 'and she's wanting to be part of Florence's life again.'

There's a collective gasp. It seems Ivan may be a serious contender. I wonder if this competition—who has it hardest—is something I can be part of. But I get a strange feeling that their sympathies might not extend to me.

'After being absent for so long?'

'I'm sorry, but no mother leaves their baby.'

'I hope you told her where to shove it.'

'What about you?' Georgina turns to me. So does everyone else. 'What's your story?'

I'd come to terms with my position in the group as nothing more than an extra in the background, so the question catches me off-guard.

'Well,' Georgina prompts, 'are you still with Coral's father?'

Does she presume that of everyone, I wonder. Did she ask Yolande the same question when she started? But I know the answer.

A truth and a lie both come to my lips simultaneously, and I hesitate for a moment between them.

'Yes, we're still together.'

'Oh.' She sounds surprised. I'm surprised too. 'What does he do?'

'He owns a cafe, so he's pretty busy.'

Around the circle, I notice a few impressed nods. I see Yolande and another woman, Mei, exchange meaningful glances. We were wrong about her, they seem to say.

Instinctively, I reach up and touch my necklace. It feels cold.

Lottie falls asleep in her pram a few minutes into our walk back to the bus stop, and even though it adds over an hour to my trip home by not catching the bus, I don't want to risk waking her so I decide to walk the entire way instead. Plenty of time to mentally berate myself.

I don't know why I lied about Heath. For approval, I guess. I wanted to see Georgina flustered, eating her words and her assumptions. But the sad thing is, it seemed to work. For the first time since falling pregnant, I felt like I had some kind of value. A stay-at-home mum being supported by her husband is worthy. A single mum being supported by the government, not so much.

The only problem is my newfound value isn't attached to reality.

There is a river that cuts through the city, dividing it. Here, where playgroup is held, the streets are wider, leafier, greener, and sheltered by large trees. There seems to be a surplus of red post boxes scattered around. The cars are newer, and although the houses on both sides are the same age, on this side they're more likely to be raised and built in underneath. As I get closer to the bridge crossing the muddy, brown river, the trees thin out to nothing and the houses are replaced with small shopfronts: a carpet warehouse, a kitchen showroom, a little takeaway that specialises in fried chicken.

With the sun beating down, it doesn't feel like winter anymore. Coral is protected by her sun visor, but I am overheating. I pull over to the side of the footpath to remove my jacket. There's another bus stop across the road, and even though I'm not even halfway through the walk yet I don't detour to it. It feels important somehow to push on; some kind of self-imposed punishment.

It's not lying to the other parents at playgroup that's making me feel guilty—I don't owe them anything—it's lying to myself. From the moment they heard about him, Aisha and Lionel had distrusted Heath, but it didn't take long before I stopped caring about their opinions. All my thoughts and attention shifted, focused only on him.

At work, all my shifts were with him.

When the cafe was busy and full of customers, he would let me know I was on his mind even when we had to be on our best behaviour. His fingers would brush over my arms as we squeezed past each other to get to the register and sometimes he would stand behind me, his breath heavy in my ear, as though it were physically draining him to be so close. Once the cafe was closed and the lights were down, he would lift me onto the bench, kissing me softly as though I were delicate and easily broken. Then quicker, harder, ravenous.

'Lottie, you're like a drug to me.'

I liked the thought of it. Of being something addictive, something dangerous—but now, in hindsight, I saw the opposite was true. I was the one addicted. At home, I often felt as insignificant as a piece of furniture, but that feeling of being seen was all-consuming and I couldn't get enough of it.

Heath was worried about how it would look and asked me not to tell anyone. 'You get it, don't you?' he said. 'People only see what they want to see. They wouldn't understand.'

Despite his warnings, I couldn't help but share my frenzied excitement with Aisha and Lionel. But he was right—they didn't understand, and though they gradually resorted to mild disinterest instead of outright disapproval, over time I told them less and less.

Something about it being a secret made it feel more exciting. All the other girls at school were chasing lanky, awkward boys with fumbling hands while I was sleeping with my boss, who owned a successful cafe and drove a black BMW.

Who bought me gifts.

One night, he presented me with a diamond necklace. The receipt was still in the bottom of the bag. A thousand dollars.

'He left it in there on purpose,' Aisha said, always the cynic.

Lionel agreed. 'It's so you feel indebted to him.'

But neither of them had dated anyone yet: they were just jealous.

Another time, he booked a room on the coast, and I pretended to my parents that I was having a sleepover with Aisha. She reluctantly agreed to cover for me if they checked—a disapproving friend, but still a loyal one.

Heath picked me up a few blocks away from school and got me to change out of my uniform into a short velvet dress in the back of the car. He'd correctly guessed my size. 'We can't have you showing up in this thing,' he said, tossing my uniform into the paper bag.

On the street, I saw some boys from my class walking along the road, their shirts hanging out and socks uneven. One was on his skateboard. He tried to do a trick and fell, barrel-rolling onto the grass, while the rest jeered.

'One of your love interests?' Heath asked. The dress had made me feel grown up, but the feeling quickly dissipated. I shook my head, mortified, but Heath just laughed. 'Their loss.'

A three-car crash on the highway had all the cars crawling, so it was dark by the time we arrived. The hotel was lit with golden lights, making it look like something out of a fairy tale, with valet parking and water fountains at the entrance. I'd never been on holidays before, never been anywhere like this.

Heath tossed the keys to one of the staff and led me inside. Everything sparkled. As we walked into the lobby, my doe-eyed reflection stared back at me from every angle. Hastily, I pulled my shoulders together and straightened my back, trying to look confident, like I belonged, but when I glanced back I was still a fireweed that had inexplicably popped up in a rose garden.

Even the elevator was beautiful. I could have set up a bed and stayed in it quite happily.

'You've really never been on holidays?' Heath asked incredulously as I bounded around the room, squealing over the king-sized bed as fluffy as a marshmallow and the spa bath that overlooked the glittering lights of the surrounding high-rises. 'Not once?'

'Mum hasn't left the house in years, remember?'

His eyes crinkled in concern and his mouth became a hard line. The same troubled expression always crossed his face whenever I talked about my family—and there was something about that expression I couldn't get enough of. I wanted to photograph it or paint it, turn the moment into something concrete that I could pull out and look at whenever I needed to feel understood.

Health came and stood behind me, his arm around my waist, as we looked out the window that spanned the entire wall. I'd spent my whole life on acreage; I didn't know nights could be so full of colour and light. Reaching out, I put my hands against the cold glass, feeling like it could break at any moment, sending us sprawling to the road below. Knowing it wouldn't.

'I wish I could take you away from there.'

I wished he would. No more tiptoeing around, a chameleon in my own life. I imagined a shiny new life with someone who saw me, understood me and loved me.

He had seemed like my ticket out.

But I was stupid and naive.

Still am.

There's only one bridge. I've heard there are plans for another, further along, but the people on the nicer side have petitioned against it. They're worried that linking up the suburbs will affect their house prices. It would drive the crime rate up, they argue.

I've been over the bridge countless times in the bus, but walking it is different, and the bridge is longer than it appears from the bus window. By the time I reach the opposite side there's a burning sensation in my calves, and blisters have sprung up on the heels of my feet. I'm forced to step on the backs of my shoes and shuffle awkwardly, painfully, the rest of the way home.

It's enough to finally drown out the sharp edge of self-loathing.

Can opener.
Photo frames.
Candles.
Plants.
A jacket.
A driver's licence.
A car.
Flowers or vegetable seeds.
A pet.
Beach toys.
A sense of direction.
~~A five-dollar note.~~
Mobile data.

f/5.0

I WAIT UNTIL there's no one around before I slip inside. It's ridiculous really, sneaking into a thrift shop the way a married man must approach a brothel, but I know people must look at me and think I can't afford to provide for Coral. It's like everything I do I now see through *their* eyes: a crudely stitched-together caricature of every person who's ever looked down their nose at me. Only they are always there, even if I'm alone. Always whispering in my ear.

Mum would see thrift shopping differently. Most of my clothes growing up were hand-me-downs from my cousins, and whenever I'd complained about it she'd begin one of her lectures about fast fashion and how our materialistic attitudes are killing the planet. I try to focus on that. I'm doing a good thing, I tell myself, reusing instead of buying new. But *they* just shake their heads at me, unconvinced.

The shop is less of a shop and more of a huge warehouse. It isn't the cute kind of thrift shop they have in upmarket suburbs, with only brand-name clothes passed on from other people in those same suburbs. This warehouse has everything, including the things no one really wants. Down one end there's furniture: cupboards, drawers, desks, and beds. In the middle are rows upon rows of clothes, sorted by occasion and size. The far end is everything else: a wall full of books and a smaller section of DVDs and CDs, a jumble of faded kids' toys in one corner, kitchenware in the other, and scattered around the registers are bins of miscellaneous stuff: tennis racquets, flippers and light fittings.

I walk slowly, holding Coral with one hand and pushing the pram with the other. She's tolerating being confined to the pram less as she gets older—and unfortunately also heavier—preferring to be in my arms, looking around at everything and trying to see what she can grab as we pass by.

The pricing here always seems sporadic, as though they've given the job to a kid who has no idea about the cost of anything. I suppose someone like me, a year ago. For instance, I have in one hand, a baby carrier. One of those material ones that wraps around your body like a cocoon. It looks barely used, and I know they sell new for a couple of hundred. This one is only $20. But when I went to admire the bed frames, even the cheapest one—a hideous heavy timber frame covered in claw marks, presumably from a cat—still cost more than the flatpacks you can get from Ikea. There are amazing bargains, but I've also learnt that you can't just presume everything will be a good deal.

In the kitchen section I begin my hunt for a can opener. There are all kinds of weird and wonderful things. An avocado saver, with a raised sphere right where the seed would be. Plastic cups with glitter that floats around like a snow globe. Measuring cups in the shape of Matryoshka dolls. But no can opener. I guess I'll just have to avoid the home-brand tuna.

There's a squeal, and I look up to see two girls around my age in the clothes section. They rifle through the hangers with a kind of easy carelessness that is unfamiliar to me. Occasionally one grabs something and hands it to the other. 'This is so you.'

It might sound silly, but it makes me feel better being here. Justified. Like maybe it's not so bad buying things from a second-hand shop. The people I usually see here are pretty varied, but they all seem to have something in common—a kind of hopelessness in their eyes and a lethargy in their bodies. Each person is completely different to the next, but they all know what it's like to be swimming against the current.

These girls aren't like them.

Like me.

The taller one picks up a white satin dress and holds it against herself, pouting and batting her eyelashes. 'Lil, what do you think?'

'Yes!' The other girl pushes her towards the changing room, which is just a rectangular area surrounded by a sheet. 'You have to try it on!'

Feeling emboldened, I venture into the clothes section and start peering through the hangers. I find a denim jacket. A black woollen scarf. A turquoise pullover jumper, tag still attached. And the best thing—an extra warm and fluffy sleep suit for Coral.

The pile of things in the pram grows, but I calculate as I go and I've only spent just over thirty dollars. It's on the more excessive side, but my parenting payment would've landed in my account last night, so I'm feeling more optimistic than usual. And besides, we need all these things.

Behind the counter is a woman who looks too old to still be working. She squints at the price tags, even through thick glasses, and keys in the amounts slowly, but she also asks me about my plans for the day and smiles at Coral, which makes up for it.

'You're very lucky,' she says to me. 'And young enough that the two of you will have a whole lifetime together. My mother is still one of my best friends.'

I baulk at the idea of this old woman still having her mother alive, but she isn't wrong. When Coral's seventy, I'll be eighty-seven. Barely a difference. I picture us shuffling around together with walking frames, bitching about young people and reminiscing about the past.

'Thirty-two dollars fifty,' the woman says, pushing an EFTPOS machine towards me. I tap.

Insufficient funds.

A buzzing sound fills my head.

'Oh. Maybe I did something wrong.'

The woman smiles kindly. 'Let's try again.'

This time I check the amount on the screen to make sure it's correct before tapping.

Insufficient funds.

I'm suddenly aware of the people queuing behind me. What they must be thinking.

I don't think they're surprised.

'I'm sorry,' I stammer. 'There should be money on the card.'

It's Friday. My payment always goes into my account just after midnight. I didn't think to check before I left but it's always been there. Not enough to live off, but reliable at the very least.

In my bag, I search frantically and find a few loose coins. I know I should probably save them just in case but walking out empty-handed feels even more humiliating.

'Can I just grab this?' I say pointing to the sleepsuit.

The woman folds it carefully and places it into a plastic bag.

I want to disappear.

Once outside, I park the pram around the corner and lean against the cool bricks. I feel flushed, despite the crisp breeze in the air. My face has always given me away like that, any minor embarrassment displayed loudly on my cheeks. Mum once told me it would go away as I got older, but as usual she let me down.

I notice in the bag the stuffed hedgehog Coral had fallen in love with, resting on top of the sleepsuit. The elderly woman with the elderly mother must've snuck it in after my card declined the second time. It's a nice gesture—one of those pay-it-forward things, I guess—but somehow it makes me feel worse that someone working in a down-and-out second-hand shop pities me. Whatever that says about the state of my life, it isn't good.

But it happens sometimes, right? Cards decline. There could be a mix-up with the bank. The payment could be delayed, floating in the ether, waiting for the bytes to sync.

I fumble in my bag and find my phone, a squashed sultana on the screen.

It comes to life and a text is waiting for me.

Your payment has been suspended...

I don't read the rest. My chest feels tight and my vision swims. I kiss Coral's head over and over to distract myself. All I can think about is our pantry, almost bare. Our empty fridge, empty bank account. And it's Friday. Nothing gets fixed over the weekend.

Melodic laughter fills the car park, and the two girls with the silky white dress walk past. They talk loudly. Confidently. Swaying their hips as they move.

'That was such a good find.'

'Right?' The other pulls out a key and a little silver sedan lights up with a friendly beep, ready to take them wherever they want to go. The absolute freedom makes my head swirl. I wonder how often they drive to the beach just to dip their toes in the water. Or up Mount Coot-Tha to see the twinkling city lights.

'You just need to find a blonde wig now, and you'll be the best Marilyn Monroe ever.'

Of course. Of course, they were only here shopping for a dress-up party.

As soon as I get home, I call the phone number at the bottom of the text message. Almost instantly, a robotic voice answers.

Please be advised there are longer than usual wait times.

Elevator music.

Your call is important to us.

Coral is tired, overdue for her midday nap. I put the phone on speaker while I pace around in circles, trying to rock her to sleep.

The music is slow. Calm. Be patient, it seems to say. Don't be frustrated just because you're on hold with a cranky baby and an empty fridge.

Just as Coral's eyelids start to flutter closed, the music cuts off suddenly, making them fly open again.

Your call is important to us.

More music.

'Shhh, shhh…' I bounce around, trying to get into a rhythm with the music and the rocking. Again, Coral begins drifting off when the music cuts out.

Your call is important to us.

One hour and forty-five minutes later, there's a muffled sound of someone picking up the phone. Then a loud click, followed by the dial tone.

I've been disconnected.

Fuck.

Straight away I redial the number, but already the message has changed.

You are calling outside of business hours. We are open Monday to Friday, eight a.m. to—

I checked my account, and I have a total of $3.15 left to make it through the weekend. My pantry is nearly empty. There's a tin of tuna sitting right in the middle, taunting me, that I can't get into without a fucking can opener.

I'm not an angry person, but it takes all my willpower not to hurl the phone across the room.

That night, the temperature drops dramatically, making Coral cling to me more than usual, and every time I attempt to put her down she wakes up crying and desperately clutching at my shirt.

Admitting defeat, I lie down beside her. I haven't finished my nightly routine, but I give up on trying to untangle myself from her millimetre by millimetre until I am teetering half on, half off the mattress in some complicated yoga position. There is still washing hanging outside that I didn't get to bring in, and dirty dishes on the sink. I imagine the wind picking up during the night and tossing the clothes horse over and waking up to find my clean clothes lying on the wet concrete below covered in pearly fish scales. I know I should bring it inside; I know I should do the dishes, but tonight I can't bring myself to care. Can't even muster the energy to grab the blanket from the end of the bed and pull it up around myself.

At least Coral is warm in her new onesie.

I think about the denim jacket. Five dollars and I couldn't buy it. I may as well get used to the cold. Try to acclimatise.

f/5.6

I AM SICK of pumpkin.

All weekend it's been the primary thing I've eaten, as well as finishing off the frozen bread in the freezer. I'll need to recheck my account tomorrow morning when the work week starts up again, and probably spend more time waiting on hold and pleading with bored voices on the other end who pretend to care but actually don't give a fuck. They will be shitty because it's a Monday, annoyed at needing to drag themselves back to work after a lazy weekend. The last thing they want is to deal with someone who gets paid to sit around all day and do nothing. What a luxury! If only someone paid them to do nothing. But the thing is, they could if they wanted. They could quit their jobs. Leave their marriages. Fill out the novel-length forms and jump through the endless hoops to apply for a pension. Live below the poverty line. Cancel their Netflix subscriptions. Move to an unappealing postcode. Trawl second-hand shops instead of David Jones. Catch public transport instead of driving everywhere. Eat nothing but pumpkin for days.

Late in the afternoon, I raid Coral's little ceramic piggy bank for money. Whenever I have loose change, I put it in there. Some babies have trust funds and savings accounts; Coral has a pile of predominantly silver coins. I hoped it would be a start at least.

'Sorry,' I say out loud as I pull out the rubber stopper, tip the contents onto the benchtop and count the coins into my palm.

Just over seven dollars. It works out to be around a dollar per month of her life. If I continue like that, by the time she's eighteen she'll have—I calculate in my head—just over two hundred dollars.

Lucky her.

'I promise I'll pay you back,' I whisper into her hair while pocketing a two-dollar coin, 'with interest.'

Once Coral is rugged up in her warmest jacket, I carry her downstairs to get some hot chips. I don't like chips much, but I'm desperate for something that's not pumpkin, and I need to get out of the flat, even if it's just downstairs to sit undercover and watch the rain.

Frank looks relieved to see me, see someone. 'It's been a slow day,' he sighs, and I have to agree. He gives me a staff discount, as though just by living in the same building I am one of them.

Coral and I sit at one of the rickety silver tables out on the footpath, and I unwrap the butcher's paper, careful to keep them just out of Coral's reach until they cool. Sprinkled on the top are some chicken nuggets, a potato scallop and a seafood stick. Extras I didn't pay for.

My initial reaction is undiluted happiness—the extras are things I would've ordered if I had the money—but nipping at its heel comes wariness. I've been tricked by kindness before, not seen what was beneath it.

Eventually, every girl learns that nothing nice comes without strings attached, no matter how invisible that string is.

A compliment demands a smile. A drink at a bar demands a kiss.

A lift home is a finger slipped into your underwear. A necklace, sex on the side of the road.

What does an undeserved staff discount demand? What about three chicken nuggets? A potato scallop? A seafood stick?

I bite the end off a chip for Coral, putting it to the side to cool down. You're being silly, I think. Overdramatic. Frank is older than me. Too much older. And married.

But.

'You aren't vegetarian or anything, are you?' Frank has come out to stand at the doorway and assess the clouds.

I shake my head, no. 'Thank you,' I say, trying to keep my voice a safe kind of neutral—not too grateful, not too rude. 'You didn't need to—'

But he waves me away. 'It's nothing,' he says, walking back inside as though it's nothing. Probably because it is.

I shake my head at myself. There are genuinely lovely people in the world, and some nice gestures are just that.

f/6.3

Aisha was with me when I went to the chemist and bought the pregnancy test. 'Oh my God,' she whispered repeatedly as we stood in front of the selection of boxes, all pink and blue packaging. *99% accurate. First to detect. Results within a minute.* 'Oh my God.'

I nudged her. 'You aren't helping.'

'I think the woman behind the counter is looking at us. I think she knows what we're looking at.'

'She'll know when we take it over to pay.'

We had crept out of school during the last lesson and walked up the hill to the small cluster of shops nearby. It was a first for us. We'd never snuck away from school, but Aisha had a tight schedule and parents who were always around, always there—the opposite of mine. Every day they dropped her off and picked her up from the front gate. School hours were the only time I had her to myself, and I needed her for this, although I was beginning to wish I'd asked Lionel instead.

'I think I recognise her.' She pulled her dark hair around her face, her head down. 'I think she might know my mum.'

I looked over and the woman behind the register looked back, her face hard.

'What if she—'

'Do you want to wait outside?' I said, frustrated. 'You're stressing me out.'

'Sorry.' She squeezed my arm and retreated quickly towards the front doors. 'But Mum would kill me if she knew I skipped school.'

Without Aisha, I felt calmer, more in control. We had been growing apart lately. Her consumed with band rehearsals and music practice, me consumed by Heath.

Maybe I didn't need her after all.

I picked a box at random and walked over to the counter, where the hard-faced woman was waiting. Her fingers tapped against the counter, a steady drumming.

She looked at the box and back at me, her eyes roaming over my school uniform. Her lips formed a thin line.

I shrugged off her judgement, the way ducks shake off water. She didn't understand. Heath wasn't some dropkick high-school boyfriend.

'I hope for your sake it's negative,' she said as I handed her the money.

I smiled at her and grabbed the box.

Results within a minute.

I sat hunched forward on the toilet, my school dress bunched around my waist, and Aisha cross-legged on the floor. The pregnancy test was on the tiles between us, time suspended as we stared, waiting.

Aisha reached out and touched my knee, but I was somewhere else, watching the scene from far away. 'How are you feeling?'

'Nervous.'

Nervous for what it meant if I was.

Nervous for what it meant if I wasn't.

'We'll sort it out.' I could hear her voice shaking, and was suddenly overwhelmed with gratitude that she was with me, sitting in a dingy toilet block at quarter to three on a Monday.

The urine crept across the test window. A single pink line to show it was working.

'What does that mean?'

I handed her the leaflet. I'd read over it several times, waiting for the instructions to sink in. 'You need two lines for positive.'

We both leaned forward, our foreheads nearly touching as we studied the window. Was there something there? A second line? Maybe. But then I blinked and it disappeared like an apparition, teasing me, playing with my emotions.

Aisha gasped. 'Is that—?'

I snatched the stick off the floor and held it up, trying to use the light from the window to illuminate it. I thought I could see a second line, but it was so faint it was hard to be sure.

Aisha grabbed it, her eyes going wide. 'Oh my God. Oh my God!' She turned to me, awaiting my reaction, but it was as though she'd sucked all the feelings from the room, leaving nothing for me. My mind travelled around my body, testing for happiness, anxiety, relief, fear, panic, something, anything.

There was nothing.

'Are you okay?' she asked tentatively. We both froze as we heard the soft tap of shoes walking in. Beside us, the cubicle door closed, and there was a pause, followed by trickling.

Aisha looked at her watch.

The toilet flushed. The door squeaked open.

'I'm sorry, Lot, I have to go. We'll sort this out though. Don't worry.' She kissed my forehead.

Everything seemed fuzzy. My emotions seemed to lack clarity, bleeding into one another. My immediate thought was that this was all wrong; that having a baby was not part of the plan—or at least not for a while—but another competing thought was fighting its way to the forefront. I knew I could look after a baby. Ironically, Mum's absence had prepared me for that. But more importantly, this would tip the scales in my direction with Heath. For months he had been reassuring me that he wanted us to be together, but something was still stopping him from taking that final leap. Perhaps this was the gentle nudge he needed.

When I finally emerged from the toilet block, the world looked different somehow, sharper and more vibrant. I noticed things I hadn't seen before. A dropped ten-cent piece in the corner, melted chocolate ice cream running down the edge of the trash can, how the afternoon sun reflected off the car windshields in the car park. I rested my hand lightly over my stomach, imagining the baby in there, already fully formed in my head. In the front pocket of my school bag was the pregnancy test. A piece of urine-soaked plastic that held the future.

ƒ/7.1

IT'S DESPERATION THAT drives me to get on a bus and head home.

Home.

It's weird that I still naturally call it that, even after I've tried so hard to leave it behind. It isn't my home anymore. It's like scratchy clothes, or shoes that are a size too small; familiar but wrong somehow. But then my flat doesn't quite feel like home either. Just a temporary stop.

Has any place ever really felt like home, really?

It's a long trip. Just over an hour by bus, with a changeover midway. Apparently only half that in a car. Whenever Mum complains she doesn't see enough of me, this is the excuse I give her. And as far as excuses go, it's a good one. Only it's not quite the truth. Even if she lived down the road, I would still avoid visiting.

It feels grossly unfair that it's all up to me. Surely it shouldn't be my responsibility—the one with a baby—to do all the running around? She just sits around all day.

If she cared, she would make the effort.

But she doesn't.

I quash the thought as quickly as it comes. It's a familiar one, a well-worn track in my mind. Like a passive-aggressive friend who tells you they wish they had your confidence to pull off those clothes.

I get to the driveway and turn the pram towards the house, pushing it over the loose gravel. It's on acreage, set far back from the road but surrounded on both sides by new estates filled with identical homes: smooth and modern, all painted grey and white. Our house looks out of place now. It's small and dilapidated, with a messy garden and a tyre swing out the front.

When I was young, all properties around it were the same—hobby farms, with chickens, cows, maybe a couple of horses, and machinery scattered around—but they all sold up, one by one, choosing money over endless space. Dad says holding onto it will set him up for retirement. A few years back, Aunty Lou made the move to a little coastal town half a day's drive away and she swears the coastal air has helped with everything from her asthma to her arthritis. Ever since, Dad has talked about eventually following her there.

Never mind the fact that Mum hasn't set foot out the front gate in years.

Never mind that his daughter lives in the opposite direction.

Coral had been starting to grumble and whine on the bus, but she quietens now. The bumpy, uneven surface seems to soothe her. For me, though, my heart starts to beat just a little faster as we approach the front door, never quite sure of what I will find when I get there.

I pause outside and take a few deep breaths, grounding myself. It's been months since I last visited, but nothing has changed. One half of the house is painted cream, the other half is still wearing its original paint, a dull avocado-green, chipped and peeling. It was one of Mum's projects, but she got bored of it before she finished and it's been a work-in-progress for seven years now. Unfinished projects are her speciality. She's like a paper aeroplane that starts off with so much promise but is too light, too fragile and gets tossed around by every puff of wind. Even on a calm day, when

conditions are perfect, she can nosedive suddenly, spiralling down-
wards without warning and crashing to the floor.

From inside, I hear a vacuum cleaner turn off. A good sign.

The door opens seconds before I can knock and Mum appears,
wearing an olive sweater that makes her eyes look bright, loose
black pants and slippers; the same ones she's had for years. Her
hair is brushed—not always a given—and her face breaks into a
smile as she sees me.

She looks towards Coral. 'She's grown!'

I realise my hands are clenched into balls by my sides. I shake
them out.

'Yeah, getting big,' I agree, even though I can't see it. To me,
she looks the same as yesterday and the day before that. Change is
sneaky in that way.

Mum lowers her head towards the pram, cooing to Coral, but
when she reaches to lift her out, Coral whines and bats her away,
eyeing her with suspicion.

'I told you she won't remember me, Lottie. You've left it
too long.'

I want to answer back sharply. But instead, I bite my tongue,
unclip Coral, and follow Mum inside.

In the small cavity of the kitchen, I perch on a bar stool while
Mum potters around. The kitchen is old and dated, obnoxiously
loud with mustard cupboards that demand attention for all the
wrong reasons.

It always feels strange to be here. I'm not a member of the
household anymore but not quite a guest either. I have no possessions here, and my room was reclaimed as a study almost as
soon as it was empty. Admittedly, it looks better now. It was always
slightly too small and claustrophobic to be a bedroom, whereas it
seems cosy and inviting as a study. But selfishly, I had hoped my
presence—or lack of it—might be missed for a few months at least.

They didn't even wait a week.

'Do you want a drink?'

I can tell she's been busy cleaning. There are dishes on the drying rack with water pooled underneath them, and out on the clothesline bed sheets are waving in the breeze. But there is the smell of something rotting, and the kitchen bench is covered in junk.

Mum opens the fridge and peers inside. 'I have apple juice, lime cordial—?'

Drinks that eight-year-old me loved.

'I'll have a coffee.'

I say it quickly, without thinking, just to prove a point. I don't really drink coffee, but I love the smell. I bought a jar once, on a whim, and sometimes I will make myself a weak one. Half a teaspoon. Lots of milk and too much sugar, barely a coffee at all. It's like using training wheels. I plan to eliminate the sugar and increase the amount of coffee over time and in a few years I'll be drinking espressos. I know it's ridiculous, but I've always correlated the strength of someone's coffee with how successful they are.

Heath drank double-shot espressos —several per day —and success seemed to ooze from him. You could see it in the way he walked, with a kind of bounce in his step, and how he held your eyes when he spoke, like he was examining your soul and wasn't afraid for you to know it. I wish I could have that confidence, but I look all over the place when I talk. I remember conversations by what object I was staring at during them. My pregnancy being confirmed by the GP is a small cactus in an echidna pot. Getting the keys to my flat is a pair of brown loafers. By the time I graduate to espressos, maybe I'll have mastered the piercing gaze as well.

Mum pauses, as though I am some stranger who has wandered in, someone she doesn't recognise. 'Coffee. Right.'

She flicks the kettle on and busies herself getting out milk, sugar and, from the cupboard, two mugs. One is her usual mug that she has been using for as long as I can remember: larger than average, now chipped in the corner with brown staining the inside.

The other is a spare I don't recognise. It says 'Best Mum Ever' printed in gaudy pink bubble writing, with a picture of a chubby bear hugging a baby bear. It's too pink and too cutesy—something I would've picked out at the Mother's Day stall at school. The kind you don't want to use but can't get rid of either. She measures out a teaspoon of sugar into hers, then pauses.

'How do you have your coffee?'

I don't want to say weak, full of sugar and milk. 'Same as you.'

'Black?'

'Yep.'

There goes my theory about the correlation between coffee and success.

She shrugs, scoops a heaped teaspoon of instant coffee into both mugs and puts the milk back in the fridge. Steam rises, miniature clouds as she pours water from the kettle and pushes the Best Mum Ever mug towards me. I hesitate to take it, thinking of my empty fridge, and raiding Coral's piggy bank for coins. Surely those words can't apply to me.

Maybe that's why Mum never used it either. Or maybe it's just ugly.

'Thanks.'

The coffee is too hot, too bitter. It burns my mouth, and I wish I'd just asked for lime cordial. Mum nurses her cup and watches me with amusement, the way you might watch a kindergartener attempting to tie their shoelaces.

My tongue throbs painfully. I can't believe people drink this stuff every day.

She puts out a plate of Arrowroot biscuits, and we make small talk. She tells me about a vegetable garden that she's been building and how she's been busy researching companion plants. 'I joined a permaculture group on Facebook.'

'That's good, Mum,' I say, even though I'm sure I remember her undertaking the exact project years earlier and never finishing it.

Edward, she continues, has given up soccer after all those years of weekly training and Saturday games and decided to learn the guitar instead. 'He's pretty good actually. A natural.'

I can't help but feel resentful. I'd asked to learn the clarinet in primary school, but Dad wouldn't even entertain the idea. 'We don't have the money,' he'd said firmly.

Their financial situation must have changed.

'Your dad wasn't too impressed at first, you know how much he loves his sport, but even he can see Eddie's talent.'

'That's great.'

When she asks about me, I tell her I've started going to a weekly playgroup. I don't mention it's mandated or that it caused my payment to be cut off.

'Oh?' Mum looks up at me. 'How is it?'

'Good.'

'The other parents are nice?'

I nod. 'Yeah. Kind of. I mean, they can be a little competitive sometimes.'

Mum nods knowingly into her mug. 'Don't remind me. You think that other parents are going through the same things as you, that they will get it, but somehow they seem to judge the harshest. I never got on with other parents.'

'Well, I've only been twice. It might get better once I get to know everyone more. I mean, it's always a bit difficult, starting something new?' What I said was meant to be a statement, but it came out more like a question, my voice turning up at the end, cautious with uncertainty.

'You know the best thing I ever did? Stopped trying. Stopped trying to fit in with people who were intent on looking for faults. Stopped trying to compete in a competition that has no winner.'

Just stopped trying.

I take another sip of coffee. It has cooled to a more tolerable temperature, but without the blinding heat the flavour comes through stronger. The acidic tang.

I may not remember the last time we went to that park with the ducks, but I do remember the first time I felt abandoned by Mum.

My first day of school.

Until that point, I hadn't spent much time around other kids—Edward excluded—and I didn't know how their lives differed from my own, but with starting school, my reality was suddenly out in the open, exposed to the elements.

On the drive there, I had a cardboard box filled with stationery supplies on my lap: wind-up crayons, scissors, a handwriting book and way too many tubes of glue. At my feet was my school bag. Mum had found an old knapsack in the cupboard and covered it with buttons of all different sizes. It was the most beautiful thing I had ever seen; I couldn't take my eyes off it.

We arrived early, but everyone else had the same idea.

'Lucky,' Mum said. 'We got one of the last parks.'

It seemed like a good start to a good day.

I wondered if my teacher would be nice. Who my friends would be. What we would learn.

But when I went to open my door, Mum reached out her hand, stopping me.

'Wait.'

Her voice was serious, and even though she was wearing sunglasses I could see her watching all the people filing in through the front gates. Groups of parents, waving, standing around to chat. Kids showing off their new shoes. Their bags.

I looked back down at mine—it looked different from theirs. Theirs were covered in shiny pictures of Disney characters, or butterflies, or jungle animals. Mine looked homemade. I picked it up and let my fingers run over the buttons, feeling the bumps and different textures.

A bell sounded. Outside the car, the crowds began moving faster and with more urgency.

'Mum?'

'Just a minute, Lottie.'

Her hands still gripped the steering wheel.

A teacher found me lost at the front gate and helped me to my classroom. It was humming with noise and activity, filled to the brim with people, and reminded me of the beehive I'd found down by the creek once.

I had expected to see lots of kids, but I hadn't expected them to be outnumbered by adults. I was the only one who didn't have someone there, to help me put all my things into the correct places, smooth my hair, take photos.

My teacher took pity on me.

'Your parents couldn't stay?' she asked, looking around.

I shook my head.

Some of the kids were crying, but I noticed some of the parents were too. They had to be herded out of the room like stubborn cattle, but still they hovered by the doorways and windows, and Miss Higgins had to use a firm voice to tell them it was time for us to start the day.

The boy beside me had a bright-red lipstick mark on his cheek from where his mum had kissed him.

I was jealous of the red stain on his face. A tangible reminder of his mother's love.

Later, during art, I got out my red Texta and drew wobbly lips on the inside of my palm.

After about an hour, Coral has warmed up to Mum enough that she's able to take her for a walk around the garden to show her the new ex-battery hens she had stumbled across on a poultry page online. While they're distracted, I creep down the end of the house and slip into the master bedroom. It always felt like a cave to me, dark and musty, but today it's unusually tidy and the curtains have been pulled back, letting the light in. At the end of the bed, I drop to my knees and reach around underneath. I'd found Mum's stash of money years ago when I'd hidden under the bed to escape one of Dad's moods. The envelope was cream and taped firmly to the bed slats, the colours similar enough to make it completely indistinguishable except to someone lying directly beneath. At the time, there had only been a handful of notes, but when I fumble my hands along the slats I can tell the stash has grown.

Even as a kid, I knew Dad controlled all the money in the house.

Some kids in my class got pocket money just for making their bed each morning. Some just for feeding their pets or keeping their room clean. Others seemed to get it for no reason at all other than just existing. I did more than all of them combined, but I'd never received any. Emboldened by having heard my friends boasting about it, one night at dinner I asked why I didn't get pocket money.

Dad had seemed annoyed. 'You don't get money for contributing to the household, Lottie. Do I pay your mum for cooking and cleaning?'

'But how does Mum get money?'

'She doesn't have a job.' His voice was matter of fact. 'So she doesn't have any money. I pay for everything around here.'

As soon as I was old enough, I started working for Heath.

I'm careful to only take what I need and nothing more. I stuff the yellow note into the back pocket of my jeans as I exit the room, closing the door softly behind me.

As I walk back out, I pass by my old room, now unrecognisable. Edward's room has changed too. His boyish bedspread, once covered in cartoon dogs, is now a simple navy. The toys lined up on his chest of drawers have been replaced with cans of deodorant and tattered notebooks for school. And on a stand in the corner of the room, his new guitar sits proudly.

Can opener.
Photo frames.
Candles.
Plants.
A jacket.
A driver's licence.
A car.
Flowers or vegetable seeds.

A pet.
Beach toys.
A sense of direction.
Mobile data.
Lime cordial.

f/8.0

Monday morning can't come quick enough, and even though I call as soon as the office opens it still takes ten minutes of proving my identity and nearly two hours of listening to the maddening hold music—again—for a three-minute conversation about why my payments have been cut off. It's because of playgroup. I went. But I didn't report back that I'd been.

'It's an obligation,' the man's voice on the line says. 'And you need to show compliance.'

'But I told you already: I went to playgroup.'

'You say that, but you didn't report your attendance on the app. Reporting attendance is part of the requirements.'

Apps require data. Data requires money.

'I don't have the app.'

'Well, you can always log into your account on your computer.'

'I don't have a computer.'

'Or you can come into our office, or you can call us, like you are doing now, and report over the phone.'

His voice is upbeat and tinny; it oozes a kind of fake nice. A perfect call-centre voice, lacking in human emotion.

'So can I report it now, to you?'

'You need to comply with your obligations,' he repeats, sounding like a disappointed parent. 'So we'll need to check you went to the playgroup, as you say.'

I imagine him to have overly whitened teeth. A weak jawline he's always been self-conscious about. He was bullied at school, I'm sure of it. This job gives him some of that power back and he wields it like a sword.

'How long will that take?' My eyes burn, and I struggle to keep my voice steady.

'We'll try to get in touch with the playgroup coordinator in the next few days.'

'But.' All the strength in my voice crumbles away, like a sandcastle being stepped on. You can build it as big and imposing as you want, but in the end it's only temporary. 'We don't have any money for food.'

'The expectations would have been laid out for you at the intake meeting. Once I've confirmed your attendance at playgroup, you'll be paid, but next time I urge you to download the app and report your attendance straight away to avoid accruing demerit points.'

'Demerit points? For not going to a playgroup?'

'So, you didn't attend?'

'No, I did! But—'

'I'm going to need you to calm down,' he says firmly. 'Abuse of staff is not tolerated.'

Down the line, I hear the smirk in his voice. He can tell the difference between abuse and distress, but he's at the top of this particular hierarchy. And I am powerless.

I imagine all the girls in high school who rejected him for more popular boys. I wonder if when he talks to me, he imagines their faces, forlorn and desperate. *Look at me now, bitches.*

'Is there anything else I can help you with today?'

f/9.0

WHEN MY PAYMENT finally lands in my account, I nearly cry. It's now over a week late. My rent is overdue, and I've already had two missed calls from the landlord. I need more phone credit, and my bus card has gone into deficit. I'd purchased a small amount of food with Mum's stolen money, but already am in dire need of more. And I need five fucking dollars for playgroup. But I don't pay anything straight away. I want to just pretend—even for a few hours—that I am not living on the poverty line. I want to be able to log into my account and see the total staring back at me.

Tom
f/10

THE MENU IS greasy, the laminate peeling at the corners, and even though I've read the entire thing twice over I can't decide what I want to eat. All the food seems heavy—burgers, fish and chips, potato scallops, fried calamari rings. It's one-thirty p.m. and I haven't eaten all day, but I'm not sure I'm even hungry.

I'd arrived early. Ridiculously so.

The shoot isn't until sunset—the premium timeslot—but Amanda's house is further out than I would normally agree to, and the highway can be unpredictable at the best of times, let alone peak hour, so I'd decided to beat the traffic. I figured I could have a late lunch, maybe a walk along the boardwalk before heading to her place.

If I can find something I want to eat.

From inside the shop, I can see the waitress peering at me with concern through the takeaway window, and I'm suddenly aware that I'm taking far too long to make a decision. I leave my camera bag under the table and trot into the shop to order, picking something at random and hoping my appetite picks up while I wait.

It's been overcast all day, but now the sun rolls out from the clouds, managing to bypass the umbrella jutting out from the centre of the table, shining directly into my eyes. The entire takeaway shop is outdated and long overdue for retirement. The tables and chairs are white plastic, the kind that dominated Australian backyards until synthetic wicker took over (always in dark grey). The umbrellas would've been brightly coloured but are now flimsy and faded. Something about it reminds me of The Corner Store, only no doubt this place has been kept alive thanks to its location. It's not the coast—more wetlands and mangroves than sand and surf—but with the same salty air and a quieter pace. Across the road is a jetty, where, according to the sign on the footpath, whale-watching tours leave from. I imagine it would be a popular spot for budding photographers.

With some reluctance, I pull my camera out of the bag at my feet to format SD cards while I wait for my food. When I first started photography, I always got prepared the night before. I'd put the batteries on charge, make sure I had enough cleared cards, and go through the camera bag checking things off a list. I'd bring all my equipment with me wherever I went. Two camera bodies, every lens I owned (and I owned too many), speed lights and adaptors, a tripod, spare batteries, a charger just in case, breath mints, Panadol, spare lens caps and cleaning cloths. Even the instruction manuals. These days I do it all last minute. Sometimes I remember to charge the batteries an hour before I leave. Other times, I forget altogether and get to a job praying I have a spare floating around somewhere in my car. Now I carry very little, but what I do carry works. I dropped all the extras. The what-ifs. The insecurities. The fear. The care. The passion.

A bell rings out from a nearby primary school, piercing my thoughts. Lunchtime is over, and kids begin trickling towards the buildings, navy dots from where I'm sitting. My school was a dust bowl, but this school has waterfront views that property developers would kill for. Do the kids even appreciate it?

Amanda always wanted children, at least two, and I wonder if she had any. If they go to that school. If Amanda comes here with them in the afternoons to get snacks before going for a walk along the jetty and letting them dip their toes into the water before heading home.

I guess I'll find out soon enough.

The waitress walks over balancing my burger, a look of concentration on her face. It's perched on a mountain of oily chips and already falling apart—too many components to be able to hold itself together. Despite there being no one else here, she checks the table number before putting it down. The whole thing collapses sideways.

She nods towards my camera. 'You're a photographer? What do you shoot?'

'Real estate mainly.'

'I want to be a photographer,' she says, hovering. 'I'm trying to get into fashion and editorial.'

I notice then, the tattoo of a vintage camera on the underside of her arm. On the opposite wrist is an aperture tattoo, barely open. 'I'm just working here while I build up my portfolio. Do you do photography full-time?'

'More or less.'

She shakes her head, staring out into the distance, a whimsical look on her face. 'That's the dream.'

When she walks off, I wrangle the burger back into one piece and take a bite. My regret is immediate: it's too much and sits heavily in my stomach.

I'm not hungry enough to finish it.

I loved Amanda; I did. But still, something dragged me back to the same spot along the river every morning. In the beginning, I was on edge the entire time, worried I might bump into Stuart—Stu— and he might recognise Floyd, but I checked the car park each day and had never spotted his Land Cruiser. Equally, there had been no sign of Adeline. But on the fifth morning, Floyd began pulling against the lead and when I looked up, she was there, striding towards us with a grin on her face.

'Fancy bumping into you here. Tom, wasn't it?'

She was less red but across her back her skin was peeling off in delicate flakes and there was a slight tang of aloe vera in the air.

'And it was Adeline, right? What a coincidence.'

She folded onto her knees and scratched Floyd behind his ears.

'I've been hoping to see you two again,' she exclaimed. 'What did you end up naming him?'

'Floyd. After the park.'

'I love it,' she smiled. 'But you should tell people it's after Pink Floyd.'

'You're probably right.' I laughed.

'And how is he going? Liking his new home?'

I ran my fingers through my hair. It had been more work than I expected. Ripped up cushions, toileting accidents, missing shoes, chewed table legs. He had even managed to chew the walls.

'He seems happy,' I told her. 'The first night I set him up in the bathroom but he wasn't a huge fan of that, so he sleeps in the bedroom now. He has a really comfortable, really expensive bed, but of course he prefers to sleep on my dirty clothes.'

'Of course. Give it a few more weeks and he'll be in your bed.'

I opened my mouth to say that Amanda wouldn't approve of that but closed it again. It seemed like an unnecessary detail and I didn't want to ruin the moment. Besides, I knew Adeline was in a relationship. It wasn't like anything was going to happen.

Coincidentally or not, we started bumping into each other every morning. It didn't feel wrong because we never made concrete plans and had no way of contacting each other. We just so happened to be two people who went for walks at the same time.

Adeline talked the whole time. She had a way of making it feel like we were close friends who had a lifetime of stories to catch up on, rather than strangers who'd only recently met. Just listening to her made the world seem more vibrant somehow. Like there were colours I hadn't noticed before, sounds I hadn't paid attention to.

One of the things that surprised me most was her lack of any clear direction for her future. Like most twenty-somethings, she was working a menial job to pay the bills, but she wasn't studying anything or working towards a proper career. Not because she didn't have anything that grabbed her interest but because she had too many things.

'Maybe you should write down the things you enjoy and do a pros and cons list.'

'A very sensible suggestion,' she said. 'You will make a good accountant.'

I pretended her words didn't sting.

'But I *want* to do everything,' she continued, biting on her bottom lip. 'It all gives me enjoyment, on different days and in different moods. I don't want to be stuck in a box.' We stopped under a tree to let Floyd sniff around the trunk. 'How did you decide what you wanted to do?'

I told her about my accounting course. How my dad had drilled into me the importance of financial security and being able to provide for your family. How he had bought the shop when he was only a bit older than me and it had given them the stability they wanted.

'Will it make you happy?'

I shrugged. 'I suppose so. I can hopefully earn enough to live comfortably.'

She shook her head as though I had failed to understand the question. 'But do you love it?'

'No,' I admitted. 'But it's a job. You don't really need to love it.'

'I'd rather die with nothing than spend my life doing something I don't love. Imagine lying on your death bed, looking back at your life, and realising you lived entirely without enjoyment and every day was just a drag to get through.'

It seemed like a nice concept but wildly idealistic; the kind of plans a child would make before they had come to understand the realities of the world. Life would be disappointing, I thought, for someone like her, with such grandiose expectations.

'I don't think I'd look back with regret,' I said, 'because I don't really have anything I love that much.'

Adeline stopped walking and looked at me sadly. As though it were me who would have a disappointing life.

f/11

ONE MORNING, AMANDA decided to tag along. She had the day off for a dress fitting in the city, and when I woke she was already up, sitting at the dining table and writing out a to-do list for the day.

She was a morning person. And a daytime person. And a night owl. One of those people who can be productive regardless of where the sun is situated in the sky. She never seemed to need downtime and was often puzzled by my need to just do nothing.

'No, I want to come,' she reassured me, sitting on the outside steps and pushing her foot into sneakers while I fastened the collar around Floyd's neck. It was a new one; red with a silver tag hanging off it and his name engraved on the front. I'd thrown away the metal choker chain as soon as I got him home and he had already outgrown the puppy collar I'd bought him. 'Do you not want me to come along?'

I'd run out of excuses. 'Of course I do.'

There were only two other cars in the car park when we arrived. One I didn't recognise. The other, I did.

During the drive I'd been troubleshooting in my head. I knew I'd have to do everything in my power to avoid Adeline. Not because anything untoward was happening, but because I'd lied to Amanda from the very beginning about Floyd, and I'd lied to Adeline about the existence of Amanda. They'd seemed like innocuous deviations, barely worth a second thought, but with time they had grown in size and power. I'd misjudged them and was suddenly faced with the reality that neither Adeline nor Amanda were likely to view them the way I had.

Slowly, I pulled my car into the parking spot, taking my time to centre it perfectly between the two white lines.

'I'm not feeling too well,' I said to Amanda. 'Maybe we can skip the walk this morning.'

She spun towards me. Not with concern but with the excitement of a nursing student putting her newly acquired knowledge to use. 'Not well how?'

'My stomach.'

It was the truth. My stomach had begun churning on the drive over.

Floyd was bouncing around in the backseat and Amanda turned towards him. 'Well, you stay here, and I'll take him for a quick walk.'

The idea of Adeline recognising him and talking to Amanda without me was somehow worse, so I valiantly refused and hopped out of the car. 'I'll be fine. Let's just make it a quick one ...'

Floyd jumped out of the car and immediately headed towards the hill, but I pulled him back. Adeline and I had taken to meeting in the little cluster of trees down beside the river, where we had hidden with Floyd that first day. If I could just avoid that area, there was a chance we wouldn't bump into her.

'This way.'

Before Floyd, I'd not been someone who spent a lot of time in nature, but our morning walks were something I'd come to love— not just because of Adeline, although that certainly helped—just because of being outdoors. The landscape seemed to change every day, and I felt as though I was constantly noticing different things.

Not on that day.

The lead was slippery in my hand, and although Amanda was talking, I couldn't take any of it in; all my attention was focused further afield. Every time another walker appeared in the distance my heart seemed to skip a beat. Each time it was a false alarm but, still, I was relieved when we started heading back to the car. Tomorrow I could explain to Adeline that I'd been sick.

As we got near the car, I unlocked it and reached down to unclip Floy's lead so he could jump into the back seat. I saw it happen in slow motion. Floyd, realising he was free, spun around and took off running towards the hill.

'Floyd! Where's he going?' Amanda turned to me in surprise.

He must have known his favourite person was waiting just out of sight.

'I'll get him.'

But Amanda had already taken off, running after him.

I was the last one to reach the bend. Adeline was sitting on a rock beside the water, her shoes kicked off to the side. Floyd was trying to climb onto her lap, licking excitedly at her face. Beside her was a thermos of coffee with two cups.

'Floyd!' Amanda ran over and pulled at his collar, dragging him away. 'I'm so sorry!'

Adeline turned towards Amanda, her eyebrows furrowed together.

'Sorry about him,' Amanda said again. And then to me, 'Tom, can you grab him? He's too heavy.'

Adeline looked back and forth between us for several seconds, her face unreadable.

I stepped forward and bundled Floyd into my arms. 'Sorry,' I murmured.

Not about Floyd.

I held my breath, waiting for the fallout, but Adeline's expression had changed. It was as though a curtain had come down over her eyes and she was someone I didn't recognise. Just a stranger at the park.

'It's fine,' she said. 'I love dogs. What's his name?'

'Floyd,' Amanda said. 'Tom found him here actually, wandering around lost.'

Adeline's expression was painted on. A pleasant smile that didn't reach her eyes.

'Wow, that's an incredible story.' Her voice was too animated.

She looked at me.

I looked away.

'It was a surprise, for sure,' Amanda continued. 'Tom went to go and get us ice creams and came back over an hour later with a dog. I was beginning to think he must've forgotten me. That maybe all the wedding talk had scared him off.'

'Wow. Yeah. Wow.' Adeline blinked at me slowly. 'So, when's the wedding?'

Her attention had turned fully to me now. I prayed Amanda wouldn't notice and she didn't seem to: she was onto her favourite topic.

'Five months. I mean, it's not really the best time for a new puppy. There's so much to do and now we'll have to organise a kennel or something for the honeymoon but Tom's in love, so I guess we'll have to adjust.'

'It's really nice of you two to take him in.' Adeline gave Floyd a final pat and stood up. 'Well, good to meet you, but I've got to go—'

Floyd started sniffing her shorts. Jumping up. Nuzzling into the pocket.

'Oh!' She fished out a handful of dog treats. 'Sorry, I think this is what he's after. Is it okay—?'

I nodded.

She looked at us both, her gaze direct. Sharp. 'And congratulations on the wedding.'

I found her at the toilets pacing back and forward, her hands in her hair. When she noticed me walking towards her, she rolled her eyes.

'Where is she?'

'Taking Floyd back to the car.'

Adeline turned towards me. 'What the fuck, Tom? You're getting married? You never even mentioned her.'

Every day, for over a month, we'd talked about our lives. About our childhoods. How she had grown up a spoilt only child. How when she was a teenager her mother was diagnosed with ovarian cancer and her dad befriended a woman from the hospital who was also there taking her husband to chemo. How their spouses had both died within a few months of each other, and he had remarried within the year, Adeline going from being an only child with a big bedroom and whatever she wanted to having two step-siblings. I told her about growing up and working in the shop. Our whole lives, existing between school, work and church, never time for anything else. She talked about her new job as a second shooter to a well-known wedding photographer, and I told her about mine working at the Video Ezy while I finished university.

But I never mentioned Amanda.

'I'm not sure.' I said weakly. 'It just never really came up in conversation.'

'Bullshit.'

She was right. There had been plenty of opportunities, so many times I'd cut a story short or omitted pieces altogether.

And I couldn't really explain why.

There was nothing going on between us. I knew she had a boyfriend. We were just people who bumped into each other on morning walks; that was it. Like seeing someone regularly at the gym.

It didn't mean you had to share everything with them. Did it?

'You're in a relationship too—'

'Exactly! But I didn't try and hide it from you.' Adeline's shoulders slumped forward. 'I just don't get it. We are both in relationships, so if we're just friends, you should have mentioned her to me.'

I didn't know what to say.

'And if we aren't just friends—' She closed her eyes. 'Then you *really* should have told me.'

I couldn't explain it to her.

Couldn't understand it myself.

'Does Gerard know about me? About Floyd?'

Adeline stared at me through lowered lashes. 'No.'

The world paused. Her green eyes on mine. Neither of us wanted to press play.

Her voice was low when she spoke again.

'What are we doing, Tom?'

What were we doing?

'We aren't doing anything.'

Then.

'I don't know.'

Back in the car, Amanda turned to me, frowning. 'That girl today, that was a bit weird, right? She had dog treats in her pocket, but no dog…Does that seem strange to you?'

I shrugged, trying to be casual, composed. Focused on the key in the ignition. Turning it. Putting the car into first gear. Releasing the clutch. Normal, everyday actions. 'I don't know, I'm sure there's plenty of reasonable explanations. Maybe she has a dog at home.'

In my periphery I watched Amanda mull over this. Then she smiled, 'Yeah, you're probably right.'

Only then did I realise I'd forgotten to breathe.

ƒ/13

FROM THE OUTSIDE the house has a similar look to Mayfield, neater though. Instead of wild, scraggly gardens threatening to overtake, they are manicured and the plants sit obediently within the confines of the garden beds. It looks freshly painted—grey with white trimmings—and a glossy black letterbox.

I grab my camera bag and make my way up the front steps, running my hand along the balustrade as I go. No splinters, what a treat.

The front door opens before I get to the top and a woman appears wearing jeans and a knitted jumper. I don't recognise her at first, but even as a teenager she hadn't been particularly memorable. She was the kind of person who would've made a perfect movie extra. Pretty, but not enough to distract from the leads. Not someone who you would really notice.

'You're a bit late,' Amanda says, checking her watch, but her smile is beaming.

'Yeah, sorry I got lost.'

Lost. Procrastinating.

'Come in, come in, I'll give you a tour.'

The layout of the house is also similar to mine: the main living at the front, kitchen at the back, and bedrooms down one side, only hers are taken up by children.

'Tabitha, my eldest, just turned thirteen.' The room in question has a queen bed with a plain rose-coloured cover. There's a desk in the corner with stacked plastic shelves beside it, all labelled. *Art. School. Homework. Miscellaneous.* 'I still can't believe I have a teenager. She hasn't hit the moody part yet, thankfully, and still seems to like being around me.' She laughs. 'What about you? Kids?'

'It's just me,' I say a bit too abruptly.

Amanda looks embarrassed. 'Oh, sorry—'

'It's fine,' I say, but the conversation has died.

I feel like I should elaborate, add something funny, maybe, but nothing comes.

We move on.

The younger two share a room, one side decorated with horses, the other overrun with Lego.

'Grace keeps asking for a pony,' says Amanda, following my gaze. 'She's dreaming, of course.'

She shows me the kitchen last. It is cluttered, like mine, but in an organised way. Herbs grow on the windowsill and an array of appliances are lined up on the counter. On the fridge is a giant calendar with multiple columns, one for each person in the house. Events and dates are highlighted in some kind of colour code. Above the sink is a laminated chore chart, covered in stickers. *Weekly Meal Plan* is on the pantry.

'I think I need you to come and organise my house.'

I say it without thinking, and immediately regret it. After all, she'd once organised our house that way. But she just laughs.

I go through the house systematically, beginning at the front. In the main room is a U-shaped lounge, grey and lumpy, bought for comfort not looks. An old piano sits in the corner, well used. Beside it, a rectangular fish tank with coloured stones and three goldfish, for three kids. On the wall above is a wedding photo, taken by an amateur. The white balance is off, giving everyone a blueish tinge, and the crop is wrong, but the moment has been captured perfectly, Amanda and her husband laughing as they exit the church, confetti raining down around them.

The master bedroom has a queen-sized bed with a ridiculous number of pillows. On the dresser there's a collection of hand-made keepsakes—a lump of clay moulded into an uneven heart, a pasta necklace and a box made from Paddle Pop sticks.

Amanda appears at the door and sees me frowning at it. 'Oh, should I have moved that stuff? I wasn't sure?'

'Probably best. You know, people like to be able to imagine themselves living in the house ...'

She nods, grabs a shoe box from the wardrobe and begins carefully piling everything into it.

'Just some of the creations the kids have made us over the years. And these are the good ones, you should see the boxes under the bed.' She says it jokingly, as though she too can see how ugly it is, but she places each item delicately, as though they are some of the most precious things she owns.

It's then I notice the painting hanging above her, an abstract piece, with brown and golden hues.

'Do you need me to move that too?'

'It's fine,' I say, struggling to tear my eyes away.

'My friend painted it,' she explains, mistaking my interest in it.

I nod, but I already know. The exact same painting had hung in our room.

Being here feels like I've stumbled into a parallel universe where time has skewed. It feels thick and gluey like soup.

I try to keep my mind on the mechanics.

The shutter speed. The ISO. The aperture. Keeping the door frames straight. Things that usually come naturally and I do every day without thinking.

This could've been my life.

My house, with googly-eyed goldfish and unsightly declarations of love scattered all around.

There was a time when I knew Amanda better than anyone else. I knew she didn't like driving in the rain, and that she wasn't a confident swimmer. I knew she always woke up at the crack of dawn and would sometimes drive back home from work in her lunch break to make sure she had turned off the iron or locked the front door. How bizarre, to have known someone so intimately— so completely—but to be now almost strangers.

Does she still avoid driving on wet roads?

Does she still wake before anyone else in the house?

Does she still worry about appliances left on, fires starting, doors left unlocked?

Floyd and I kept going for our daily walks but Adeline did not. We had agreed to stop whatever it was before it became something.

The first few days, Floyd looked for her when we reached our spot. He'd bolt ahead and when I arrived a minute later he'd be standing in the place she used to be, but within a week he'd forgotten and was back to splashing in the water and chasing sticks through the long grass.

As for me, well, I was getting married. I had a gorgeous puppy and a gorgeous fiancée to focus on. And a wedding that was closing in.

'Have you started writing your vows yet?'

We were standing in the kitchen doing the dishes. I always washed and Amanda always dried. She didn't like touching discarded food, and I didn't put things away neatly enough for her, so it worked well.

Her vows were already finished. Had been for months.

'I've made a start.'

I'd progressed from pre-contemplation to the contemplation phase.

'Oh, have you? I can't wait to hear them.'

I put a glass on the rack and Amanda held it up to the light, inspecting the quality of my washing. I always did a thorough job, but she checked every time. Satisfied, she wiped it with the tea towel and placed it into the cupboard, upside down, so dust and bugs wouldn't settle in the bottom. I scrubbed at a plate with cheese stuck to it from our lasagne.

Later that night I got out a notebook and opened it to a blank page. No doubt Amanda had written something beautiful and heartfelt.

I stared at the paper.

The page seemed to stare back, waiting. The blue lines aching to be filled.

Anticipating.

I drew some swirls into the corners.

ƒ/14

'So, WHAT DO you feel like? Tea? Coffee? Cordial? Soft drink? Water?' Amanda opens the fridge and checks it. 'Beer? Apparently these ones are really good. From a brewery in the hinterlands.'

'Sounds great.'

She gets herself a bottle of sparkling water, passes me a pale ale and sits down on one of the stools at the island bench. I follow suit.

It feels awkward to be sitting here with her, but she seemed excited by the prospect of catching up. I owe her that, at least.

'So, where are the kids?' I ask, eager to fill the silence.

'Damien picked them up from school and took them out for dinner. They shouldn't be too much longer. I figured it would be easier. They're always leaving shoes on the floor and stuff on the tables.' She rolls her eyes but is smiling: I know her complaints about the mess are empty.

'So, photography? I must admit, I'm surprised. You seemed so set on becoming an accountant and photography is...well...not accounting.'

'I like the flexibility. And accounting still comes in handy when it comes to tax time. What about you? Nursing?'

'Yeah, but I've moved on from working in a hospital to aged care. It's a different pace. The hospital was fine before I had kids, but it became tricky once they were born. Now I just work part-time.' As she talks she picks at her fingers, little flecks of polish falling onto the table. The same Amanda I remember.

For a moment, I allow myself to wonder what it would be like living my life with her.

I almost knew the answer.

There would be no real highs. No moments of intense passion or dizzying excitement. No moments of feeling so in love that the idea of being apart, for even a night, seemed like agony. But equally no despairing, devastating lows. Black holes that suck you in and spit you out, completely hollow. How different my life could've been. Stable. Content. Orderly. Everything labelled and in its correct spot.

Nice.

Amanda and Tom.

Tom and Amanda.

'So, where are you moving to?'

'Up the coast. My parents are getting pretty old and need a lot of help but we're just too far away here. The kids are excited about it. I think they fancy themselves as surfers.'

At that moment the front door bangs open and loud footsteps echo through the house.

'Mandy?' A deep voice.

I jump up from my seat as though I have been caught in a compromising position. It's just a drink. But, still, heat creeps into my face and I feel the back of my neck start burning.

'Oh, that'll be Damien and the kids.'

Amanda and Tom. Tom and Amanda.

Amanda and Damien.

I wonder if I should leave. I want to.

A man walks in carrying a white plastic bag, flanked by two girls and a younger boy. He has a round face, a round stomach and a beaming smile. Older than her, although it's not obvious. He wears Converse to try to look younger, and she's stopped dying her hair to look older. Their ages bleed together somewhere in the middle.

The little boy runs over and slides into Amanda's lap, kissing her on the cheek. The oldest girl eyes me with suspicion and folded arms. The middle one runs off. They all have dark hair and brown eyes, just like her. Round faces like him.

'Violin practice, Grace!' Amanda yells out.

There is an audible groan from somewhere in the house.

Damien comes towards me, his chubby hand outstretched and a smile on his face. 'You must be the photographer.' He shakes my hand warmly. 'Damien.'

He has no idea who I am.

'This is Tom,' Amanda says.

'Nice to meet you, Damien.' I try to smile back, but it feels plastered on. Stiff and flaky.

'Tom Woods,' Amanda says, slowly. Meaningfully.

He continues smiling.

Nothing.

He pauses for a moment, and his eyes flick to Amanda. 'Oh! *Tom!*'

I'm glued to the spot, unsure of what to say or what to expect. Jealousy, no matter how deeply buried, can be a dangerous beast. But Damien just laughs, a booming laugh that ricochets around the kitchen. 'That's right! Amanda told me weeks ago, but I forgot!' He slaps me warmly on the shoulder and goes to the fridge to get himself a beer. 'Ready for another?'

He's just like Amanda. Level-headed and calm. Friendly and warm. A *nice* person.

'No, thanks. Got to drive home.'

'True that. True that.' He leans against the countertop and pops the lid off the beer against the bench.

'Use the bottle opener!' Amanda sighs. 'I don't know how many times—'

'Sorry, sorry.' He puts up his hands in surrender.

The boy is twirling his fingers around Amanda's hair absent-mindedly and she kisses the top of his head. 'Where did you guys end up going?'

Damien doesn't answer but rolls his eyes.

They both laugh.

An inside joke. The kind people have after decades together when they know the other person intuitively. When there are no surprises left.

I've never had that.

'Sushi,' Damien explains to me. 'It's meant to be cheap, but the kids inhale it. Ends up costing more than it would to go somewhere nice. I think William had about six plates. I put some in the fridge for you too,' he says to Amanda. 'Chicken and avocado.'

Chicken and avocado. The sushi for people who aren't really into sushi.

'Can I watch TV?' William asks.

Amanda nods. 'Just for a bit. But make sure you feed the Three Musketeers first.'

'Okay.' He races off.

'Goldfish,' she explains. 'They couldn't tell them apart, so Tabby gave them a collective name.'

'Pretty creative.'

'We also have had a bird named Birdie, a guinea pig called Piggie and a cat called Kitty, so it's pretty hit-and-miss.'

I don't have anything to add—no funny stories of random pet names, so I just smile. 'Lots of pets.'

'Haven't had a dog yet, though,' Damien says. 'The kids and I have been begging for a puppy but Mandy isn't much of a dog person. Says they're too much work, but they can't be worse than cleaning out tanks every weekend. I think we're slowly breaking her down.'

Amanda glances at me. A silent understanding.

I guess we have inside conversations too.

From the other end of the house, a violin starts playing. It's like a wild animal being beaten into submission, scratching and whining in protest.

'So,' he says, 'the photos went okay, then?'

'Yeah, great thanks.'

'You know, I always wanted to be a photographer,' says Damien. 'I used to sneak off with my parent's camera and use up the whole roll of film taking photos of blue tongues down the bottom of our garden. They used to get so angry.' When he laughs, his whole body rocks. He is like a younger, brown-haired version of Santa, bearing loyalty and chicken and avocado sushi. 'They would come back all dark and blurry. And I was normally too far away to even see the lizards.'

'We all have to start somewhere,' I say.

'And end somewhere. I think they hid the camera from me after that and my interest died off. I became a plumber instead, as far away from creativity as you can get.'

'Probably not a bad decision.'

'Photography not all it's cracked up to be?'

'It's fine, but it's just a job for me too.'

He nods. Amanda nods. But their eyes are blank. Creativity to them is paddle pop stick frames. And I don't think any of us know passion anymore. It's something nostalgic—a feeling we knew once but now can hardly remember; something for the young and optimistic. Damien and Amanda may be able to recapture it vicariously through their children, but there's no hope for me.

When I look up, I notice Damien staring at me. He shakes his head. 'It's so crazy to be meeting you after all these years. It's like meeting someone famous. I heard so much about you in those early years when Mandy and I first met, I was honestly sick of hearing your name.'

I take another sip of my beer. A gulp. It's still half full, the one time I want it to be half empty. 'Sorry about all that.' My voice fades off. Is that what I'm meant to say?

'Oh, mate, don't be. Everything turned out exactly how it was supposed to.' He winks at Amanda. 'I'd be lost without this one, although I had to ask her to marry me three times before she said yes.'

They both laugh at that. What was once a painful barrier now a funny story.

'Did things work out for you too? Did you end up with that girl, I can't remember her name.'

'Adeline,' Amanda says.

I feel myself freeze up.

Damien is watching me expectantly. I look at Amanda. I'd broken her heart, but here she is, looking content. And all of a sudden I realise none of the what ifs have ever crossed her mind. She loves her life with her plastic shelves and stuck-on labels. She's happy and the past is well and truly behind her, where it should be.

'No, it didn't work out.'

Amanda reaches over and touches my hand.

'That's too bad,' Damien says, and it sounds like he means it. Genuine. *Nice.*

The conversation shudders and stalls.

I skull the last of my beer and go to pack up my things, folding the tripods down into unobtrusive sticks and slotting the speed-lights into their padded cases. The kids begin arguing over what to watch on TV. The eldest daughter is the manipulator, her voice low and smooth. The son yells back, emotional and out of control, and I know it will be him who gets sent to his room.

I put my bags by the front door and pop my head back in to say goodbye. Amanda gives me a quick hug. 'So nice to see you again.'

Damien is in the bedroom but comes out and shakes my hand. 'Thanks, mate. All the best with everything.'

As I pass, I notice he has been putting all the little trinkets that were hidden for the photos back on display. It's only been a few minutes, but already the chest of drawers are again bursting with sentiment. Like I'd never even been there.

f/16

On the way home, I buy three bottles of shiraz.

I hadn't thought about Amanda in years; seeing her again has destabilised me and taken me right back to a time I prefer not to venture. It is like peering through a magic door with an alternative reality and I suddenly see my life for what it is, without the beautiful veil of denial over it. Empty. Grey. A bleak, dull shade, where there was once so much colour.

When I arrive home, Mayfield sits silent and cloaked in darkness, while all down the street the houses hum with the chatter of people and swell with activity. Everything seems too still, too quiet, after being around noise and *life*.

I walk through the house, turning on lights. The dull overhead light in the fan above me, the cheap lamp on my bedside table, the dim light of the rangehood in the kitchen. I find my wireless speaker and put some music on, slightly too loud for a weekday. To someone passing by, Mayfield would look like any other house on the street, glowing with warmth, music escaping out from the open windows. But it's not the same. Not the same as laughter, and stories, and mindless chatter. You can't substitute the wonderfully chaotic with something recorded in another time and another place. I know all the words, the parts where the music rises and falls and where the bridge hits the chorus or falls away again. No suspense, no spontaneity.

It feels dead.

I scroll through my phone and find another playlist; a new one I haven't heard before. An unexpected voice flies into the room, deep and gravelly, and the peculiarity of it calms me for a moment.

Just like that, one day she was there again.

She looked different to the last time I had seen her. Instead of her usual ponytail, her hair was down, spilling over her shoulders in waves, and rather than walking clothes she was wearing a dusty pink dress that floated around her thighs. No longer any pretence of fitness.

'I hope you put on sunscreen,' I said, and she spun around, smiling. My breath caught for a moment. I wasn't sure anyone else had ever smiled at me in that way.

Floyd went mad, jumping, licking and zooming around in loops.

'He's so big,' Adeline exclaimed. Since the last time she'd seen him, he had nearly doubled in size. 'He has really grown into his feet and ears.'

We sat down, side by side, as Floyd ran down to the river, scaring off ducks and herons from the water's edge.

'So,' she said.

'So.'

My whole body trembled, with nervousness or excitement, I couldn't tell. Over the last few weeks, I'd begun to believe I would never see her again, but now here she was, right there. The whole situation felt delicate, like spun sugar, and all it would take was a single teardrop to have it dissolve into a sticky puddle, right in front of me.

'What now?'

'I don't know,' I told her. 'But I've missed this.'

'Me too.'

We sat in silence for a long time. It seemed like there was too much to say to each other.

But we said nothing.

There was no point.

I was marrying Amanda. She was with Gerard. But it, whatever it was, quivered in the air between us.

'I can't leave Gerard,' she said finally. 'He isn't perfect, but he was there for me at a time in my life when I had no one else.' Her voice cracked.

'I don't want to leave Amanda either. She's such a sweet person, she doesn't deserve it.' I reach out to Adeline and touch her hand as a way to show support.

The faintest touch.

But electric.

I could hear her breathing deepen. Neither of us moved.

Adeline looked down, my fingers on top of hers and nodded slowly. 'Okay. So, we can just be friends. People are allowed friends, right?'

'Of course they are.' I moved my hand back, but it tingled as though the skin had been branded.

Friends.

'But…if the timing was different…'

'Yes,' I agreed. 'The timing is all wrong.'

f/18

You ALREADY KNOW what happened, so I won't drag it out.

Our friendship snowballed into something else altogether, one incremental step at a time. At first it was exchanging numbers (just in case), which led to hushed conversations late into the night. Then on top of the morning walks, we started taking other opportunities to see each other. If Amanda was out, Adeline would come over (just to talk), or we'd accidentally sit next to each other in a cinema. But we hadn't had sex, so I took great comfort in reassuring myself it was still an innocent friendship.

An innocent friendship my fiancée knew nothing about.

Gerard was also in the dark, yet Adeline had a good reason for that. She had slowly opened up to me about their relationship and how he was highly jealous. I'd learnt how he'd stripped away her friends by causing explosive fights each time she spent time with them, until it became easier for her to stop doing so. And when she finally landed her dream job with the well-known wedding photographer he'd become so riddled with insecurity about them spending time together that he'd forced her to quit.

'I just don't understand how you ever ended up with someone like that.'

She shrugged. 'I was young and just so angry with Dad for letting Daria and her kids move in after Mum died. Straight away, too. I just hated being there so much, and I think they hated me too. She had different rules for me and was always trying to tell me what to do, but she had no right. When I met Gerard through a friend and we clicked, it made sense for me to move in with him. And I loved how protective he could be, but—'

I waited.

'But what?'

'Well, it's a fine line, isn't it? Between protective and possessive.'

It was Adeline who eventually suggested we break off our relationships.

Of course, the thought had crossed my mind—multiple times—but I had set my path, and even though I had my doubts I didn't have the strength to deviate from it.

Adeline had never liked sticking to the beaten track.

'We can't keep doing this forever,' she said.

I knew she was right. I hated the lying, but—always the peace-keeper—I was avoiding the inevitable.

'We need to make a decision, one way or the other.'

I broke the news to Amanda over breakfast, while the light was streaming through the windows. Warm and golden.

I barely noticed.

She didn't ask for details, but I gave them to her anyway, from when I first met Adeline right up until that very moment in the kitchen. I wasn't sure whether I was trying to give her closure or absolve myself from guilt—but it didn't seem to do either.

Amanda cried as I talked, but she didn't yell or explode in anger like I expected. She didn't beg, or plead, or throw a plate at my head. When I finished talking, she crumpled into herself, shaking her head.

'This isn't you, Tom,' she said with a sob. 'You aren't a thief, you're a good person. She's clearly crazy and has gotten into your head, turned you into a different person, and convinced you to do things that aren't you. We are getting married. This doesn't seem like a decision you would ever make.'

'It is my decision.'

Amanda shook her head furiously. 'It's not. Tom, you stole a dog!'

Saved. I saved a dog.

f/20

I CANCEL ON Freya.

When she asks why, I tell her I think I'm getting a migraine. That my vision is blurring in the corners and my head is beginning to throb. Her reply is almost instant, full of understanding. Telling me to lie down and make sure to take painkillers.

But the truth is, I just can't pretend.

Even with the lights out.

III. Light Sensitivity

Tom
ISO 100

IT'S FUNNY, ISN'T it, how we can be so certain about our memories until we see physical proof that disconfirms our reality.

Inside a notebook, I found that photo.

The first one I ever took of Adeline—possibly the first photo I ever took of anyone. It was folded into quarters, and fell out, right at my feet.

I opened it carefully, as though uncovering some precious artefact, which I suppose in some way I was. I stared at it for a long time. Floyd, a blurry splotch in the background. Adeline's eyes screwed shut, her mouth open in laughter. And I swear for a moment I could smell the lightest tang of aloe vera float in on the breeze.

But I had been wrong about something.

She wasn't wearing a white top, the one with the lace, like I'd thought. It was a pastel dress, soft colours running into each other. I'd been so sure about that top I would've made a bet on it. A few hundred maybe, not enough to risk losing everything—I, of all people, understand how fallible we can be—but enough money to confirm my absolute certainty. But looking into the past is like trying to coax details out of shadowy depths. The past is grainy. Hard to make out.

The same theory would propose the present is clearer, but I disagree. The present is even more problematic. It's all new territory that we don't yet know how to navigate. We can only use maps we've already drawn.

When we look back, we might not be able to get all the small details correct—the exact order of events, the words just as they were spoken—but hindsight gives us the distance to see the whole picture.

We are too close to the present.

ISO 125

SHE ANSWERS THE door wearing sheer lingerie—a black chiffon slip flecked with red roses, her nipples visible between embroidered flower buds, stiletto heels, and thin black stockings held in place by a garter belt. Her eyes are smoky, her lips red, and her expression is dark. Grabbing my hand, she drags me inside and pushes me down onto the couch. I am cautiously obliging as she kneels down in front of me, unzipping my pants. Her eyes lock with mine as she takes me in her mouth. I have to force myself not to look away.

Afterwards, Freya goes into the bathroom to have a shower, while I pull my clothes back on, pick up the cushions from the floor and straighten the coffee table. When she comes out, she's wearing a blue satin gown tied firmly at the waist, and her damp hair is twisted up into a clip. There is no evidence of the dark eyeshadow from earlier, the red lips are gone, but her lashes are thick with freshly applied mascara and her lips sparkle with gloss. It looks like she's been crying.

'Gin and tonic?'

She doesn't wait for a reply, is already in the kitchen reaching for a chopping board and a knife.

'Sure.'

She's quiet as she concentrates on cutting the lime into perfect wedges, keeping her hands busy and her eyes diverted while I sit up straight on the same couch we just fucked on, trying to think of a conversation starter.

The lingerie thing was new. And the eye contact. Her usual barriers were down, but somehow they seem to have gone up even higher now. Reinforced.

'Is everything okay?' I ask after an uncomfortable few minutes of silence.

Freya nods but doesn't speak.

'Are you sure? You just seem a little—' Not yourself. 'Off.'

'Actually, I'm not really.' She is filling the glasses with ice cubes and I strain to hear her over the noise. 'Remember my ex?'

'Yeah, of course. The one who took off with the French bulldog.'

'And our neighbour. I found out today they're expecting a baby together.'

I can hear the pain in her voice, cracking through her words.

'Shit, Freya, I'm sorry.'

'I'm just surprised, you know. I really didn't think it would work out. I thought he would've got bored with her, like he did with me, but then for some reason I searched his profile and there was a photo of him with his hand on her stomach. They did a pregnancy photoshoot! You must think I'm ridiculous, still caring about his life after all this time.'

'Not at all.'

She picks up the two glasses and I follow her out onto the balcony. It's dark, lit only by a small citronella candle that she puts under the table and the traffic lights from the intersection across the road. We sit side by side, watching them changing from green to yellow to red.

I take a sip of my gin and tonic. It's weak. Far too much tonic, not enough gin.

'You know,' she continues, 'I asked him about kids, and he said he didn't want any. He was adamant.'

'Maybe it was unplanned?'

'I don't know.' She passes me a cigarette. 'When we were together, I fell pregnant on accident once. Scott really pushed for me to have an abortion. Like, really pushed. Threatened to leave me if I didn't. I was so torn up about it. I'd always wanted a baby, so aborting seemed nonsensical to me, but at the same time having a baby with someone who has strongly expressed their disapproval from the beginning...Well, it's just setting you up for failure. I think I called the abortion clinic and cancelled three or four times.'

I want to reach over and touch her, but oddly, we don't have that kind of relationship, so instead I take another drag of the cigarette.

'In the end, I had a miscarriage, which was a blessing in some ways; it took the decision out of my hands at least. I still don't know what I would've chosen to do.' As though suddenly regretting what she said, she adds, 'Please don't judge me.'

'Of course not. Kids are such a huge responsibility. I don't think it's a decision people should make lightly or do just because it's expected.'

'You never wanted kids?'

'I used to. It just didn't work out.'

'It's not too late for you,' she says. 'You're in your forties, men can have kids forever. Time will be running out for me soon, though.' She puts her palms up to her face and presses them against her eyes. 'Anyway, Scott has a little boy due in a few weeks and I don't know why I'm so upset, but I am. Why wasn't I good enough, but she is?'

'I don't think it's that,' I say. 'Maybe he just changed his mind over time.'

'Maybe. Or maybe she brings out a side of him that I could never reach.'

The traffic lights continue to cycle.

Go. Slow down. Stop.

On the drive home, I thought about what Freya had said. From the moment she'd told me about her ex, I'd disliked him. He'd taken the coward's way out, sneaking off while she was at work, without so much as an explanation. But when I thought about it, Adeline had done the same thing to Gerard. She was too afraid of the fallout to tell him she was leaving, so she'd waited until Amanda had moved out of our rental, then left one day while Gerard was out, all her possessions in a single suitcase. She'd moved straight in, running from her issues with her family to Gerard, then from Gerard to me.

We were naive, Adeline and I, to believe we could disrupt things the way we did without any consequences. With the exception of Lena, my family took the break-up badly, as though I had personally cheated on each of them.

Dad had called me one night, his voice low and disappointed. 'Tell me, Thomas, that you haven't committed one of the greatest sins in the Bible.'

Adultery.

I hadn't known how to respond to that. Objectively, I'd always known that what we had done wasn't *right*, but it didn't feel wrong either. I'd never planned for things to go the way they did, and I certainly had never intended to hurt anyone; I'd simply fallen in love with someone else. Wouldn't the bigger sin have been staying with Amanda for the rest of my life, purely out of obligation? Didn't she deserve better than that?

Didn't we all?

'Do you not realise how this looks, Thomas?' he yelled, so loud I held the phone away from my ear. 'What are we meant to tell people? We raised you better than this! We raised you knowing right from wrong.'

I could hear Mum sobbing in the background, and I could just imagine how mortified she would be, having to explain the situation to her friends at church. My life choices were a direct reflection of her parenting. A direct reflection of her.

'*She* is not welcome here!'

She. As though Adeline was a temptress who had tricked me into biting a forbidden apple. It wasn't that I expected everyone to

forget about Amanda and immediately accept Adeline with welcome arms; but I thought there would be a sliver of understanding
that the situation wasn't simply black and white. Good or evil.

My mind cycles through my previous conversations with Freya.
I'd always said the right things. I'd assured her that her ex was an
idiot for not appreciating what he had. That she deserved better.

He'd hurt Freya, and therefore he was a bad guy in my eyes. I'd
never paused to consider the grey.

The truth was, he and Freya probably just weren't right
together.

I guess people can always justify their own choices, even if
those choices are replicas of things they despise in others.

A dandelion is still a weed, even if you display it in a beautiful vase.

You're probably doing it now. Judging me, for leaving Amanda in
that way. But what should I have done, I wonder?

I was so young. How was I supposed to know what I was looking for when all I had experienced was my own, small, insignificant
speck of a life? Does anyone really know in their first relationship?

Let me ask you something. How did your first love turn out for
you? Do you still love them?

Chances are, probably not.

Did you ever really love them at all?

ISO 160

It's late. Too late to be cleaning the house, yet here I am.

It's almost eleven p.m. and my bed has been stripped of the slightly yellowed sheets that smelled of old sweat and been remade with a spare set that instead smell faintly of dust. The empty wine bottles and dirty takeaway containers have been taken outside to the bin, the smashing of glass bottles shattering the night's serenity. The scattered mess of clothes on the bedroom floor has been swept up into a small mountain and shoved unceremoniously into the wardrobe and all the random, loose papers—bills, community newsletters, pizza coupons, and who knows what else—have been piled in a stack and moved from the dining table to the office desk where they should've been all along. The room at the back of the house is the only one I haven't touched, its door remaining firmly shut.

Mayfield hums. I didn't do a perfect job by any means—there wasn't enough time for that—but she's tidier than she has been in years. Timber floorboards that have been covered with clutter are exposed, the kitchen looks spacious instead of crammed, and a candle someone gifted me years ago has finally found its calling.

Funny how we will put in effort for others that we wouldn't for ourselves.

Mayfield feels welcoming. Almost homely again.

I hear a car pull up outside and turn on the patio light. The engine cuts out, and a few seconds later there's the sound of a door slamming, followed by flashing orange lights as the car is locked with a soft beep. The neighbour's new sensor light comes on with a burst as the front gate squeals open, illuminating Freya as she walks towards the stairs, a small suitcase dragging behind her.

'You found it okay?' I ask—one of those stupid, yet polite questions.

She's wearing long-sleeved pyjamas with a cartoon cat across the front and beige Ugg boots. Her eyes are tired and her hair is hanging limp. Nothing like the perfect, manicured version I normally see.

'Well, the GPS did,' she says as she nears the top of the stairs. 'Fuck!' She lifts her hand from the railing and I see blood pooling on the tip of her finger.

'Oh, sorry, they really need sanding.' I grab her bag and lead her inside. Freya follows with her hand outstretched.

'Do you have a tissue or something?'

'Sure.'

I throw down the bags and run into the bathroom. I stopped buying tissues long ago but tear off a few squares of toilet paper. When I go back into the lounge room I see her eyes flickering around, taking everything in, trying to decode some kind of meaning—from the books piled on the shelf, the painting on the wall, the heavy ornate chest in the corner. I wonder what my possessions say about me.

She turns and smiles. 'It's nice. Tidier than I expected.'

I hand her the toilet paper and she blots her finger, her blood spreading over the white. The cut is deeper than I first thought.

'Thanks.' She slumps onto the couch heavily. 'I think your house hates me,' she says with a weak laugh.

I laugh too.

A cold breeze blows and Mayfield rattles.

Freya puts her suitcase in my room, right in the doorway. It's one of those shiny ones with a hard outer shell, and she clearly packed in a hurry. There are pieces of clothing bulging out from the top where the zip wouldn't quite do up, and it takes up most of the limited floor space.

But it won't be for long.

I bring out a bottle of shiraz and two glasses. 'I figure you might need this.' I pour eagerly, a little higher than I should.

'I really do. Your house is so cold, do you have a throw or something?'

'Um—'

'You know, like a blanket.'

'I know what a throw is, and no, I don't have one.' I go to the bedroom, stepping over her suitcase, and pull the quilt off the bed. 'Will this do?'

Freya smiles as I drape it over her. 'I can't believe you don't own a throw.'

'Why would I need one when I have a quilt?'

Freya rolls her eyes. 'Such a bachelor.'

She takes a sip of the wine. 'This is really good,' she says, picking up the bottle and studying the label. 'Ah, that explains it. It's from the Barossa. You know my family live less than an hour's drive from there?'

'I'll admit it, I'm a bit jealous. Did you go there often?'

'Not really.'

Despite her praise for the wine, Freya drinks like a cat, as though she has all the time in the world. I twirl the stem in my hand impatiently, trying not to finish my first glass too quickly. I bet she's one of those people who can happily sit on one glass all night. Or worse, someone who owns a bottle stopper. I've always wondered how there can possibly be a market for them—she might be it.

After a few minutes, I give in and pour a top-up.

As the night crawls on, Freya tells me more about what happened. How she'd gotten home from work and gone to have a shower when she heard a noise from the bedroom and crept to the door to investigate. Her voice shakes as she describes seeing a shadowy figure moving around in the dark, riffling through her drawers. Her gasp had alerted him and he'd darted out the sliding door and jumped over the balcony.

'Thanks for letting me stay, Tom. I know you like your space, but I didn't have anyone else I could ask.'

'No, don't be silly. Anytime.'

Although not too often.

Sleep evades me. My thoughts seem messy, like spidery splotches on a Rorschach test. From one angle, a harmless butterfly; from another, a demon. I can't make sense of them.

Freya, it turns out, is a light sleeper. Finicky in the same way she picks at her salads and sips her wine, and every time I shift in bed she mirrors me. I'm not used to having to be aware of someone else and I find myself overanalysing each move I make, uncomfortable in every position I choose. My body itches. At first just my jawline, but when I scratch it, it shifts to under my nose. Then the point of my elbow. Along my Achilles tendon. The middle of my back. Between my toes. Until I want to scratch at my whole body with a fork.

I decide to sneak out of bed in stages, so as not to wake her. Fragile increments.

There is more wine in the kitchen.

Normally I wouldn't, but it's been a stressful night and an extra glass won't hurt. Rather than taking it to the couch, I sit up at the kitchen bench. It gives me more notice if she gets up, more time to hide it—I wouldn't want her thinking I have a problem, and I don't, but wine soothes me. Helps my thoughts to soften and separate so that I can bring them out one at a time and inspect them.

For three years I've kept her at arm's length, not allowed her into my space, into my life, but I have to admit it's been nice to sit on the couch and talk the night away. Nicer than sitting alone staring at fictional lives on a screen while creating fictional photos. No one to talk to. Except Mayfield, of course. A house.

Her finger, dripping blood.

I think your house hates me.

Would my life be different if I'd sold up and started over again?

Probably. I could've moved on. Maybe married someone like Freya. Had kids.

People move on from tragedy all the time, if they want to.

But I don't want to, I realise. I don't deserve it.

ISO 200

I WAKE TO the smell of toast and the sound of someone moving around the kitchen. I can hear the gas clicking on, a frypan being put down on the stovetop, the kettle bubbling. Adeline hates cooking. Hates it. She avoids the kitchen like the plague, but she loves breakfast more, so sometimes she makes an exception in the morning.

'Oh, you're awake.' The voice is wrong: too high-pitched, the vowels too rounded.

For a moment I struggle to orient myself. Not physically—I know I'm at Mayfield, lying across my faithful couch—but in time. The years wobble and shimmer before me, like heat waves dancing above the ground in summer.

Freya.

'Good timing! I've almost finished breakfast.'

Disappointment settles over me, a well-worn blanket.

She comes out, balancing two plates and cups on a serving tray that I didn't realise I owned, unearthed from the depths of the kitchen cupboards. She's already dressed in gym clothes, her hair up, her make-up done. The Freya I'm used to seeing, not the vulnerable version from the previous night.

She moves towards the dining table, visible for the first time in years, but it feels unnatural to sit there.

'I usually eat outside.'

Freya has made poached eggs on toast and two mugs of Earl Grey, which I study with apprehension. The teabag, I notice, has a small split in the side and little pieces of debris swirl around the mug before settling down the bottom. It looks like water from the creek behind the house, and I imagine it to taste similar. The teabags were only bought for the rare occasion when my parents visit—I hope they haven't expired.

'Thanks for this.'

'I would normally cook some mushrooms or tomatoes, maybe some wilted baby spinach, but your fridge was pretty bare.'

'I haven't had a chance to go shopping yet.' A part truth. The full truth is that the fridge, even after shopping, is still fairly sparse. You don't really need much for one person, especially when most of my diet consists of caffeine and non-perishables in the form of various flavours of chips.

I hesitate with my cutlery over the eggs, white and wobbling. Poaching is easily the most unappealing way of cooking eggs. And what for? Just to avoid a little butter? I push the knife down into the jiggling blobs, the egg white oozing out, undercooked and the consistency of mucus.

'I've taken a few days off work,' she tells me. 'Just while I deal with the police report and everything. Is it okay if I stay a bit longer? I don't feel safe to go home right now.'

'Of course, stay as long as you need. I have a couple of shoots this afternoon, though. Will you be okay here on your own, or should I cancel them?'

'No, don't cancel, I'll be fine. I might duck out and get some more groceries while you're gone. Pick up some ingredients for dinner.'

'You don't have to cook.'

'I want to.' She smiles. 'It makes me feel better about intruding. Any special requests?'

'Whatever is fine,' I say. Although I want to ask her how long she's planning on staying. How long until she will feel safe enough to go back home.

I don't know what answer I'm hoping for.

There's a flapping of wings and Judge lands gracefully on the handrails in front of us. Freya lets out a high-pitched scream and jumps to her feet, waving her arms around in circles like a human windmill. 'Shoo! Shoo!'

He flies lazily over to the nearby jacaranda tree and watches her antics from a safe distance.

'He's fine,' I tell her. 'He's been coming every morning.'

Freya lowers herself slowly back into the chair, her body stiff and her eyes alert, trained on Judge.

'I don't think you understand,' she says, her voice serious. 'I used to get attacked by magpies riding my bike to school every morning. They're horrible birds.'

'I get it. I did too—but not every day, surely? They only swoop when they're nesting.'

Freya looks unconvinced. 'Well, it certainly felt like every day.'

There's movement from across the street, and the guy from twenty-two walks out onto the footpath to check if his bins have been emptied. He's wearing plaid boxer shorts with greyed socks and sandals, a large beer gut hanging over the elastic band.

I have a theory. There are two reasons why people stop making an effort. Either they are so comfortable in life that they become lazy and complacent, smug in their good fortune, their lives so safe that they turn their attention outwards, towards others, just to have something exciting to talk about. Or they have lost enough that caring starts to seem pointless.

He is definitely in the former group.

I wonder what they've said about me. The middle-aged guy living on his own in the house overrun with weeds and desperately needing a paint. I will him to look up and see me sitting on the veranda with Freya, give them a new topic for the dinner table, but he peers inside the bins and turns around, pulling them both behind him.

Clive and Claire. The couple who lived across the road.

Before.

Before the guy with the beer gut.

Not quite a year into our relationship, the last of my paternal grandparents died, leaving me an inheritance that allowed me to get into the property market a few years earlier than planned, and we made the move to Mayfield.

It didn't take long for Adeline to make friends. When one of Claire's parcels was incorrectly delivered to our address, Adeline dropped it over and came back an hour later telling me all about them.

She guessed they were only a few years older than us. Claire had been running a wildly successful business for years: French knitting. She sold necklaces and knitted coasters at some of the local florists and gift shops, but her main income was from custom orders. Clive was an animator who worked on medium-budget productions, mostly from home, with short stints to the Gold Coast here and there. At that point Adeline was desperate to get her photography business off the ground. Afternoons were spent doing family portraits for free, and on weekends she was shooting weddings for pocket change. Whatever she made went straight back into the business in the form of advertising.

I could tell she found them both fascinating.

'I've invited them over for coffee,' she said a few days later.

I was the odd one out. The only one who worked regular hours, who didn't have the freedom to catch up for coffee at ten a.m. on a Tuesday.

'If she can make a full-time wage French-knitting coasters, surely I can do the same as a photographer. It would just be nice to chat to them. See how they did it.'

It was as though Adeline believed some of their success would shed from them and land on her so that she might absorb it. A form of osmosis.

'Are you sure it's a good idea?' I asked. 'To befriend your neighbours?'

Adeline gave me a strange look. 'Why would it be a bad idea?'

I remembered the drama that used to come into our shop. How the gossip would lurk in the corners, growing until it was almost unrecognisable.

'What if we have a falling out? Then even going out in your own yard becomes awkward. We'd have to move.'

Adeline just laughed. 'That's a very pessimistic way of looking at things.'

Stale air. Kitty litter. And *stuff*. So much stuff.

The house is bursting with it.

I let my eyes travel around the room, taking everything in. A huge eight-seater dining table in the middle, a half-completed puzzle of Machu Picchu across it. Romance and fantasy novels stuffed into a sagging bookshelf. An aquarium that spans one entire wall.

Plants in various stages of the life cycle.

Photos pegged to strings of fairy lights.

Unexpectedly, a life-sized cardboard cut-out of a man in a suit.

It's not a small room, but the clutter makes it feel pokey.

Opal looks horrified. 'I'm sorry, Tom, I didn't think it would be immaculate, but I hoped it would be in a better state than this. I suggested they hire a storage container, but I suppose they decided against it.' She stands rooted to the spot, looking around the room without moving her head as though the house is some untamed animal that could attack at any moment. No quick movements. No eye contact. 'You'll just have to do what you can.'

A mottled-looking cat pokes its head out from behind the lounge. A tortoiseshell.

I remember Adeline telling me tortoiseshells are almost always female. Males are rare; a genetic mutation making them sterile. She always wanted to adopt one.

Topaz sneezes. 'Sorry, I'm allergic to cats.' She glares towards it and backs away from the door. 'I'll just be waiting out here.'

Carefully, I pick my way from room to room, pulling back curtains and opening windows as I go. With light and fresh air the house starts to seem less wild, more domesticated.

Yes, they own a lot. But the magazines on the coffee table are in a crisp, straight pile. The fish all appear to be thriving. Even the books are arranged alphabetically.

Spending so much time in houses that have been meticulously cleaned and styled can start to mess with reality. I find myself relieved to be photographing a house that feels lived in, that doesn't smell of bleach, and where they haven't hidden every possession away, crammed into cupboards, slipped under beds or locked away in storage containers.

Like something shameful.

It's strange really. The acquisition of stuff is something to be proud of. People get self-worth from the car they drive, the phone they have, their clothes, their shoes. But only if those things are constantly getting replaced with something better and newer.

The people who own this house have fallen victim to growing attached. It's not the shopping and collecting that makes them odd, it's the fact they don't throw things out the minute they become faded and old. They've got the newest version of Monopoly, but they've also kept the tattered-looking original. And they own far too many books. Books that are dog-eared. Yellowed pages. Dust covers with rips or curled around the edges. Many missing dust covers altogether.

All the paperbacks have broken spines.

There's a photo collage on the wall.

The couple appears to be in their late thirties, but they've clearly been together a long time. High-school sweethearts perhaps, although there are no wedding photos anywhere, so they still aren't married.

I'm guessing it's all anyone asks them about.

I place my bets. He wants to be a game designer but is a reluctant insurance broker. She's a singing teacher. They've both experienced loss. A parent maybe, or a friend. And they've travelled a lot—the photos show that—collecting souvenirs as they go.

They don't buy things to keep up with the Joneses or to show off their disposable income but as tangible reminders of experiences they've shared. But now the stuff is taking on a life of its own, threatening to overwhelm them. They know they can't keep it all, but they aren't quite ready to get rid of it either. Where would they start?

I know the feeling all too well.

That giraffe statue was from a market in Thailand. The pool table they bought on a whim. The books are all meaningful, each one capturing a different life, a different world, like owning a collection of souls. Everything is attached to treasured memories.

But no one sees that.

People only see clutter.

ISO 250

Dɪᴅ I ʀᴇᴀʟʟʏ love Adeline so completely? So absolutely?

The truth is, I didn't love her enough. The attributes I loved about her were equally the things I struggled with. Initially, I'd been drawn to her outgoing and determined nature, but while I admired it, I fought against it too.

Although I had agonised over the decision for far too long, Clive didn't even glance at the label on the bottle when I presented it to him.

'Thanks, mate,' he said putting it on the kitchen bench. 'Dinner should be about half an hour.'

Adeline had caught up with Claire and Clive a few times for an informal coffee, but so far my work hours had meant I was excluded. Now they'd invited us over for dinner—her dream and my nightmare simultaneously but I'd swallowed my apprehension.

Clive led us out to the back deck, where we settled into the outdoor chairs and he ignored most of my attempts at polite conversation. Adeline and Claire sat next to each other, giggling away like old school friends. Adeline had an uncanny ability to fast-track friendships.

No one, I noticed, seemed to be watching the dinner.

Claire pulled out a joint from inside a tin box that was sitting on the windowsill. 'You guys don't mind?'

My mother's voice was immediately in my head: her warnings, her disapproval.

'Not at all,' said Adeline.

I shut the voice down.

Clive retrieved the bottle of red I had so carefully selected and passed it around, everyone taking turns swigging from it in between drags on the joint.

When it came to me, I tried to look casual, like I knew what I was doing.

'He has no idea what he's doing,' Adeline said with a squeal.

I gave her the finger. Put the joint between my lips and sucked back.

Smoke burnt my throat, tickled my oesophagus, and I coughed. Too much.

'You have to hold it in your lungs for a bit,' Claire said, with a pitying smile. 'Don't exhale straight away.'

Everyone was laughing while I tried to suppress a coughing fit.

The accountant who hadn't smoked before, who had spent his teenage years serving behind a shop counter instead of getting high.

I tried again, to nods of approval. Better.

'How long does it take to work?' I asked.

Claire snorted. 'You'll know.'

'Tom has a fun side,' Adeline told them, retelling the story of how we met. 'It's just repressed under years of Catholic shame.'

'Anglican,' I corrected.

She waved me away. 'Same, same.'

'And he's actually a great photographer. I think he should quit his job and we could go into business together. Heaps of photographers do.'

'That would be cute.'

'So cute. But he won't. He's risk-averse.'

'What's the worst that could happen?'

'Right?'

I didn't feel any different; perhaps I hadn't inhaled right.

'Is that what got you into accounting?' Claire asked. 'Your religious upbringing, the whole idea of men being providers? Or you just really love numbers and helping people decrease their taxable income?'

Hanging out with creatives felt like a topsy-turvy world. I was used to them justifying their career choices to everyone, but since meeting Adeline I'd found I was often the one needing to explain myself.

'I'm just realistic. It's great you have all managed to do things you love, but we can't all do that.'

'True. But we only have one life. I want it to be meaningful.'

'What's meaningful about knitting? Or coasters, for that matter?'

Immediately, I felt guilty. They'd invited me to their house, cooked for me. But Claire didn't bat an eyelid.

'I enjoy it. It's something I'd do for fun, so it's a bonus to be able to make money from it. I also knit beanies for babies in special care. It ticks my philanthropic box.'

'That's so beautiful. Maybe I could do something meaningful with photography.'

'Yes, so many options.'

'Chickens.'

'Chickens?'

'You should knit jumpers for chickens.'

'They have feathers.'

'But what about the ones who are rescued? Battery hens. They lose their feathers. They need jumpers.'

I could picture them. Running around with Christmas-themed jumpers. Bare legs. Half-naked. 'What about their legs?'

Laughter.

'What about them?'

'They need pants.'

'How would they shit?'

I hadn't thought of that. It hadn't occurred to me that they couldn't pull their pants down if they needed to.

'Fuck.' Clive stood up and barrelled past, his footsteps echoing.

Running. Did someone just leave?

'Where's Clive?'

'He burnt dinner.'

'Is it working yet?'

Claire's face was in front of mine. She had so many eyelashes. More eyelashes than people should have. Like a shark, with layers upon layers of teeth.

'You want to put pants on chickens, so I think so.'

Dinner was ruined.

There were stale Doritos instead of the promised pasta bake.

Adeline licked the cream from inside Oreos and passed me the chocolate biscuits, wet from her tongue. She didn't want to waste time on them. Just the cream.

When the Oreos and Doritos were gone, someone found a box of Corn Flakes. A rooster without clothes on the box.

I took a handful. 'They are better this way.'

'What way?'

'Sans milk.'

My thought, but not my voice. Someone else had answered for me. Read my mind, perhaps.

'Everything is better without milk.'

'Not coffee.'

'Especially coffee.'

My voice. I recognised it.

'Why do we have cows' milk? For calves.'

'We are stealing from baby cows.'

'We should have human milk. But people are grossed out by it.'

Claire jiggled her breasts. 'Only because men think boobs exist purely for them.'

My mind was too sharp. And too fuzzy. I noticed things I never had before, every individual mosquito buzzing around me, the fibres in my clothes, the beats in the music. But the minute I had the thought, it was lost.

'Will this,' I waved the joint, 'make me jump off the balcony?'

Laughter.

'I don't want to break my arm. Or impale myself on a garden stake.'

Adeline was suddenly on my lap, her hands on either side of my face.

'Stop stressing.'

The osmosis worked.

A few days later Clive popped in to speak to Adeline. One of the producers he worked with was getting married and Clive had recommended Adeline.

'They are interested,' he said, 'so be prepared with your prices and availability, and whatever you do, don't undersell yourself. They already love your work.'

After that first wedding, Adeline's business took off. Every weekend she was booked out, as well as most afternoons. I was gone every weekday, while she was home editing and doing book-work, and when I got home she would be heading out. Many times I'd pass her car turning out of our street just as I was turning in.

We became ships passing in the night, and Adeline renewed her campaign for me to quit my job. 'You're a great photographer,' she said, 'and it's becoming too much for just me, and I could really use a second shooter. Or you could take over the paperwork. You know how hopeless I am at that.'

My answer was always the same. 'I can't.'

My job was stable and secure, whereas hers fluctuated depending on the weather, the season, and sometimes on nothing at all.

'Why not, though?'

We had a mortgage, cars, bills. 'It's not a sound financial decision.'

'But we're fine, we have savings as a buffer.'

The thought was out before I could stop it: the savings were thanks to me.

'Some months might be tougher than others, but we'll figure it out. And imagine how much time we would get to spend together.'

I would've loved nothing more than to skip around the countryside with her—I hated my job—but we couldn't both run around with our heads in the clouds.

ISO 320

When I get home, the guy from across the road is out the front again, checking his mailbox. He has a shirt on this time, stretched too tight. He makes no move to go inside but leans against the fence while he cycles through the mail, inspecting the names carefully. Every now and then he glances into my yard.

I follow his gaze and see Freya, crouched down in her sports bra and bike pants, pulling weeds from the front garden.

He's never even looked at me before, but today as I climb out of my car he nods in my direction.

Acknowledgement.

Finally.

Before I was just the weird guy across the road who lived on his own, but now I'm the guy across the road with the hot girlfriend.

Fuck him.

'It was a bit of a jungle out here.' Freya stands up as I open the gate. She rubs her hands on her thighs, leaving a streak of dirt.

'Sorry. Gardening isn't really my thing...'

It was Adeline's domain; cooking was mine. Although that's just an excuse, isn't it? I don't bother with cooking anymore either.

'No, no, I'm loving it. It's kind of a novelty for me, coming from an apartment. I'd love to have a garden.' Her voice is almost wistful, and I don't say anything, not wanting to give her any ideas.

She carries the bucket over to the bin and shakes it out, watching the weeds rain down. 'There,' she says with satisfaction, like she has achieved so much. And she has, but they'll be back within a month. A never-ending battle—one I can't be bothered fighting anymore.

'I was going to trim back the lilly pillies along the fence, but I couldn't find any shears. I tried to get into the carport around the side but—'

'Don't go in there,' I say, too abruptly. I pause. Try again. 'There's nothing in there but I have some tools under the house.'

Freya folds her arms and smirks at me. 'Far out, is that where you bury the bodies?'

She laughs. I do too.

I begin walking up the front steps when something bright flashes into my eyes, momentarily blinding me. Dazed, I search for the source and discover Mayfield is shining—not in the metaphorical sense, but literally. There are mirrored disks hanging along the veranda, swaying and rotating in the breeze. As they spin, the setting sun bounces off them, shooting bursts of light around haphazardly.

'What's with the new outdoor decorations?' I yell down to Freya.

'Oh, I got them today! Magpie deterrents. The guy at the shop told me birds don't like the sunlight being reflected.'

There's a white circle in my vision every time I blink.

'No, I'm sure they don't.'

While I edit the photos from the day, Freya takes control of the remote, and we end up watching a reality dating show where all the girls are fake and all the guys are toxic. It's utter crap, but I have to admit it's fun to watch Freya's dismay whenever they act like the arrogant fuckwits they clearly are. I wouldn't have described her as an expressive person, but I'd never seen her watch reality television before.

She asks me who I would choose to date, and when I say none of them she looks offended.

'I'm sure they wouldn't be interested in you anyway.'

She's made a quinoa salad for dinner, and gets us both glasses of water with ice. The salad is better than expected, and she looks pleased when I go and get myself a second serving, as though she's converted me to healthy eating.

I pick up both our bowls and take them to the kitchen, washing them immediately under running water with a squirt of dish soap. It takes all of fifteen seconds, such a simple task, and I wonder why I usually avoid it so vehemently. I vow to do better.

'Want a glass of wine?' I yell out, although I've already uncorked it and got out two glasses.

'Again?'

Even through the walls, I can hear the disapproval dripping from her voice. I put the bottle back down reluctantly and instead refill my water glass at the sink.

When I sit back down, Jayda is crying into the camera after finding out Hayden kissed Phoebe at the reunion dinner.

Freya is watching me. 'Do you drink every night?'

'I might have a glass or two most nights. You know what they say about a glass of red wine...'

She sits up straighter, her eyes still on me. I wish she'd turn her attention back to the TV she was so engrossed in only seconds ago. 'I know there are a lot of studies about the benefits of red wine, but more than a glass is not recommended. People tend to twist those studies to justify their drinking.'

'That's not what I'm doing.'

'So, you don't drink more than one small glass a night?'

'Not usually.'

'And you could stop drinking if you wanted to?'

'Of course.'

'Okay.'

I pretend to be asleep when she comes into the room. It's far too early for me to go to bed, but Freya doesn't know that. She lifts the covers and slides into bed beside me, letting in a cool breeze with her. I feel her breath on my cheek as she leans over, looking for signs of life. Her arm snakes over my body, and her hand runs down underneath my boxers, reaching for my limp cock, already out for the night. I try to think unsexy thoughts.

The upcoming election.

The weather forecast.

Emails I need to send.

But her hands are warm and persistent and the traitor responds. Surrendering, I pull her down onto me and close my eyes.

It's quick, quicker than normal. The frame of the bed bumps against the wall, the floorboards creak. Freya rocks back and forth, moaning so loudly I feel certain the whole street will hear. Finally, she collapses beside me, breathing heavily.

'That was amazing, Tom,' she sighs, as though I had anything to do with it. And although it was, I can't bring myself to agree with her.

Instead, I sit up. 'Want a smoke?' It's always been her idea, but tonight I'm feeling restless.

'I think I'm good.'

Once Freya is asleep, I find the pack of cigarettes in her hand-bag and take one, sneaking outside with it and a bottle of red, as though I'm still a teenager living at home rather than a grown adult in my own house. On the veranda, everything is quiet and bathed in silvery light. I sit on the top step overlooking the newly tamed garden, the flame searing into my vision as I flick the lighter. The air is cold, but the smoke warms my mouth and lungs, the cloud expelled dissipating before me. I breathe in, soaking in the peace and solitude. Freya has never declined a post-sex smoke before, and although this sudden change unsettles me, I'm relieved to be alone.

Once the first cigarette is exhausted, I sneak back inside and steal another one, then another. Mayfield has always been a kind of haven for me, but tonight the walls feel too close, too claustrophobic.

There's the tinkling sound of a bell and a cat slinks along the fence line, its white fur glowing in the moonlight. It stops at the bottom of the stairs, daintily grooming itself, aware of yet unbothered by my presence. When it turns its gaze towards me, I lift my glass in acknowledgement and it moves on, unperturbed.

'Doesn't it feel strange, shooting all these weddings when you don't believe in marriage?'

'Do you believe in the tax system?'

From the moment I'd broken off my previous engagement, I had been planning my next one, but at Clive and Claire's one night, while getting stoned, Adeline announced she had no such plans.

'It's just the transfer of ownership,' she mused. 'The way brides get given away by their fathers to the groom, it's transferring a woman from one man to another.'

'But,' I said, 'no one sees it that way anymore. It's a symbol of love.'

'A symbol to who?'

'Everyone?'

'Why do we need everyone's approval? I don't speak to my family, and yours already don't approve.'

'They might if they can see how serious we are.'

'If the only way they'll accept me is for us to spend a fortune on a wedding, then I don't want it. Besides, white doesn't suit me.'

Claire and Clive were married, and I looked towards them for back-up, but Clive shrugged. 'She's right. We would've been better off spending that money on a holiday.'

'Or buying a car.'

'Putting in a pool.'

'Donating it.'

'Why does it matter so much to you?' Adeline asked.

Suddenly I wasn't sure. Because it was what I had always planned? Because it seemed important? 'Because I love you so much, and I want everyone to know it.'

Adeline nuzzled into my neck. 'That's sweet, Tommy, but I already know it. I don't need some outdated ceremony. I've felt like a possession before, I have no desire to be one again.'

Possession.

A memory. That first day at the river. *The dog is his possession.* I couldn't understand how someone as strong as Adeline could've ever felt that way.

Adeline watched the smoke coming out of her mouth. 'I'm a dragon.'

ISO 400

MOST OF THE mail is junk—pizza coupons and catalogues. A kid on the street is offering dog-walking services for ten dollars. Stephanie Stevens has sold a few houses, one within *TWO HOURS* of being on the market!!! *And now she can sell yours!!!* A couple of envelopes look deceptively personal, but it's just election material. One of them is full of promises, outlining all the incredible changes that will happen if you vote for Harold Spencer, another lists all the ways Harold Spencer is utterly incompetent. The invitation Rebekah promised me is at the bottom of the pile, in a small navy envelope. As soon as I see her writing—sharp and slanted, in metallic silver—I recognise it.

'What's that?' Freya asks. She's eating muesli topped with Greek yoghurt and raspberries, all things that had magically appeared in my fridge in recent days. Last night, I noticed her toothbrush was sitting in the glass alongside mine, and her bottles of skincare products seemed to be breeding on the bench.

I realise I've been staring at my name on the front of the envelope but made no move to open it. 'Oh, just an invitation I think.' I unfold it and give an obligatory glance. 'My nephew's birthday.'

I throw it back down on the pile of junk mail, and Freya picks it up, scanning it carefully. 'I didn't know you had a nephew.'

'I have four of them, actually.'

'You've never mentioned them.'

'I don't really have anything to do with them.'

She looks bothered by this new information, as though it's something I've been purposefully withholding from her.

'It just seems weird you didn't tell me when I've been talking about my nephew with you.'

An uneasiness prickles beneath my skin, and I get the distinct feeling that something has shifted within our dynamic.

There's a flash of black and white and Judge lands in the jacaranda tree, eyeing the spinning discs with apprehension. He makes no move to come closer.

Freya looks pleased with herself.

'Good! Seems like the mirrors worked.'

ISO 500

THEY STUFF UP my pizza order—instead of a pan-base supreme, it's a thin and crispy cheese. The mix-up of toppings I can handle but I despise thin and crispy bases. It's like eating cardboard dipped in grease. I'm just glad I realised when I got to the car, not after getting all the way home.

Freya had offered to cook again, but I suggested takeaway. She had cooked breakfast both mornings, plus dinner. I knew she was worried about being a burden and didn't want to feel indebted, but I was beginning to worry the pendulum of indebtedness was now swinging too far the other way.

In front of me a woman opens a box and jabs her fingers towards an array of vegetables. 'This isn't what I ordered. Do you think my kids will eat this?'

The boy behind the counter looks young, almost too young to be working, but I'm getting that feeling more and more. A few months back I went to a medical centre and my doctor looked school-aged; I don't particularly want to deconstruct the reason for that.

The kid pushes his glasses up his nose and blinks. 'I'm sorry, but, um, we can make you another one if you're happy to wait?'

He glances around, looking for some support from the other staff, some kind of confirmation that he's allowed to offer that, but they're all busy and all look equally clueless.

I jump forward. 'I think our orders might've been mixed up.'

The woman turns to me, her eyes ablaze.

I continue. 'You ordered thin and crispy cheese?'

'Yes. My kids won't eat anything else.'

I hold out the box towards her. 'I accidentally got yours. We probably just have similar names or something.' The receipt is still in my hand, and I glance at it. S. Thomas. 'My name is Tom; your last name is Thomas. It seems like a harmless mistake.'

I smile and the kid looks relieved, but something about that statement seems to fire her up again.

'It's not though, is it?'

She turns back to the boy, whose eyes are wide.

'It's not just a harmless mistake. What if my child was allergic to something on this pizza?'

She taps her foot. Waits.

'I—I don't know,' he stammers, glancing around again. An SOS with his eyes, pinging around the room.

'They could die,' she says pointedly. 'Because of your carelessness.'

I snort. 'That's a bit extreme.'

The boy looks at me gratefully. A few short years ago he was probably in bed at this time. Now he's being accused of negligence causing death. Once the years start gaining speed, they don't slow down.

'If my child was anaphylactic—'

'Of course,' I say, 'but I don't think death is the most likely outcome of a mixed-up order. The most likely outcome is probably exactly what happened—both of us noticing it wasn't what we ordered and having it swapped back or a new pizza made. This is clearly the first job for most of the kids here. I'm sure they're doing their best.'

A girl comes out from the back, still young but with an air of authority about her. 'I'm sorry, it seems like there's been some kind of mix-up?'

'Yes,' I say. 'But it's sorted out now.'

The woman looks at me from the corner of her eye, not convinced.

'We can offer you both a voucher for a free large pizza of your choice and garlic bread for the next time you visit.' She produces two shiny slips of paper. 'We're also happy to remake your pizzas tonight.'

'I don't have time to wait around,' the woman huffs, passing her pizza box to me. 'My children will be waiting and hungry.' But she snatches the voucher from the girl's hand. She turns to the boy. 'I expect you'll be more careful in the future.'

He nods quickly.

She looks as though she has more to say but glances my way before turning and marching out the door.

'Sir.' The girl holds out the voucher.

'It's fine.' I wave her away and smile at the boy. He already looks far too stressed; there's a whole lifetime of that ahead of him. 'Mistakes happen.'

We watch Freya's show and she nibbles slowly on a single slice of pizza while I try to hold myself back from demolishing the whole box. I show constraint with my drink too, still sipping on my first glass of wine, when normally I would be up to my third.

It feels warmer inside than usual, stuffier. Mayfield herself, quieter. I look around. All the windows have been closed against the cold. Against the fresh air.

On the screen an orange woman is screaming in the middle of a restaurant at a man who is built like a boulder. I missed what the catalyst was but it's usually a simple misunderstanding, something completely minor.

Freya finishes her slice of pizza and doesn't go for a second. I'm already up to my fourth.

I want to ask her when she will feel safe to go back to her apartment. If there's anything I can do to speed along the process.

But I don't. It's only been three nights, which isn't much, really. Not in the big scheme of things. And I don't want to seem insensitive.

'You done?' I say, picking up the pizza box. 'I might put the leftovers in the fridge.'

She nods without looking at me. 'Yeah, there's more calories in that one piece than I normally have in a day.'

In the safety of the kitchen, I take out another slice and eat it quickly. I'm desperate for a drink but don't want to deal with the insinuation that I'm an alcoholic. But I can't relax when she's around, so I'm craving it more than ever.

'Tom, I'm going to have a shower. Can I grab a fresh towel?' Her voice floats through the doorway.

Hurriedly, I toss the pizza slice behind the coffee machine, trying to swallow quickly. A criminal hiding a murder weapon.

'Of course! There are some towels in the linen cupboard, you can grab yourself one.'

I wait, listening for the sound of the shower turning on so I can return to my discarded pizza slice, maybe skull a glass of wine or two while it's safe. Hopefully she has to wash her hair. Shave too.

But the shower isn't turning on. Were there no towels in the linen cupboard?

'What the hell?'

Her voice is high-pitched. Alarmed.

My vision swims for a moment, the edges becoming dark and unfocused. I don't need to walk out into the hallway to know she's gone to the spare room instead of the linen cupboard nearby. Don't need to see her puzzled face as she takes in the scene before her. The soft green walls with white trim. The rocking chair underneath the window. The timber cots in the corner. Shelves lined with stuffed animals, picture books and trinkets. Framed paintings of farm animals on the wall: a duckling, a lamb, a piglet, a foal.

She appears in the kitchen doorway, her eyes searching my face for some kind of reasonable explanation. 'I don't understand. Do you have a baby?'

I shake my head.

'This makes no sense.' Her voice trembles. 'Explain it to me, Tom!'

'I can't.'

'You can. We've spoken about children before. I confided in you about my pregnancy, and now it's your turn. I have a right to know what's going on.'

But that's the thing—she doesn't have a right to know. We aren't dating, and I don't owe her anything, a very deliberate decision on my part.

'I'm sorry.'

It's the best I can offer.

'Without honesty, we're nothing,' she says. Her words are intended as a threat, but when she realises she won't get anything more from me she goes into my room and begins frantically stuffing all her clothes back into her suitcase. She looks scared now, anger turned into panic, and part of me wants to reach out and reassure her, but I know there's nothing that will fix this. We don't say anything to each other as she gets to the front door and pauses momentarily to look back. Her expression is one of confusion, as though she doesn't recognise me.

The door slams loudly behind her.

Once she's gone, I retrieve the pizza slice and finish it off as I walk around Mayfield, opening all the windows that Freya had shut. The breeze feels refreshing on my face. In my room I can see the floor again. I notice a collection of bottles on my bedside table. Face serums of some description. In the bathroom I find her toothbrush and a roll of floss on the bench. Bottles of shampoo and conditioner in the shower. Freya had packed in such a hurry she'd left anything behind that wasn't immediately within reach.

It should feel like rejection, but it doesn't. It feels inevitable.

Lottie
ISO 640

AT THE GROCERY store, there's a tray bursting with succulents prominently displayed. I come to a stop in front of them, thinking of the empty pots on my balcony. I'd always loved nature and it would be nice to have something green to look at rather than being surrounded by iron bars, grey carpet and bitumen. I glance at the prices and recoil. It feels extravagant to spend money on something that could just die. Surely the money could be put towards something more sensible. More necessary.

But still, I hesitate.

I can't remember the last time I've done something selfish, something for me. I love Coral with everything I have but we are so enmeshed I can no longer tell where I end and she begins. My every choice revolves around her, my every dollar, my every minute. Did Lottie the person—not just Lottie the mum—even exist anymore? Who was she?

Suddenly, doing something for me, however small, seems critical.

The whole bus ride home, I am obsessively attentive to my little succulents. To avoid them being crushed, I put the heavy groceries in the mesh basket at the bottom of the pram and carefully place the plants in the seat, surrounded by soft items—bread and toilet paper—to keep them from tipping over. It means I have to carry Coral the whole way, not that she minds.

In the end, I'd selected three, one for each of the empty pots. I needed all the help I could get, so two of them were the biggest and healthiest ones of the bunch. The third was small and spindly with browning leaves and a yellow sticker announcing 50 per cent off. It was a risk, but it deserved a chance too.

When we get home, I sit Coral beside me while I repot them into their newer, bigger homes. I don't have any potting mix and the dirt in the pots looks dry and lacking in nutrients, but I moisten it with water and dig a hole for the new occupants. Coral runs her hand under the jug while I carefully water them. I read the information on the tags aloud, trying to memorise their requirements. Full sun. Water sparingly.

It seems doable.

Can opener.
Photo frames.
Candles.
~~Plants.~~
A jacket.
A driver's licence.
A car.
Flowers or vegetable seeds.
A pet.
Beach toys.
A sense of direction.
~~Mobile data.~~
~~Lime cordial.~~

ISO 800

DUE TO WINTER sickness, the amount of people at playgroup the following week is cut in half. Coral is coming down with something too. Since starting solids she's been sleeping through the night more and more regularly, but last night she was up every hour and this morning she felt unusually warm. The thermometer confirmed she had a slight fever, but after the debacle with my payments last fortnight I didn't want to risk another issue. Before we left, I squirted some Panadol into her mouth and embraced denial.

Georgina looks frustrated by the amount of food she's bought. She paces around the kitchenette, muttering about people not showing.

'Just keep the biscuits in their packet,' says Mei in a soothing voice. 'They'll keep fresh until next week. We can eat the fruit today.'

'I just wish people would give me more notice. Lisa only messaged me twenty minutes ago. I'm sorry, but surely she knew Toby was sick earlier than that.'

Mei shrugs as she cuts a kiwifruit into wedges. 'She probably just forgot.'

'Can't be bothered, more like it. At least there's one person I can rely on to always turn up.'

At first I think she is talking about Mei, but then her eyes meet mine. Heat rises up my neck as I realise she must know that attending playgroup is a requirement for me. The employment provider confirming my attendance had clearly given it away.

The first half hour is spent discussing the absent people. One baby's come down with hand, foot and mouth disease. Another has a cold. Yolande, who last week had been referred to as a superwoman, is in hospital with her toddler, who had fallen from his highchair and was being monitored for a concussion.

Mei shakes her head sadly. 'Yolande feels awful. It's just horrible when she's already dealing with so much.'

Georgina exchanges a glance with another mother, a blonde-haired woman named Alison, who appears to live in gym clothes. 'And so she should. It's completely her fault.'

'Exactly. That's why highchairs have straps. She obviously wasn't using it safely.'

Mei is frowning. 'She did have him strapped in, but Benny slipped out of it while she was in another room. You know how she had to get him a Houdini strap for the car? He's an escape artist.'

'Which is exactly why she should know better than to leave him unsupervised. I would never!'

'Same here. There's really no excuse.'

'She's got two other kids she needs to be supervising,' Mei says. 'I'm sure she was doing her best, but accidents happen.'

But Georgina's expression is resolute. 'I have three kids too. None of them have ever had a concussion,' she says sternly. And that seems to settle it.

Again, in the car park I try to make myself as inconspicuous as possible, but with so few people it's immediately obvious that the car-to-people ratio is wrong.

'Where's your car?' Mei asks me suddenly, sounding concerned. She swivels her head around as though it might suddenly appear in one of the empty spaces.

Georgina raises her head inquisitively from the boot of her own car.

Alison looks genuinely puzzled. 'How did you get here?'

Clearly they've never heard of public transport.

'Public transport, I'm guessing,' says Georgina, raising an eyebrow at me.

But this explanation doesn't sit well with Mei. 'The nearest bus stop is too far. No one is going to walk that kind of distance. And with a baby!'

I laugh along with them as though it's a ridiculous suggestion. 'Don't worry, I got dropped off. They're just running a bit late to pick me up.'

'Your partner?' asks Georgina, amused.

She knows.

'Want us to wait with you?' Mei offers.

'No, no, you guys go. I need to make a call anyway.'

For a moment, I think they are going to insist—Mei out of concern, Georgina to catch me out in a lie—but waiting around in a car park is too inconvenient. I'm relieved when the last of their cars disappear at the top of the driveway, but the anxiety that had washed over me remains, sticky on my skin.

Without thinking, I touch the diamond necklace around my neck, only this time it doesn't comfort me. Now it feels ridiculous and childish. Like stick-on earrings. I wonder why I'm still wearing it.

I'd thought Heath was the one and that he felt the same. The necklace was evidence of that. But I had been wrong about him. When I excitedly showed him the pregnancy test, well...I guess I don't need to tell you what Heath's reaction was when he found out.

It turns out that sometimes you never really know people at all.

ISO 1000

HE IS THERE today when we go past. The homeless man in the park.

Two women in pencil skirts and a man with a button-up shirt are walking down the hill towards me, laughing. They all have lanyards covered in pins hanging from their necks, and in their hands are large plastic cups filled with iced coffee and cream.

'Remind me not to go there again,' one of the women says, tossing her cup into the bin as they pass. 'Gross.'

It's still half full.

The homeless man stands up from his bench and pads over to the bubbler, resting one elbow on the lever, and using the other hand to splash some water on his face.

I notice them notice him.

How they glance his way quickly, then away again, and as they pass by they swerve off the path, careful not to get too close. It's as though there's an invisible force field putting distance between him and everyone else.

Or between everyone else and him.

As they pass me, I see one of the women look me up and down. Her eyes flick to Coral, for a second, then quickly away.

I put my head down and walk faster.

Unintentionally, I arrive at the library right on Story Time, so the kids' section is packed with prams and people. Coral and I had spent the last few days housebound while she battled a fever, and the sudden crowd of people feels especially suffocating.

One of the librarians is sitting in front of a small crowd dressed as a pig. She is wearing a pink onesie complete with a curly tail, and has a plastic snout over her nose, the elastic leaving deep grooves in her cheeks. She holds up a picture book, which she moves around after each page so all the children, no matter where they are sitting, can see. Some of the kids have dressed up too, all as various farm animals, and I spot a lamb, a cow and two dogs. They jostle to be sitting right at the front, and every now and then she pauses to gently direct them off her feet. A few parents sit cross-legged at the back of the circle with smaller toddlers on their laps, but most stand in small groups further back, talking to each other in hushed voices. It's clear this is a regular activity for most, and they seem familiar with each other. I spot an overabundance of linen, iPhones, and Birkenstocks; all clear signs I won't fit in, and instinctively I shrink back around the corner until I'm out of sight.

'Are you hiding?'

Startled, I look up to see Ivan before me, an amused expression on his face. It takes me a minute to process where I know him from.

'Of course not.'

He glances towards the other parents. 'I get it can be a bit intimidating,' he says, and I realise then he is also the odd one out—they're all mothers. 'But Coral will love it. Odette is amazing.'

Although the librarian has been a constant in my life for months now, I never knew her name, and feel almost guilty about it, but he's right, she is amazing. For the entire half hour she keeps all the kids (and parents) enraptured with her Oscar-worthy voices and expressions. When she closes the final book, there's a moment when everyone blinks around the room at each other, slowly coming out of whatever trance she put them in.

A few women give Ivan a friendly wave as they leave, which somehow extends to me. I can't help but look for the judgement in their eyes as I smile back, but it doesn't seem to be there, and I wonder what kind of spell Odette managed to weave.

'You don't have to look so worried,' Ivan says, 'they're all pretty nice here. A few of us have started our own little unofficial playgroup.'

I remember then that he wasn't at the last session. 'You aren't going back to the Wednesday one?'

'No. I didn't like it there, but Florence enjoys playing with other kids so I wanted to replace it with something a bit more relaxed. You should come along.'

'I'm surprised,' I say. 'Everyone seemed to worship you.'

'Yeah, that was kind of the problem.'

I think back to all the times everyone had gushed over him: for cutting up grapes, for doing Florence's hair in piggy tails, for remembering to bring her jacket, for carrying Band-Aids in his nappy bag.

For *having* a nappy bag.

'You didn't like being put on a pedestal?'

He gives me a strange look. 'Definitely not. To be honest, it's kind of demeaning.'

Demeaning seems like a strong word for admiration. What I would give to have even half that.

'It just feels like the expectations of me are so low that even doing the bare necessities somehow deserves praise.' His eyes meet mine. 'I'm sure you can relate to being underestimated.'

I might've been wrong about him.

He checks his watch and groans quietly. 'I might need to get going soon.' Florence is tottering back and forward happily, selecting picture books for Coral. At my feet, a literary mountain is forming. 'I hate dragging her away when she is having fun, but I have a meeting at midday and need to get Florence down for her nap beforehand.'

This surprises me, even though I feel it shouldn't. 'What do you do for work?'

'I run an online store.' He bends down to wrestle shoes onto Florence's wriggly feet. 'I do most of the work at nights, or around her naps, so I'm pretty lucky in that way.'

From the outside, Florence appears to have the best of everything, and I'm equal parts impressed and envious that Ivan can provide that for her as a single parent without sacrificing time together. His world feels light years away from mine, scrimping and stressing over the purchase of three little plants.

He seems to sense my thoughts.

'I did a business degree straight out of school and had it set up and running smoothly before she was born; it's not as impressive as it sounds. Anyway.' He scoops Florence up in one arm and slings the nappy bag over the other. 'Will I see you at our new playgroup? We meet on Friday mornings at the park across from the fish and chip shop. It's just down the end of Nicholas Street.'

'I know it.'

How convenient would it be to walk directly across the road instead of the mammoth journey I currently undertake. And I certainly have no desire to see Georgina again, but I tell him I'll think about it. I'm worried an unofficial playgroup won't be enough to prove my worthiness to the powers above, and I'm scared of messing up my obligations. I can't risk losing my payment again.

Once Ivan left the library I jumped onto one of the spare computers. My next appointment with the employment provider was coming up again, and I knew they would ask me if I'd looked into study options. I wanted to be prepared this time.

Business degrees were offered at universities everywhere, on campus, hybrid or online, and I printed as many as I could to look at properly later. The end result is twenty-four course outlines, now spread out on the kitchen bench before me. I pick one at random and hold it under the light to read the details. I'd always thought I lacked direction, but as I skim through the information, I realise that's not quite the case: I might not be able to pinpoint precisely where I want to go and the path to get there but I know exactly what I *don't* want. Which it turns out, is almost the same thing.

Can opener.
Photo frames.
Candles.
A jacket.
A driver's licence.
A car.
Flowers or vegetable seeds.
A pet.
Beach toys.
A sense of direction.

ISO 1250

USUALLY I AVOID public transport during school hours, but my appointment has been booked early this time, leaving me no choice. They're around the same age as me and have overtaken the whole bus stop. One boy is doing pull-ups from the roof of the shelter, his biceps straining against his school shirt. Others stand around in groups, laughing, pushing each other, swearing and talking in a language I no longer understand, their school bags tossed carelessly on the ground.

I stand a metre or so down the hill, bouncing Coral on my hip and trying to look as inconspicuous as possible, but they've noticed me. The girls pull their shoulders back and hold their heads a little higher to look at me down their noses. The boys snigger, their eyebrows raised and smirks on their faces.

We are peers, but we're not.

I twirl my fingers through Coral's hair, making each of her ringlets more pronounced. 'Shhhh, it's okay,' I murmur to her. Not that she was upset in the first place.

One of the louder boys with an acne-covered face and bulging shoulders nudges one of the quieter ones, who is standing a little away from the group, his eyes downcast. He is shorter and skinnier than the rest, still more of a boy than a man, and even though brute strength is of little value these days, it still seems to hold some kind of social currency.

'You might have a chance with her.' The big one points in my direction. 'At least you know she's easy.'

The others laugh. The skinny one kicks at imaginary stones, and I play with Coral's hair.

When the bus arrives, I don't get on. I pretend I'm waiting for another one, even though I know it will be at least ten minutes away.

I'm a few minutes late for my appointment, but it doesn't really matter—they're running behind schedule again anyway.

It's someone different this time—a middle-aged man with a rodent face and hair receding slightly at the sides. He grins and makes small talk as we walk over to the desk, asking about Coral and commenting on the weather outside. It seems like a good start.

'So,' he says, leaning back in his chair, one foot resting on his knee. 'You and I are going to be working together for a while, but I want you to know I'm here to help, not judge. I want this to be a safe space where you can be honest with me. Sometimes we might not see eye to eye, but like any relationship—working relationship,' he clarifies with a wink, 'we can sort it out and come to a mutual understanding. Sound like a plan?'

'Sure.'

I notice he has a gold necklace around his neck, and I get the feeling he's one of those guys who hasn't quite realised his own age yet. I imagine him at home in the evenings with his wife—if he has one—telling her about his day. *I just connect with these young, disadvantaged parents. It's so rewarding, you know?*

He toggles his mouse, waiting for the computer to come to life.

'Okay.' He squints at the screen. 'There's a note here on the system saying you've accrued some demerit points and your last payment was suspended.'

As I explain what happened, he frowns, nodding along. 'I can see you're upset, but the requirements are that you must report your activities.'

I've heard it all before.

'I know it was a misunderstanding last time, but just make sure you report back in the future so we can be sure you're meeting your obligations.' He waggles a finger at me as though I'm a disobedient child, and I almost miss the stuck-up woman from last time.

'The last woman suggested looking into study,' I say, trying to steer the conversation in a more helpful direction. 'I think I've found a degree I'd like to do.'

I have the information folded up in my bag, and I slide it across the table to him with a sheepishness that gives the illusion of it being a bribe instead of a course outline. For days I'd poured over the printouts, weighing up all the options until it had become almost an obsession. 'There's a bridging course I could do to get in.'

He barely glances at it before handing it back. 'That's going to be quite a long undertaking, especially once you factor in the bridging course. We usually recommend short courses with good prospects. There's no sense in slogging away for years at university when you could do a six-month certificate and walk straight into a job.'

Coral reaches forward and snatches the paper off the table, stuffing it into her mouth, but I'm too numb to care.

'I come across a lot of young mothers in your exact situation,' he continues, 'and if I may be so bold as to make a suggestion, most of them have found working in childcare the perfect fit. There are plenty of vacancies, you can work while gaining a qualification, and you don't have to worry about finding someone to look after bub. She can come to work with you.'

Looking satisfied, he taps away at his computer, before running off to grab some papers from the printer. 'When you get home, have a look at these.' He lays the printouts in front of me as though they are the only choices.

When we get home, I run myself a bath.

Coral sits in between my legs, splashing at the water and bab-bling away, but I feel too drained to pay much attention. Squeezing my eyes shut, I press my palms into them until black spots appear. The message was clear. If you're unfortunate enough to be a single parent requiring government assistance, there's no room for ide-alistic dreams.

When I was encased in the tranquillity of the library, going to university had seemed like an exciting possibility, but now, back in the cage of my flat, it just seems foolish. Of course I can't spend years studying. Too many barriers loom before me. I don't even have an office desk or a laptop. No wi-fi. I've heard textbooks cost hundreds of dollars. And who would watch Coral?

Once again, I'd fallen prey to my own naivety and erroneously believed they wanted to help me. But it was clear that, to them, I wasn't a person with my own hopes and dreams; just a customer reference number being pushed towards whatever future is easiest for them to meet their KPIs and get their bonuses.

When would I learn?

Sighing, I sink down lower into the water. Coral squeals excit-edly as it surges around her.

Ivan had set himself up before Florence was born, before his relationship fell apart. My time for planning out a future had passed a long time ago. Now I just had to take what I could get.

A feeling of hopelessness creeps over me like a vine. It starts at my toes, climbs up my legs and weaves around my body. Up around my neck and over my face, tightening until the world around me becomes grainy like trying to see a solar eclipse through a pinhole.

Coral stops splashing and lies back against me, her head against my heart. Her body relaxes, and I wonder if my heartbeat sounds to her like home. I suppose there must've been a time I felt the same way about Mum, although the thought seems bizarre. She's always seemed like a foreign landscape—unfamiliar terrain for which I've never been able to acquire a map. I watch as Coral's eyelids flutter closed, and I want nothing more than to close mine too. Instead, I brush my finger softly over the curve of her cheek to keep myself awake. Her eyelashes are dark brushstrokes against dewy skin, her hair a gentle wisp of velvety strawberry blonde.

Sometimes when I look at her, I get the feeling of standing on the edge of a mountain admiring the breathtaking views: clusters of emerald trees below, a patchwork of fields in the distance and clouds so close you could almost skim them with your hand. The beauty of it causes your eyes to mist over and your breath to catch in your throat. But then you look down and realise how close the edge you are and that all it takes is one loose pebble under your shoe and you could slip.

Tom
ISO 1600

THE NEXT MORNING, I'm up unusually early.

Two eggs are sizzling on the frypan, surrounded by way too much bubbling butter. The coffee machine is whirring. A cold breeze is floating through the open windows.

Everything feels right with the world.

While I wait for the toaster to pop, I heap some sugar into my cup and swirl it around. When it does, the bread is barely toasted but I don't put it on again—that's only asking for trouble.

I spread on a thick layer of butter and pop the eggs on top. Balancing the plate in one hand and the cup of espresso in the other, I grab a knife on my way past. A big one, with serrated edges.

Judge is already there when I get outside, sitting high in the tree, far from the spinning mirrors that are twirling in the breeze. He always seems unimpressed, but today he looks particularly so. I put my breakfast on the table, before using the knife to hack at the cords the mirrors are suspended from.

I did some research on magpies after Freya left.

They're highly intelligent. When scientists tried to tag some for a study, the magpies worked together to free each other from the contraptions, a rare display of animal altruism. And you can befriend them. They're capable of memorising up to thirty individual faces, and during swooping season won't attack those who they recognise aren't a threat.

Six weeks.

Only six weeks out of fifty-two, and even then only a small percentage of magpies will ever swoop, yet everyone avoids them for life, their reputation preceding them wherever they go.

It doesn't happen instantly, but as I eat Judge edges closer and closer, until he is back in his usual spot on the veranda. I flick a small crumb of toast in his direction. Just a crumb. A token. Judge cocks his head, weighing me up, deciding if it's a gift or a trap.

After a moment, he flies over and stabs at it with his beak.

ISO 2000

FREYA FEELS BETRAYED. She thinks I lied to her. But I didn't.

Not really.

No one ever tells another person everything. I'm confident I don't know everything in her past, just like I haven't told her everything in mine.

Twins. That's what they said at the ultrasound, both of us squinting at the grainy grey blobs on the screen. Identical.

The sonographer paused for effect, the transducer still pressed low into Adeline's abdomen, smiling at our shocked faces.

'Double the trouble.'

I squeezed Adeline's hand. Twins!

He pointed them out. One fuzzy splotch. A second fuzzy splotch.

I'd always wanted kids, but the overwhelming love I felt surprised me. I hadn't realised how fast it could happen—when they're nothing but marks on a screen.

Not even babies yet. Embryos. The only evidence of them, a grainy black-and-white picture.

ISO 2500

THE CAFE IS one of those places that doesn't quite know what it wants to be. There are several signs dotted along the road out the front. *Cafe!* one says. *Books! Plants & Pots! Thursday night trivia!* As though too many people were involved in its creation and couldn't quite agree on which direction they should take.

Lena's already there, sitting at a wooden table in the garden, her greyhounds lying at her feet. In front of her are two cartons of eggs.

'You said you'd pick somewhere halfway,' she says accusingly, standing up to kiss me on the cheek. 'It only took me twenty minutes to get here; it must've taken you ages.'

I bend down to give the dogs a pat. 'It looked about halfway on the map.'

Lena glares for a moment. She doesn't believe me, and she's right not to. I purposely found somewhere closer to her. Didn't want to add anything to whatever was weighing her down.

A lie, but a white one.

It was Danielle who initiated this impromptu lunch date. She called a few days ago and I could hear her concern, even down the line. It had been a month since the funeral, and still Lena wasn't herself. She had barely been eating and was missing deadlines at work. And she was smoking daily.

We order. Bruschetta and iced tea for Lena, a burger and doppio for me. My third for the day.

Lena checks her watch pointedly when the waiter retreats. 'That's a lot of caffeine for the afternoon. Not planning on sleeping tonight?'

'I sleep poorly, regardless.'

She nods. 'Touché.'

We make small talk, about my work, Danielle's work, her work. I don't know how to progress the conversation towards deeper topics. A catch-up at a bar might've been better. Alcohol is helpful in that way.

Lena steals chips off my plate to give to the dogs.

'So,' she says, 'what else have you been up to.'

I say it almost without thinking. 'I've been sleeping with someone for the past three years.' A personal disclosure to encourage a reciprocal one from her. 'Her apartment was broken into recently, and she came to stay at my place for a few days.'

Lena stops eating. 'Wow, Tom. That's huge. Why didn't you tell us earlier?'

'Because I didn't want people thinking it was more serious than it was.'

'But now you've realised it's serious?'

'The opposite, actually.'

Lena laughs at that. 'Are you planning on ending it then?'

'She saw the nursery and left. I don't think I'll hear from her again.'

'Oh. Sorry.'

I stab at the side salad, struggling to get the lettuce on the fork. 'It was nice at times, but overall I couldn't wait for her to leave, so it's a relief, honestly. Is it bad to say that? We were just two lost people who came together to distract ourselves. But we never clicked. Not really.'

A couple comes down the stairs, struggling under the weight of a large fiddle leaf. They both shuffle sideways, each holding onto one side of the pot and looking proud of their new purchase.

Lena pushes her plate away and takes a cigarette out of her jacket pocket. 'Do you think I can smoke here?' she asks, before shrugging and lighting it anyway. 'I think I have the opposite issue.'

'You and Danielle have just always clicked? Yeah, your sickeningly happy twenty-year relationship is testament to that.'

'You're a dick.' She kicks my shin under the table. 'No, I thought I would be relieved when Dad was gone. He wasn't even part of my life. But I'm upset. And then I'm upset with myself, for being upset.'

'You're allowed to be,' I say.

She shakes her head furiously. 'We haven't spoken for most of my adult life, not since I met Danielle, and I was okay with that. But now he's gone, I feel ripped off. Somewhere deep down I guess I still wanted his approval and still clung to hope that one day I would get it. Which sounds stupid.'

I shake my head. 'No, not stupid at all.'

'I was even resentful of you for a while.'

I'm surprised by this. Lena and I have never clashed, ever. 'Really? When?'

'Well, it felt like you and Adeline were in the same boat as me and Dani. Mum and Dad disapproved of your relationship just as much as mine. I know the black sheep of the family is usually the odd one out, but for a while we were both rejects together. It was nice to have someone on the outer with me. But then they patched things up with you when they found out about the pregnancy.'

The sun, which has been hiding behind clouds all morning, comes out at that moment, as though to emphasise Lena's words.

'I felt like you guys managed to get the acceptance I always wanted. And because Dani and I weren't giving them grandkids, we couldn't have that.'

I'd never considered it from Lena's perspective before, but it's true. One day Mum and Dad had showed up unexpectedly at the house. After I left Amanda, my relationship with them deterio-rated. We had seen them only sporadically, usually at Rebekah's events—her being the only one who had not yet managed to bring shame upon them—but things were tense, and they had taken to giving Adeline the cold shoulder, as though by ignoring her existence she would fade into oblivion. But that all changed with the pregnancy. After years of stubborn refusal, they showed up unexpectedly one weekend, laden with gifts. A bribe for them to be active in their grandchildrens' lives—and for us to ignore the way they'd treated Adeline. They had exaggerated smiles painted on, as though nothing was wrong.

When Adeline saw them, she placed her hands protectively in front of her growing bump. Our eyes met, hers puzzled, mine pleading.

I could see the indignation on her face.

But they were my parents.

Please.

I sighed as I saw the fire in her eyes extinguish. She turned towards them and smiled.

'Can I have one?' I nod towards the cigarette hanging from Lena's lips. At the opposite end of the garden, a family with two young kids glares in our direction.

Lena raises her eyebrows but hands the packet over without comment.

Adeline had never understood how I could let them back into our lives just like that—brush things under the carpet as though it were all okay.

'I get why you felt that way, but I hated myself for not being more like you. For not having better boundaries and not demand-ing more. The apology we were hoping for never came, but I let it slide because I was so desperate for their approval again. But their acceptance of Adeline was fake and self-serving.' It was something I'd always known but never said out loud until that moment. 'I chose to believe the lie because I wanted it to be true.'

The waiter approaches again, this time looking nervous. 'Sorry, but you can't smoke here.' He indicates to a sign displayed prominently on the fence. Moments earlier, I'd noticed the mother from the nearby table calling him over. Now she sits with her head turned deliberately away.

ISO 3200

EVEN THOUGH I'M fifteen minutes early, Sapphire has beaten me to the house and is waiting at the front gate, pacing around in small circles as she talks on her phone. She hangs up when she sees me.

'This should be an easy one for you,' she says. 'The owners agreed to have it professionally styled.'

No *Phantom of the Opera* masks to hide. No family photos to replace with a generic landscape in Photoshop. No cats lurking in the corners. No clutter.

'Doesn't it look amazing? Not everyone is open to the additional cost, but we always reassure them they'll recoup the money in the sale price. Styled houses sell themselves.'

In the entry is a vase of flowers, a thick card propped beside them. The flowers are fake, of course, although I reach out and touch them just to be sure. The card is blank. In the lounge, the sofa is pristine—no stains from pizza nights, no dog fur—with plump cushions and a woollen throw. A travel magazine is lying open on the coffee table, as though someone was just flicking through it before they got called away. A jug of water sits on the island bench in the kitchen, slices of plastic lime bobbing on top. The clothes in the walk-in wardrobe are sparse and loosely colour-coded.

Everything magazine-worthy.

Crystal stays out of my way while I go through the house capturing each perfect room. She's like a ghost, always just out of my sight—a flash in the doorway, an echo of footsteps, lingering perfume. I appreciate being able to work without the pressure of a forced conversation, and it isn't long before I'm out on the street taking the final shots of the exterior, the sun obediently bathing the street in a warm light.

If only all jobs could be so straightforward.

Back inside, Amethyst is sitting at the kitchen bench, absorbed in her phone. I glimpse a game on the screen.

'All done,' I say, and she jumps. The screen goes black.

'Oh, that's great.' She's flustered, her neck pink. 'Sorry, you startled me.'

'Hope you didn't lose the progress on your game.'

'It wasn't—' she begins, before changing tack. 'There's just not a lot of emails to reply to at this time.'

'It's fine. I think the world would be a better place if everyone had more time to recharge during the day. No one can be productive every second.'

'Everyone else seems to be.'

I glance around the kitchen. 'Appearance often isn't reality.'

Her face relaxes into a smile and transforms her. She needs to smile more often. Really smile.

'Thanks, I needed to hear that. It's been a stressful week.' She blinks rapidly, and I realise she's holding back tears.

I pick up the jug from the bench. 'Can I offer you a water?'

She snorts. 'That would be great.'

I open the cupboard to find a glass, but of course it's empty. 'I don't have a glass, I'm afraid. But feel free to skull from the jug.'

There's a moments hesitation before she takes the jug from me with two hands. 'Like Oktoberfest.'

'Sure.'

'I don't know about you, but I kind of wish I could just stay here forever. All that's waiting for me at home is more work.'

'You do realise whoever buys this place will also have dishes and laundry to do?'

'Not like me. I'm drowning in them.'

I'm surprised to hear that. Turquoise seems so organised and polished, like Freya on speed. My expression must show my disbelief because she puts her head in her hands. 'Sorry, but my partner and I had a huge fight last night. I've been letting the housework slide lately, but only because I'm behind on work so I've been trying to put in extra hours to catch up.'

'That sounds hectic.'

'It is. I just can't keep on top of everything, it's relentless.'

'Does he help out much?'

She shakes her head. 'No, he pulls a lot of extra hours too.'

'So you're both in the same position then?'

'Kind of, but his job is more important than mine. The house stuff's meant to be my domain, but sometimes I just want to hop in my car and drive away from it all. Forget about everything.'

'That makes sense. Denial is a coping mechanism, after all. Not a healthy one, but it's my poison of choice.'

'That's good enough for me.' She takes another sip of the water and tilts her head, considering. 'This would be better with vodka.'

'Yeah, sorry, I don't have any on me right now.'

'Damn.' She holds out the jug to me. 'Want some water?'

'Sure.' I take a gulp.

It tastes like plastic.

Instead of going straight home, I take a long and inconvenient detour by the cemetery. Rather than going to the usual florist, I'm forced to stop at a supermarket, where I buy the last bunch of sad-looking flowers, sitting alone in a bucket.

It's ten minutes before closing when I pull in through the double gates and creep my car along the little laneway at a respectable speed, although there doesn't appear to be another living soul around. I leave the car running; the lights illuminating the rows of plaques before me. Usually, mine are the only flowers in the stainless-steel vase, but tonight there's an impressive bouquet of mixed natives already there. I slip my little bunch of wilted flowers in beside it.

I don't bother to recount the tales from my day or explain why I'm later than planned. I know it helps some people to speak to the spirits—to put their thoughts, sadness, fears and hopes out into the ether. It would be soothing, I imagine, to have the chance to explain, to apologise, to feel less alone, but I can't feel any other-worldly presence.

I don't drag myself here to appease the dead.

When I'd told Diamond that denial was my chosen coping mechanism, it was an incomplete statement. Denial is a utopia, welcoming and safe; easy to want to visit, easier still to stay. I make myself regularly visit the cemetery as an antidote to that. To keep myself accountable.

Those first few weeks were a fog.

It doesn't matter how prepared you are, everyone under-estimates the toll of babies. For us, multiplied by two. It wasn't just the sudden, pervasive loss of time, but the combination of everything. The slow, steady financial leak. The drain of having all your emotions powered up: the senseless anxiety, the overactive tear reflex, the love so overwhelming it knocks the air out of you. Never-ending checklists. Opinions pressing in from all directions. Nipples that cry and nappies that leak. Moments that stop you in your tracks but clocks that refuse to stop ticking. Small plastic baths inside large porcelain ones. The overwhelm of getting out the front door.

Dirty clothes and dirty hair but babies that smell of lavender.

Too many sunrises but not enough sleep.

Lost dummies. Lost days. Lost identity.

But within a couple of weeks I was back at work, and life—during the day at least—returned to the usual routine.

When the girls were only a few months old, one of Adeline's images was featured in a magazine. Almost overnight, demand for her work skyrocketed. I took care of the girls if her photoshoots fell on a weekend, and during the week babysitting fell to Rebekah, who was home with Noah. He was only a few weeks younger than the twins, and she always seemed genuinely happy to have our extras. No matter how busy she got, Adeline wouldn't turn jobs away, so I'd presumed she'd adjusted to our new life with the same ease I had. Assumed she was coping.

Eventually, the bubble burst.

One afternoon I came home from work to find the girls sitting in a trance-like state in front of the TV. Ellie had taken off her nappy, Charlie was chewing on the remote, and Floyd was licking yogurt off the floor.

Adeline was nowhere to be found.

Panicking, I raced through the house checking each room, my mind conjuring up alarming scenarios. When I found her lying in the bath, annoyance flared within me.

'What the fuck? The girls are out there—'

She was crying. Her face red and shiny.

'I can't do it anymore.'

I collapsed onto the floor beside her and grabbed her hand. It was wet, the pads of her fingers shrivelled. 'Can't do what?'

'This. Motherhood. Work. All of it.'

My eyes travelled to a razor beside her. Had she been shaving her legs or—

'Ad, what do you mean? You love the girls.'

She sat up, glaring at me through mascara-streaked eyes. 'Of course I fucking love them, Tom! That's the fucking problem, isn't it?'

Loving them was the problem? I blinked at her.

'It's like once you're a mother you can only prove your love by how much time you sacrifice. How much of yourself you give up.' She wiped her nose against her wrist and swished it into the water.

'I'm behind on editing, I haven't sent an invoice in weeks, I have emails piling up. I love photography and I'm failing at it. I love the girls and I'm failing them.'

My eyes kept slipping back to the razor. How long had she been feeling this way? How had I missed it?

'Maybe we could look at putting the girls into childcare, even just a couple of days a week. Or you could cut back your work hours and—'

'It's okay.' I rubbed her hand. 'You're putting too much pressure on yourself.'

'But—'

'And I know you don't want to put the girls into childcare. My income is enough for us to survive on. Maybe it's time to fold the photography business and focus on what's really important.'

Just then, the girls wobbled into the room, as if to emphasise my point. I smiled at her. 'Being a mum is the most important job in the world, and I'm going to try harder to support you with that. You've been spreading yourself too thin—but you don't need to anymore.'

Adeline didn't say anything. I helped her out of the bath and grabbed her a towel.

At the time, I'd interpreted her silence as relief.

Lottie
ISO 4000

IT'S LATE AT night when Aisha calls, the bubbly melody abruptly jarring me from sleep. I don't get many calls, especially at this time, and my mind is flooded with images. Hospitals, police stations, and dark alleyways.

But it's none of those things, just her calling to invite me to her boyfriend's birthday party next month.

Sighing, I sink back into my pillow, offering my breast to Coral who was now awake.

'Lionel's coming too. It will be nice for us to all catch up.'

She sounds different somehow. Happier. More confident, maybe. Recently, she's been posting lots of photos of her boyfriend and he looks nice. Genuine. I'm happy for her, I really am, but I can't help but feel jealous too. 'So, are you free?'

I don't know how to explain to Aisha that I'm always free. But never free. Apart from playgroup on a Wednesday morning, my schedule is completely clear. It doesn't mean I can just go to a party.

'What would I do with Coral?'

'I don't know, bring her along?'

'To a party?'

'Or can't your mum look after her?'

I can't go back to sleep after Aisha hangs up.

Growing up, I never knew what to expect day to day. Mum could be warm and affectionate one moment, cool and aloof the next. Some days she'd come and sit on the edge of my bed, eager to talk. Others, it seemed like my very presence was offensive to her. Then there were times she wouldn't leave her room for hours.

Sometimes days.

Dad was more predictable. He always felt distant, like a mirage I could never get to, no matter how I tried. I may not have been able to reach him, but I studied him from afar. His mood, I realised, seemed to be directly linked to the state of the house. I lost count of the times he got home, saw the dirty dishes piled on the sink or the toys strewn about that Edward had been playing with, and his body became stiff, as though rigor mortis had set in prematurely.

'What the fuck does she do all day?' he'd hiss, walking too heavily and closing doors with too much force. 'Fucking useless.'

The reaction was always the same, but the timing was variable. His frustration would simmer just beneath his skin, building and building, so I would spend the evenings creeping around the house, waiting for the inevitable explosion. But the threat of his anger seemed to affect me more than it did her. It wouldn't have been that hard for her to do a quick tidy in the afternoons before he walked in the door, but even knowing what was coming, she didn't seem to care.

Eventually, it just became easier for me to prevent it.

I started looking at the house through his eyes, each thing out of place a personal affront. And soon enough, I began to understand his annoyance. The dirty dishes multiplying on the sink, the soap scum building up in the shower, Edward's toys peppered on the floor were all evidence of her apathy. He was right. What *did* she do all day?

When I cleaned up, it made a big difference to the overall mood of the house. There was no tension in the air on those nights. No walking on eggshells. And it didn't take that long, really. But I'll be honest, part of me hoped that me picking up the slack would bring Dad and I closer together, bridge the gap I felt between us. But he barely acknowledged it. He didn't seem to care who did the housework, as long as it was done.

It was still worth it, though. For the peace.

Can opener.
Photo frames.
Candles.
A jacket.
A driver's licence.
A car.
Flowers or vegetable seeds.
A pet.
Beach toys.
A babysitter.

ISO 5000

I ONCE READ an article about becoming a parent called 'How having a baby changed my perspective of my mother'. The title connected with me because I had felt the same thing—my perception had changed. But it turned out I was wrong about the article.

The woman wrote about how all the challenges she had experienced as a parent had given her a newfound appreciation of her own mother. How it had made her realise how much her mother had done to support her throughout her life. She said even the little things, like cheering from the sidelines on sports day or cooking your favourite dinner after a good report card were things that, as children, you don't appreciate. You take it for granted. It took living it to see the sacrifices yourself.

In her bio, the woman called herself a mummy blogger. Not a writer. A mummy blogger. Only someone with excess, only some-one who has never been without, would so carelessly dismiss their personal achievements to make parenting their whole identity.

When Coral was born, the woman sharing my room in the hospital had shared a similar sentiment. She'd named her baby girl Paige Margaret, after her mother—funny, I can remember her baby's name but not hers.

'We were never that close when I was growing up,' she told me one night. 'We used to fight about everything. But now I've experienced pregnancy and birth, I feel so much closer to her.'

Like me, she was young and had found herself alone during pregnancy, but her mother had been there with her during labour, and every day would show up at the hospital first thing in the morning with toys and bundles of clothes for her new grand-daughter. I'd pretended my mother was interstate and trying as hard as she could to organise flights. There had been several stuff-ups, I'd explained.

'She'll be here as soon as she can,' she'd assured me. 'She's probably on the phone every minute of the day trying to sort it out. It must be killing her, knowing she has a new granddaughter she can't see yet.'

The truth was I hadn't even told Mum when I'd gone into labour. All the pregnancy books agreed—make sure you are surrounded by positivity, but from the moment she found out about the preg-nancy, she was full of doubt. Even worse, she seemed to presume that I wasn't capable and would need her help.

The hypocrisy was staggering. Had she forgotten all the times I'd had to make Edward breakfast while she was holed up in bed? My nightly ritual of doing housework that she'd neglected?

After a particularly heated argument I realised I'd have to move out. I knew I would be welcome to stay with Lionel and his dad until I could organise something more permanent.

'Don't be so dramatic,' Mum said as I began packing my things into bags.

But it was becoming clear to me that if I was going to go through with this, I would need to prove myself. To Mum, to myself, to everyone.

On the day they discharged me and Coral from hospital, they asked if there was anyone they should contact to pick me up. For a fraction of a second, I almost considered swallowing my pride and

calling Mum. Fortunately, I came to my senses. The look of satisfaction on her face that I hadn't even gotten Coral home before I'd
needed her help would be more than I could bear. And besides, it's
not like she would've come anyway.

ISO 6400

MY EXPECTATIONS WERE low. History had taught me it was best not to have my hopes too high. Any time I slipped up—allowed myself to dream—they just ended up crumbling to pieces.

All year, my friends from school had been celebrating their eighteenth birthdays and posting the photos online. Colour-themed parties and their names on custom signs above their heads. Lionel had double the celebrations: his mum threw him an elaborate party in the city, and his dad and stepmum took him on a cruise to New Caledonia. Aisha, who'd had her licence for a year already, got a car. A Ford Fiesta that she joked about being embarrassed by.

I would've loved it.

Mum opens the door in her pyjamas, and my heart sinks. Pyjamas at midday is never good.

'Happy Birthday!' She gathers me into a hug. 'Your dad and Edward have just ducked out to pick up a few things for me, but come in.'

I step inside.

Mum has decorated the house with photos of me from when I was a baby, up to right before I moved out.

'Remember how much you loved Easter egg hunts as a kid?' she says. 'This is the birthday version.'

They're everywhere. On the front door, stuck to the TV, in the fruit bowl, inside the fridge, on the toilet, hanging from fishing line stuck to the ceiling. I didn't know so many photos of me existed. There are the typical happy snaps, but some beautiful shots—almost professional quality—mixed in as well. By the time I have found all of them, they completely cover the table.

My eyes sting. Just a bit.

'I haven't seen so many of these,' I muse, picking up one of me as a baby. 'I look just like Coral.'

I never realised how similar we looked. Like my little twin.

'She definitely takes after you.'

In another photo, I'm maybe two or three years old, in polka-dot togs, sitting in front of an elaborate sandcastle, clearly built by someone with far more dexterity than I could've possessed. My heart does a little flip—I didn't know Mum had ever taken me to the beach.

Another. Me around the same age but this time at the zoo, more interested in the ice cream in my hands than the dingo enclosure behind me.

The zoo again, only this time I'm holding hands with a little boy, and a woman I don't recognise is pointing to something out of the frame. I've changed outfits too: clearly the ice cream was a mistake.

'Who are those people?' The idea of Mum having friends, let alone close friends you would take day trips with, is almost comical to me.

Mum squints at them, and shrugs. 'Just some people we used to spend time with. I don't even remember their names now. How terrible is that?'

I pick up another. Mum is lifting me up in the air, kissing my cheek.

Mum and I laughing, our hands covered in paint.

All my childhood memories are of being alone. Invisible. But right here in my hands is the proof of another life.

We used to have fun. Spend time together. Be happy.

I want to ask her what changed, but don't want to risk ruining the moment.

'Here.' She hands me a rectangular present.

Inside is a photo album, covered in grey linen, and a collection of 4 × 6 timber frames.

'You can pick which photos to display.' She looks at the table. 'Sorry, it's kind of a DIY present.'

It's not a cruise or a car. It's even more perfect.

'I love it.'

Mum pats my back. 'Come on, I'll help you pack everything up. Dad and Edward will be back soon.'

We sit outside on a picnic blanket for lunch. Mum has made mini quiches and fairy bread, my favourite from when I was little, but Dad and Edward got Red Rooster on the way home. Coral mashes pieces of banana between her gums and two new teeth. Nearby, the chickens walk around, scratching and digging up bugs, their feathers growing in haphazard clumps.

Edward has shot up since I last saw him. He is twelve now, only wears black, and takes himself too seriously. Earlier, we'd attempted a conversation, but it hadn't gone well. I'd asked a few questions about school, to which I got monosyllabic replies. He'd asked Coral's age before we'd both run out of things to say.

'Well, finally an adult,' Dad says, even though I can barely remember the last time I relied on them. 'One down, one to go.' He punches Edward on the shoulder.

I take another bite of fairy bread. I love the sentiment behind it, but it doesn't taste quite how I remembered. The butter is too thick and the sprinkles hurt my teeth. Green ants charge recklessly onto the picnic rug in search of sugar, and I keep my eyes trained on the tartan blanket to flick them off before they reach their destination.

Once we finish eating, Edward goes inside and returns with his guitar. He sits slightly away from us, leaning against the silvery trunk of a gum tree, and begins playing a few basic chords, looking every bit the angsty tween. Though hardly the child prodigy I've been led to expect.

Dad clears his throat and hands me a plain pink envelope. 'Here you go,' he says stiffly. When I open it, two hundred dollars drops out onto my lap. Maybe I can go and get myself another jacket now. And a highchair for Coral.

I feel like crying.

'Thank you,' I manage to choke out. 'And thanks for the other present too.'

Dad's head snaps up. 'What other present?'

Instantly, I realise my mistake.

Mum starts fussing, clearing away the plates and bags of takeaway.

'Just a few photos… it wasn't much…'

But Dad is no longer paying attention to me. His eyes don't leave Mum.

Mum and I are in the kitchen cleaning up—her scraping discarded food into the bin, me searching through the cupboards for a plastic container for the leftovers. Edward had looked panic-stricken when I'd asked him to watch Coral for a few minutes so I could help.

Once, Dad storming off in one of his moods would've been enough to fill me with panic and have me rushing around, trying to smooth it over, but today I feel separated from the imminent blow-up.

I guess because I am.

I'm a visitor to their world now, and the realisation is somewhat freeing. That, and it being my birthday, means I'm filled with a confidence that usually escapes me.

'I don't know why you put up with him.' The words slip out with a careless ease before I've had time to properly mull them over.

Mum's head snaps up. 'Stop—' She puts her hand up. 'I know your father isn't perfect, but he has helped me in ways you couldn't imagine.'

She's right: between his quiet seething and his complete disconnect, I can't imagine any way he's helped her. My face must show my disbelief.

'I know how it looks,' she continues, 'but life is complicated. You just don't understand.'

'I try,' I say desperately, 'but you always keep me at arm's length. Explain it to me.'

There's a long pause and Mum stares, unfocused, out the window. I'm beginning to think she hasn't heard me when she finally speaks. 'I know you don't believe it, but I've always tried my best.' She brings her hands up to her face, kneading her forehead. There's a kind of vulnerability in the action, and suddenly I see her not as my mother—unreliable, unpredictable, disappointing— but as a person being tossed around by life's waves, desperately struggling to keep afloat. 'Trust me, Lottie, no one chooses to live like this.'

Can opener.
~~Photo frames.~~
Candles.
A jacket.
A driver's licence.
A car.
Flowers or vegetable seeds.
A pet.
Beach toys.
A babysitter.
A highchair.

ISO 8000

It's Pirate Day at Story Time. Odette is wearing a striped shirt and a bandana. She has a plastic patch over one eye and a stuffed parrot on her lap. There are plenty of pirates sitting at her feet too, although Coral and I missed the memo again. Where are they getting their information from?

Ivan is there again, cross-legged with Florence on his lap. He waves me over, and a few of the women from last time greet me as I shuffle past and find a spot on the floor. Odette begins reading and a hush falls over the room. It is only lifted by closing the final book.

'I don't know how she does it,' I say as the crowd slowly trickles out.

Ivan nods. 'Right?'

He asks about my week, and I tell him about my birthday—the photos and money, although I leave out the heated conversation with Mum in the kitchen. He tells me Florence spent the weekend with his ex, so he'd walked around the markets, taking his time to look at everything, and gone out to dinner with friends: activities that would have been difficult with a toddler in tow.

'I didn't think Florence's mum was in the picture?'

'She wasn't,' he says, 'but she's getting her life together and wants to rebuild her relationship with Florence.'

'And you're okay with that?'

'Well, there's no safety concerns, so I can't see why not.'

I'm not so sure I agree with him. What kind of mother, I wonder, walks away from her baby?

Ivan continues. 'Lisa's husband disappeared when Toby was born, and when he eventually came crawling back, no one said anything.' Then, sensing my confusion, he adds, 'Lisa from playgroup.'

I nod, as though of course I remembered Lisa.

'If anything, they seemed to think it was good he'd finally come to his senses. Surely Alex also deserves a second chance? But just like they hold me to embarrassingly low standards, they hold her to impossible ones.'

Part of me knows what he's saying is right, but the other part isn't quite ready to admit it yet. 'Do you know why she left?'

Ivan shrugs. 'It's hard to narrow it down, really. But when Florence was born she had severe postnatal depression. She tried her best, but in the end it was just too much, and I guess she just couldn't be around us.'

My eyes travel to Florence, who is lying on the ground with a book open, closely studying the illustrations. She is clearly well looked after and happy, but still I can't help feel sorry for her.

Ivan is watching too, with a kind of melancholy smile. 'Alex had a lot of unresolved stuff from her childhood,' he says finally, 'and I think something about becoming a parent herself reignited it.'

'Is that an excuse, though?' The words are out of my mouth before I can stop them.

'No,' says Ivan. 'But it's an explanation.'

When we get home Coral goes down for her midday nap, and I go outside with a jug to water the succulents.

I couldn't stop thinking about the compassionate way Ivan had spoken about Alex. Mum had said a similar thing on my birthday—that she had always tried her best—and I wonder if I've been too harsh on her.

It was true that I didn't know much about her life, but the parts I did know about weren't great. Married to a man who seemed to despise her, with no access to her own money, no support, no escape. And he was jealous. I remember him interrogating Mum once about the postman, who I don't remember us ever seeing, let alone having a conversation with, but Dad was convinced that something was going on. I could only imagine how paranoid he must have been about her going out into a world full of possibilities.

Was a self-imposed banishment easier than a daily inquisition?

My parents had always existed in separate bubbles. Until now, I hadn't linked them together; hadn't paid attention to their influence on each other.

It was like a lightbulb flicking on in my head. All this time, I'd been so disappointed in Mum for not being there, yet it was Dad's moods that made me feel the need to slink around cleaning up, keeping the peace. But my anger had been directed solely at Mum. Somehow he'd managed to avoid it.

A memory comes. Followed by another. And another. Catching the school bus at six years old when all the other kids were being walked into the classroom. Getting rides with other families when I joined the netball team; sitting quietly in the back of their cars, trying not to be an inconvenience. Walking home alone in high school; my bag full of textbooks, dragging down my shoulders.

Heath driving me home after work. Heath buying me things. Heath giving me everything I was missing.

No wonder I'd been sucked in.

But it wasn't just Mum who'd let me down.

ISO 10,000

MUM TAKES US outside to show off her vegetable garden. There's spinach, broccoli, cauliflower and carrots in rectangular garden beds, which she's made from discarded timber planks, and tomatoes and snow peas climbing up trellises. In the corner, giant leaves hide immature pumpkins beneath them, and she's put up a flimsy-looking wire fence to keep the chickens out. Another new project. I wonder how long it will last.

'I don't know why I'm bothering, really,' she says, gesturing around her. 'Your dad and Edward don't even eat vegetables, and it's too much for me. But it gives me something to do, and when I get too many I just put them in crates out the front with a sign for people to take what they need.'

For all her faults, she has a side that is pure goodness.

'Do you want to take a bag?' she says suddenly. 'What do you and Coral like?'

She starts pulling up carrots dripping with dirt and placing them into a basket on the ground. 'Tomatoes? Spinach? The pumpkins aren't quite ready yet but give it a few more weeks.'

Since we arrived at her house my betrayal has been sitting heavily in my stomach, but now I feel it creeping up my throat.

It's no secret that our relationship is damaged—possibly beyond repair—but if we're ever going to have a shot at mending it, we need a clean slate.

'I stole some money from you.'

It's out before I know it, writhing on the ground between us. Shameful and ugly.

Mum doesn't say anything, doesn't move, but her face grows dark.

'I'm sorry,' I continue. 'My payments were cut off and I was desperate, but I can pay you back.'

She stands up abruptly, dusting her hands on her jeans. 'I think it's time for a drink.'

I follow her obediently into the kitchen. This time she doesn't ask me what I want and busies herself with getting everything out for coffee. I don't want coffee but now doesn't seem like the time to mention it. She places two mugs heavily onto the bench.

'The money from under the bed, I gather?' She pours the boiling water into the mugs and gives them both a brisk stir.

I nod sheepishly. 'I found it years ago, but I've never touched it before. I swear.'

Coffee splashes over the side of the mug as Mum pushes it roughly towards me. It leaves a dark puddle on the bench, but she makes no move to wipe it up.

I take a sip of the coffee. It's bitter and muddy, and I have to stop myself from grimacing.

'I'm really sorry,' I say again. 'I don't have the full amount on me, but I can pay you back. Half today and half next fortnight. I promise it won't happen again.'

But I've clearly said the wrong thing. When I look back at Mum she's frowning.

'I don't want you to be sorry,' she says, sounding exasperated. 'And I don't want you to pay me back. I'm not angry with you, Lottie. Don't you see? I feel guilty.'

Guilty?

'Most parents would be able to help their kids out with money, but I can't. And not only that, you also felt like you needed to steal from me instead of asking.'

I'd given up on asking for things long ago. Most children see their parents as someone stable, someone you can lean against, but I'd never had that confidence.

'I just wish I could be there for you and Coral more.' Mum's face closes off, a paper aeroplane circling towards the ground. The fire in her eyes that had been there only moments before has been extinguished, replaced by a dull nothingness—if it had even been fire in the first place. I think of all the times she had seemed distant, upset, or angry and wonder how often I've misread her in the past.

ISO 12,800

THE PARTY IS in a suburb I haven't heard of before. It would've taken me hours and a complicated walk right on nightfall, on top of the bus trip to Mum's to drop off Coral, but thankfully Lionel offered to give me a lift.

It feels strange to be walking out of the house without Coral, but Mum had been thrilled when I'd asked if she'd mind babysitting. When I arrived, she was already outside waiting. 'Finally,' she said, taking Coral off me and spinning her around.

'This will have to go in the fridge,' I said, handing her a cooler bag. I'd spent the week prior frantically expressing and getting Coral to drink out of bottles for practice. 'And I've written down some instructions—'

Mum glanced at the list and laughed. 'Don't stress, Lottie. Coral and I will have a great time.'

I'd kissed Coral's cheek and hesitated at the doorway, prepared for tears, prepared to cancel my plans and take her back home, but she'd seemed completely relaxed with Mum. All the recent visits must've helped.

I wait for Lionel under the front porch. My eyes are trained on the driveway, but my attention is elsewhere, my ears alert for the sound of Coral's cry. There is a moment when I think I hear a distressed wailing. My heartbeat quickens, but when I turn towards the house there is only silence. I'm relieved—of course, I'm relieved—but I have to admit there is a minuscule part of me that is looking for an excuse to cancel.

I'm nervous, I realise. Despite looking forward to this night—to meeting Aisha's boyfriend and catching up with Lionel again—the idea of being around people my own age fills me with equal parts excitement and fear.

I'm no longer sure where I fit.

If I fit.

A small red car turns sharply off the road and begins crunching its way down the driveway towards me. Dust clouds form behind it.

The last time I'd seen Lionel was when he'd visited me in hospital, clutching a gift bag of baby clothes that were far too big—even now Coral can't fit into them—and we've barely spoken since. Our friendship had been forged through seeing each other daily at school, and I'm anxious to see what remains of it.

The car comes to a sudden stop, and Lionel leaps out with an exuberant wave. He looks different: his hair is longer now, his clothes more vibrant and his posture more confident, but when he pulls me into a tight hug, the last seven months shrink away.

'Missed you,' he says, and all I can do is nod in agreement.

It seems rebellious somehow, sliding into the passenger seat with nothing but my phone and debit card slipped into my pocket. I'd have thought travelling light would feel like freedom, but instead, I just feel paranoid that I've forgotten something.

'You okay?' asks Lionel, forever perceptive.

I focus my attention forward, towards the night ahead. 'Yeah. Just feels strange to be without Coral. It'll be the longest I've been away from her.'

Lionel doesn't seem surprised. 'Well, you have always been stubbornly independent.'

'Only through necessity,' I say, but Lionel doesn't look convinced.

We turn onto the road, and the car rapidly picks up speed. I feel certain Lionel is driving too fast, but when I glance at the speedo it is right where it should be.

Tom
ISO 16,000

I DON'T KNOW what eighteen-year-old boys are into. Money seemed safest, so I stuffed a hundred dollars into a plain card, then at the last minute decided to double it. It's still not enough to make up for all the birthdays I've missed.

Rebekah answers the door with a hug warmer and more genuine than I was expecting. 'I'm so glad you made it. I really wasn't sure if you'd come.'

'I told you I would, didn't I?' I say with a smile. But in reality I hadn't been sure either.

She glances at the Canon dangling from my shoulder. After I'd texted through my RSVP, she'd asked if I'd mind bringing it along. It's an occupational pitfall: invites often come with the expectation of free photos. Even though I'd warned her that event photography wasn't my specialty, Rebekah had assured me it didn't matter, that she would be appreciative of even a handful of photos. What was I supposed to say?

'Now, make sure you enjoy yourself tonight, Tom. You're here as a guest first and foremost.'

She leads me out to the back of the house, where there's a small undercover area and beyond it a sprawling backyard—an acre or two at least—scattered with mismatched chairs. There's a pool, a trampoline and down the very back a couple of fires burning in barrels. I'd expected it to be a small party, but there must be sixty to seventy people milling about on the grass, most of them around Noah's age.

The trampoline has been overtaken by teenagers far too heavy for it, and despite the cold, a few brave souls are in the pool, hitting each other with foam noodles.

'Some kind of dare,' Rebekah says following my gaze. 'To be young again, huh?'

Lance is standing by the barbecue with one of the younger boys, helping to flip sausages. He gives me a wave. A woman in a wintery dress and knee-high boots is sitting nearby, smiling up at him.

'Lance is here? And that—?'

'Is his new girlfriend, Marta.' Rebekah smiles towards them. 'She's quite sweet. And the boys love her too.'

I remember how competitive Rebekah was as a kid and the disbelief must show on my face.

'I know...' she says with a shrug. 'Who would've thought?' She takes me by the shoulders and spins me around to a large, brightly lit outdoor table in the undercover area. 'Anyway, this is where you belong—the family table.'

I don't recognise most of the people, but I spot Lena and Danielle down one end, their heads bowed towards each other. At the other end Mum is talking to some elderly people I vaguely recognise, perhaps Lance's parents. It's like a reverse kids' table—everyone who doesn't fit the dominant demographic thrown into a corner to amuse themselves.

I walk around methodically, saying hi. Danielle gives me a kiss on the cheek, Lena looks relieved, and Lance's parents greet me as though we are old friends being reunited. When I reach Mum I realise it's the first time since the funeral that I've seen her without Dad. Even though his contribution was usually nothing more than the occasional word or two, his absence is palpable.

'You're late,' she says curtly. 'I was starting to think you weren't going to show.'

Before I can answer, Rebekah's back, dragging a man along behind her. He has long hair, a dark beard and is easily the tallest person here. It isn't until he pulls me into a tight bear hug that I realise who he is.

'So glad you came, Uncle Tom.'

His voice is deep, and I struggle to assimilate this giant with the toddler who used to run around the garden looking for snails.

Mum walks over and touches Rebekah on the shoulder. 'You've done such a wonderful job raising this fine young man, and the other three boys too.' Rebekah's eyes flick towards me for a fraction of a second. Noah grins broadly. 'Parenting is no easy feat; you should be so proud of yourself.'

I take a few steps back and pick up the Canon, focusing it on Noah's beaming face. *Click*. He spots me and gives me an enthusiastic thumbs up. *Click*.

The camera is the perfect excuse to get away from the monotonous conversations and I'm suddenly grateful to have brought it. As I walk into the dying light, my attention shifts from my inner world to everything happening around me. The atmosphere is charged with a reckless optimism, and in every direction a story is playing out. *Click*. A boy is frozen mid-air as he cannonballs into the freezing pool. *Click*. A bedraggled girl, wrapped in a beach towel, watches on unhappily, her skin mottled and her lips blue. *Click*. A sword fight begins, pool noodles becoming weapons, water droplets suspended in arcs.

No one seems to notice me as I point the camera towards them, and I move further into the yard, melding with the shadows. By the fire, several girls stare dreamily into the flames. *Click*. Marshmallows for roasting are passed around and stabbed onto the ends of sticks. *Click*.

I pause to scroll through the images on the small LCD screen. It's been years since I've taken candid photos, and the style is different to what I've become accustomed to. With real estate photography, you have time to set up the camera, check the settings and get the lighting exactly right, but at a party every direction you turn requires quick adjustments. I'm out of practice but pleasantly surprised to see the shots I've managed to get are perfect. Not technically perfect—some are a stop or two underexposed, some have motion blur and there's grain creeping into the blacks—but they perfectly capture the moments going on around me.

A long-lost feeling begins to simmer.

When the last purple glow in the sky fades, I begin walking back towards the light of the house; even with the ISO bumped up high, it's too dark for more photos out here. I'll wait for the cake cutting.

Ahead, I see Noah bounding across the patio to welcome some guests who've just arrived. Almost instinctively my camera's back out as he throws his arms wide, and I snap the moment he embraces one of the girls. They sway back and forward for a moment before breaking apart, and he turns his attention to the other newcomers.

Click.

Everything stops.

My heart lurches.

It's Adeline, but it's not.

I can't breathe.

Over the years I've seen her everywhere. Reaching for eggs at Coles, waiting in line at the movies, stepping onto an escalator, crossing the road, behind the wheel of a passing car, nothing more than a hint in my periphery. But each time I've twisted my head around, she's warped into someone else entirely. Nothing at all like Adeline.

This time is different.

She has the same heart-shaped face. The same sprinkle of freckles. The same small lips. But where Adeline was wild, this girl is tame. Her hair is less vibrant, the curls less pronounced; more gentle waves than tangled loops.

By the time I'm able to move again, they have disappeared into the dark.

Back at the table, my mind is elsewhere. Conversations billow around my head but I don't hear a word anyone says. I just hope my responses make sense.

It's Lena who finally pulls me aside. 'Are you okay? You look like you've seen a ghost.'

My eyes travel around the yard again, scanning the undefined figures. It's too dark to see anyone, but I can't stop myself from checking. Checking. Checking.

I know I look crazy; know I'm about to sound even crazier. 'I think I have.'

Lena frowns at me and her face is a mixture of disbelief and concern. 'What are you talking about?'

'Tom!' The man I assume is Lance's dad saunters over, slapping me on the arm. 'I've been trying to catch you all night. I hear you're a photographer?' Without waiting for an answer, he barrels on. 'I've always been interested in photography, and now that I'm retired I figure, why not? So, I'm looking to buy myself a camera. What would you recommend for someone just getting started? I'm mainly wanting to photograph wildlife; we have some beautiful birds that come to our backyard: rosellas, king parrots, pink and grey—'

But I'm no longer listening.

Emerging from the darkness is a tall figure, flanked by two shorter ones. Just shapes at first, fuzzy and lacking clarity, but as they approach the light they become clearer, their features materialising. Noah and the two girls from earlier.

I reach out and grab the corner of the table.

Noah stops and says something to Rebekah, putting his arm around the shorter girl and pulling her in close, but my eyes are glued to the other.

I want to scream, laugh, cry, throw up.

'Charlotte.'

Lena whips her head around, and it's only then I realise I've spoken out loud. It was just a thought—a name that has been swirling in my head for years. 'What did you say?'

'Charlotte,' I say again, my voice barely a croak.

Lena gasps. Grabs hold of my wrist tightly. 'Oh my God!'

Rebekah glances our way, frowning, following my gaze back to the girl. Her jaw drops.

Mum's hand flies up to her mouth.

Noah is oblivious, his attention still locked on the girl under his arm. 'This is my girlfriend, Aisha,' he announces to the table with a giddy smile. He bends down to kiss her on the top of her head.

Someone is asking where they met. Their voice far away. Like hearing a conversation through a wall.

The other girl hangs back awkwardly.

'Sorry, but you look familiar,' Rebekah says. There's a slight tremor in her voice. 'Your name's not Charlotte by any chance?"

I am convinced.

But then Noah lets out a loud laugh. 'There's no Charlotte here. I think you guys might have the wrong person.'

The wrong person? My stomach drops. I'd been absolutely certain, but then it's been so long I wouldn't have any idea what she looks like today.

'This is Aisha's friend Lottie.'

'You're such an idiot.' Aisha reaches up and flicks him on the forehead. 'You do realise that Lottie is short for Charlotte, don't you?'

'Oh.'

There are several seconds when no one says anything.

Some of us are looking shocked. Others confused.

'So—how do you know each other?' It's Lance's mother, who I'd forgotten was even there. Her eyes are bright as though waiting for some kind of drama to unfold. She looks like she's at the point in life where she would welcome a bit of excitement punctuating the dreariness of her days.

'I don't know them,' Lottie says, looking towards us. 'And no one calls me Charlotte. It's been Lottie for as long as I can remember.'

I wonder when that changed.

Mum steps forward, a smile stretched across her face that makes her look slightly unhinged. 'You do know us,' she says. 'It's been a long time, but your parents—'

'Oh, you know my parents?' says Lottie, shuffling back just a little. 'Gerard and Adeline?'

The air seems to crackle and buzz around me.

It feels like I'm inside a spacesuit, my own breathing echoing back at me, my heartbeat pumping in my ears.

Gerard.

Adeline.

Gerard and Adeline.

Fuck.

Fuck, fuck, fuck.

All this time I'd believed Charlotte—Lottie—had never tried to get in contact because she didn't want to, a choice I'd understood and respected, but she's still looking at us completely bewildered, her expression unchanged this whole time. The penny hasn't dropped.

And I realise there is no penny to drop.

She doesn't know.

ISO 20,000

ONCE ADELINE PUT her photography business on hold, things seemed to go more smoothly at home.

'That's so good to hear,' Mum said. We were sitting at the table outside while the girls rode push-along cars up and down the veranda. Adeline, still not quite comfortable with my parents, had taken the opportunity to go out and have some time to herself.

Mum sat back and took a sip of her tea. 'I don't know why she even tried to keep working once the girls were born. I'll never understand women who don't want to spend time with their babies; it's such a short time. I guess some people just care more about money.'

'I don't think it's about money.'

'No, as a photographer, I imagine not,' Mum said with a chuckle. 'I guess I never had anything else in my life that I loved as much as my family.'

'You worked when we were little,' I argued, but Mum waved away my comment.

'Only because my children could be there with me. I didn't have to sacrifice time with any of you.'

Adeline had often complained to me that my parents would make snide comments to her. I'd never seen it, and usually reassured her that their comments had been misinterpreted. Now I wasn't so sure.

'Adeline loves the girls,' I said firmly.

'Oh, I'm sure she does.' Mum dug her fork into the caramel slice she had baked and brought along. 'So where is Adeline today?'

'Just out with a friend.'

It was the last weekend of a travelling art exhibition that Adeline had been desperate to see. Claire and Clive had bought tickets, but at the last-minute Claire had an urgent custom order come through and had to stay home to get it finished. They'd offered for Adeline to take her place.

'That's nice for her,' said Mum. 'I imagine catching up with friends would be harder for her now.'

'Well, the friend she is out with today lives across the road, so she sees him fairly regularly.'

'He?'

There was a high-pitched wail, followed by tears, as Elodie tipped her car over, and although Charlie seemed unaffected by the crash she started crying in sympathy. I raced over to comfort them both and check for injuries.

'You're such a good dad,' Mum said when I sat back down. 'And a good husband too. I hope Adeline appreciates all that you do.'

'I'm sure she does.'

'Yes, yes. I just can't help but worry.'

My confusion must have been reflected in my expression.

'A leopard doesn't change its spots Thomas, and she *was* in another relationship when she met you.'

'So was—'

'And now I hear that she's out with another man—Well, it makes you wonder.'

ISO 25,600

'So, how do you know my parents?'

I can hardly believe she's sitting right in front of me.

Right.

There.

Rebekah had subtly herded everyone inside to give Lottie and I space to talk. Over the years I'd imagined various versions of this conversation: her turning up on my doorstep angry, her turning up on my doorstep nervous, her turning up on my doorstep with questions. Bumping into her at the shops, at traffic lights, at the petrol station. In all my imagined scenarios the recognition was instant. And it had been.

For me.

I'd been prepared for tears, screaming, hugs, even rotten eggs pegged at my car, but never had I envisaged a situation where she didn't realise who I was, or at least suspect it. After all this time there is something devastating about sitting across from my daughter as strangers.

Something safe about it too.

Once she had realised there was a somewhat logical reason for our reactions towards her, she'd relaxed a little; even been curious to talk to me, but I can tell her guard is still up.

'I only know your mum,' I say, 'but I haven't seen her for a long time.'

Lottie gives a dismissive wave of her hand. 'Not surprising. She doesn't get out much.'

Adeline, not getting out much?

'That doesn't sound like her.'

'You mustn't know her very well, then.'

Her words feel like a knife in the chest, but I pretend to shrug them off. 'I guess not. Not anymore. It's been a long time since we've seen each other.'

Lottie frowns into her drink. 'And you've met me before?'

'When you were really little.' I pause, not knowing how to continue. 'You were shy but inquisitive.'

My words are some kind of key, and I notice her visibly relax. I'm no longer a weird stranger who once knew her mum, but someone from *her* past as well.

She sits up straighter. 'Really?'

I nod. 'And you had a toy frog you carried absolutely everywhere.'

At that, her face seems to light up.

She's beautiful. More beautiful than I could've imagined, and I have to divert my eyes away to avoid staring. Instead, I gaze into the yard at the closest barrel of fire.

'My parents don't really have any friends or family around, so it's actually pretty great to be able to talk to you.'

Someone has lodged a knife in my chest, I'm sure of it, but I plaster on a smile.

'So, how did you meet my mum?'

Greensleeves. Sunburn. A puppy that changed everything.

'We were both waiting in line to buy ice cream and got talking. She would've only been a little older than you are now.'

I want to say more. Want to tell her the whole story, moment by moment, but I stop myself. The last thing I want to do is create drama.

A girl dances drunkenly past us, pouting her lips with each move. Lottie rolls her eyes in her direction.

'A friend of yours?'

Lottie laughs, and it's the most wonderful sound I've ever heard. 'Definitely not. No, I don't know many people here; I hadn't even met Noah until tonight. He seems nice, though. Aisha's crazy about him.'

You have met him, I want to say. You used to play in the garden together as toddlers. Instead, I grab a handful of chips from the centre of the table, stuffing several of them into my mouth.

'So,' she leans in towards me, 'what was Mum like when she was younger?'

Answers race forward, clamouring for dominance. She was beautiful like you. Passionate and unexpectedly funny. Creative and impulsive. Smart but never arrogant. Disorganised, outgoing, impatient, empathic, understanding, caring, resilient, chaotic, honest, stubborn, clumsy, brave.

She made life worth living.

But I don't say any of those things. 'She could make friends with anyone,' I say instead. I point to myself as an example. 'I probably seem really together and all-round-awesome now, but I was pretty awkward back then.'

Lottie laughs again, and even though we are surrounded by darkness, everything feels bright.

'And she cared so much. About people, animals, art, the environment, injustices. If she saw something unfair, she struggled to sit back and allow it.'

At that, Lottie's demeanour changes and she stares off into the distance, her face unreadable. 'I guess she was a different person back then.' She downs the last of her drink and stands up with finality. 'Well, it's been good to talk to you—sorry, I've forgotten, I'm hopeless with names.'

'Tom.'

'That's right. I'll tell her I bumped into you.'

'You know, you look a lot like her,' I splutter.

She grimaces, and the expression is Adeline all over. 'God, I hope not.'

I want to reach out and stop her. I want to hear about every minute detail of her life.

Did she do dance lessons, soccer, martial arts, gymnastics?

What's her favourite movie? Book? Colour? Song?

Does she like Coke or Pepsi? Summer or winter? Is she an introvert or extrovert?

What are her dreams? Her fears?

Is she happy?

In the kitchen, I sit at the bench while Rebekah opens cupboard doors looking for a cake stand. Her eyes keep darting my way and although I'm sure she's bursting with questions she doesn't ask me about Charlotte.

I appreciate it. It's not that I don't want to talk to her, but I need time to process first; wrap my head around everything that was said and everything that wasn't.

'Thomas!' I glance up to see Mum marching through the screen door, beelining straight for me. 'What are you doing sitting in here,' she says, her voice cracking slightly, 'when Charlotte is right out there?'

Rebekah pauses, the fridge door open, her hands reaching out towards a cake box.

I glance down towards the camera nestled in my lap. The comforting glow of the screen, with the last photo I'd taken displayed.

'Thomas!'

'I heard you the first time.'

'Well? You must do something. We've all been without her for sixteen years!'

'I think Tom is painfully aware of that.'

It's Lena's voice, behind my right shoulder. I didn't even realise she'd walked in, but I'm grateful to her for saying what I want to but can't.

Seeing Lottie had filled me with so much of every emotion that now I feel utterly drained. All those years of hoping, wondering, stressing, only for this. For nothing to change at all.

I want to curl up in a dark corner somewhere with a warm blanket and hibernate all winter. Or longer.

Forever, if possible.

'What do you expect me to do? She doesn't know anything.'

Anything. At all.

The thought is as comforting as it is depressing.

'She deserves the truth!' Mum continues. 'And we deserve to have her back in our lives.'

Deserve.

It's an interesting word. To get a reward or punishment, appropriate for your behaviour.

I wonder what I deserve.

'Thomas! You must tell her who you are. Who we are!'

I close my eyes. Take a deep breath. 'It's not that simple,' I say. 'She thinks he—Gerard—is her dad. She wasn't even the slightest bit suspicious. And she looks happy. I'm hardly going to shatter her entire reality just like that. Can you imagine what that would do?'

I couldn't pretend to know what decisions Adeline had made over the years, but one thing was certain, whatever she had said—or not said—was to try and protect Charlotte.

'So, you expect all of us to just forget about her again? Put us through more pain?'

Lena steps forward, ready to defend me again, but for once I don't need Lena's strength. I stand up. 'I don't give a fuck about your pain.'

Mum flinches away from me.

'And I definitely don't care about mine. But I care about Charlotte, and I don't think opening her up to a whole lot of trauma is the best thing for her.'

Mum's jaw is set firmly. 'I don't understand you sometimes, Thomas.' She looks towards Rebekah, pleading for back-up. 'Would you let any of your boys just walk out of your life, forever?'

Rebekah hesitates. 'Well, it's a bit different...'

Lena snorts and folds her arms. 'You mean the way you let me walk out of your life? Didn't seem to bother you that much.'

'Oh, Evangeline.' Mum shakes her head dismissively. 'You've always had such a stubborn streak, and when you get your knickers in a knot about something there's no changing your mind. I've given up trying.'

A girl wearing an oversized hoodie and not much else walks over, her eyes darting around the room. 'Toilet?' she whispers.

Rebekah points down the hallway and she scampers off.

'My knickers in a knot? Over expecting a bare minimum level of respect? I didn't want much from you and Dad. I would've been happy with you just saying hi to Danielle when you see her, maybe asking how she's going now and then. Not changing the topic whenever I mention her. Pretending like she doesn't exist.'

'It's always about you, isn't it, but what about my respect? You were asking me to push my values to the side.'

'Adultery and divorce are against your values too, but you managed to ignore them when it came to Tom and Bek.' Lena's shoulders deflate as all the fight slowly leaks out of her. 'The funny thing is my relationship with Danielle has lasted longer than either of theirs. No wonder you can't understand Tom's decision. He can put his own feelings aside for the good of his daughter; something you could never manage.'

Deserve.

I don't know what I deserve, but I know for sure what I don't.

ISO 32,000

It was one of the few times I was eager to be at work—not even ten am and already above thirty degrees. My long-sleeved shirt and black pants always seemed wrong for this time of year, but once I got to the office with their freezing air conditioning, I was glad for the extra layer.

I wondered how Adeline and the girls were going back home; if she'd pulled the moulded plastic shell-shaped pool out from under the house for them to cool off in.

The phone on my desk began ringing, tearing me away from my thoughts.

'Hey Tom.' It was Rebekah, sounding breathless. I could hear wailing in the background.

'Is everything okay?' It was unusual for Rebekah to ring me, and practically unheard of for her to call me at work. I sat up straighter.

'I don't want to bother you, but Elodie's sick. I've been trying to reach Adeline but she's not picking up, and I thought if you spoke to her, you could let her know.'

'The twins are with you?'

It had been a while since Adeline had needed to rely on Rebekah for babysitting, and she hadn't mentioned any plans before I'd left that morning.

'Yeah, she asked if I could watch them for a few hours. I don't want you to stress. Elodie's okay, but she'd probably be more comfortable at home.'

Already I was standing up, throwing my things into my bag. 'I'll come and grab them.'

Before I left, I tried to call Adeline, just in case.

The phone rang and rang and rang.

Until it stopped.

It's strange, isn't it? How many life-changing moments seem to happen on the days that people do something out of the ordinary.

When I arrived at Rebekah's, she was standing out the back rocking a lethargic-looking Elodie while Noah and Charlotte danced around the sprinkler, squealing.

'I'm heading in your direction later this afternoon, so I'm happy to drop Charlie off,' Rebekah offered. 'I'll just take the spare car seat from Lance's ute.'

'Are you sure?'

'Of course! That way you can focus on Elodie for a bit, and besides, Noah loves the company.'

Back in the car I tried calling Adeline several more times. but each time it rang out, and each time my anxiety increased. It seemed strange she hadn't told me she had plans. Some kind of emergency must've come up, but she hadn't mentioned anything to Rebekah, and it was stranger still that she wouldn't have contacted me if that were the case.

Unless it was something she didn't want me to know.

Leopards don't change their spots.

When Mum had expressed her concern over the friendship between Clive and Adeline, I'd immediately dismissed it. What had happened between us all those years ago was completely different;

we were outliers, not statistics. She couldn't be herself with Gerard, and after only a few years together Amanda and I were already in a rut. My connection with Adeline was something special. It was the kind of love that only happened once in a lifetime; not easily replicated.

Leopards don't change their spots.

The words looped around and around in my head like a carousel.

ISO 40,000

Soon after the cake cutting, people started to trickle out. Back home for most, but off to other parties—probably with less parental involvement—for others. Mum left first, giving me a terse goodbye, and Lena and Danielle soon after. By eleven, the only ones left were Noah and a dozen or so of his friends, Lottie included, laughing and roasting marshmallows around the remaining fire. I stayed back to help Rebekah do a sweep of the yard with garbage bags, picking up plastic cups and empty cans of premixes. It was unlike me to be the last at an event. Usually, I would be desperate to get home and relax with a drink, but I wasn't going anywhere while Charlotte was still within my orbit.

'Thanks for your help with cleaning,' Rebekah says once the house is almost back to normal and we've collapsed at the kitchen bench, eating leftover cake. Despite the huge number of people that had attended, barely any of them had touched it. Lottie was one of the exceptions. I'd seen her sitting in the corner taking small, careful bites, as though savouring every morsel. 'It sure was an eventful night.'

I can tell she has more to say but is holding back. Our relationship is still fragile. It'll take time for us to redefine the boundaries and get back to how we were. Almost as soon as the thought comes, I realise it's flawed. Time doesn't work that way. We can never get back to how we were, but maybe we can get to know these new versions of each other.

Outside, I notice the boy Charlotte arrived with rummaging through an esky for another drink, his entire body veering sideways. I hope he isn't planning on driving. I nod in his direction. 'How are all the stragglers getting home?'

Rebekah takes another spoonful of cake and shrugs. 'I daresay they'll crash here tonight.'

I blink at her. I know it's been a long time since we've seen each other, but this whole laissez-faire attitude still feels out of character.

'With four boys you've got to become adaptable, or you'll go insane trying to hold onto your control,' she says. 'It took a while, but eventually I learnt. Although sometimes I want to just grab my younger self and shake her. She was so opinionated and smug for someone with so little life experience.'

It's a familiar feeling.

'Which is why I regret all those horrible things I said to you. No wonder you wanted nothing to do with me.'

'No,' I cut her off. 'You only said what I was already thinking. It was more than that.' On my plate is still half a slice of cake, but I don't want it anymore. 'They were meant to grow up together. I just—couldn't.'

Rebekah nods sadly. It looks like she is about to say something when a jumble of voices float in from outside, and a moment later Noah appears in the doorway, looking concerned. 'Hey, Mum, Lottie needs to get home and has missed the last bus.'

'She can stay here if she wants?'

He shakes his head. 'No, she has a baby. Her parents are babysitting, but she really needs to get back tonight.'

'Oh!'

I try not to let my mouth drop open.

'Can you drive her?'

All night Rebekah has been a whirlwind; fussing around the house, topping up snacks, chatting to everyone. I hadn't seen her take a single sip of drink.

She glances at me. 'I've had too much to drive, but Uncle Tom was about to head home. I'm sure he can drop her on the way through.'

Noah turns to me. 'Would that be okay?'

I pretend to consider it briefly before giving my answer. I don't want to seem too eager.

It's been a long time since I've cleaned out my car, and even longer since I've vacuumed. After a while you stop noticing the mess, but when I open the door and the internal light comes on I suddenly see it through the eyes of a stranger.

I reach across into the passenger seat, desperately tossing empty soft drink cans and serviettes into the back

Lottie slides in stiffly, looking around. I see her subtly kick a scrunched-up Hungry Jacks bag away from her foot. 'Um, do you need this?'

She's holding up a long-lost lens cap.

'No, just throw it in the back.'

Lens caps are like pens. Or socks. Always missing.

'Thanks so much for driving me. I hope it's not too far out of your way.'

It's the complete opposite direction, but I shake my head. 'No, not at all.'

The conversation at first is stilted but that doesn't last long. By the time we've made it out of the bendy streets and onto the main road, Lottie's posture has relaxed and she's talking happily about her daughter.

'It must be a lot, raising a baby at your age. I found it difficult enough and I was twenty-six.'

'Oh, you have kids?'

For fifteen years I've been telling people no. No, I don't have kids. But tonight, I nod before quickly changing the subject back to her. 'Do your parents help out much?'

'Not really.'

'Oh?'

Up ahead is an intersection. I want the traffic lights to change, but they're stubbornly on green. I want this drive to last just a bit longer.

'I don't really need them, though. I had a lot of practice when Edward was born.'

'Edward?'

'My younger brother.'

It takes everything I have not to react to that. Adeline had another baby? My hands grip the steering wheel tighter. 'Do you and Edward get on?'

It feels like I'm driving on autopilot, barely aware of what I'm doing. My mind is so caught up in her stories, trying to piece her life together.

'Not really. I was only five when he was born, but I always felt responsible for looking after him. I guess Mum had postnatal depression or something, although at the time I didn't realise. I just remember she was in bed a lot. Sometimes it seemed like she hated him—like she didn't even want him near her—so I suppose Dad and I both overcompensated for that in our own way. Dad always favoured Edward, whereas I ended up resenting him.' She pauses. 'Sorry. I don't know why I'm telling you all this.'

'But you and your mum are close. Right?'

The answer has to be yes. Adeline had always been able to connect with anyone. Surely that included her daughter.

'Not really. She hasn't left the house in years, so she's never been there when I've needed her.'

I feel it in my chest, a heaviness. The person she's describing can't possibly be Adeline.

It can't.

Perhaps there's some kind of mistake, another Adeline, who happens to be with a different Gerard. But even as the thought comes, I know it's ridiculous. The Adeline I'd known has been broken.

ISO 51,200

THE DRIVE HOME from work was a blur. Concern without perimeters becomes unbridled panic, and my mind went wild conjuring possible scenarios I would find when I arrived back at the house. Adeline and Clive kissing at the front door. Adeline kneeling down in front of Clive in the living room. Or worst of all, Clive fucking Adeline in our bed.

I couldn't put my finger on it, but over the last few months something had shifted in her. Since closing her business she'd certainly seemed less overwhelmed, but her usual spark was missing. Clive was right there, right across the road every day. Perhaps she'd been taken in by his attention? Maybe she craved the rush of excitement from our early days.

Then, another more ominous thought began to take hold.

The razor.

When was the last time I'd seen her truly smile? Or heard her laugh?

I couldn't be sure.

Finally, I turned into our street, and Mayfield came into view. And movement. A tall figure was pushing through our front gate out onto the footpath. I wasn't close enough to see the features of the person who strode across the road and into the house across the street, but I didn't need to be.

A leopard doesn't change its spots.

Without thinking, I was out the car and climbing the front steps two at a time, but before I got to the top Adeline appeared in the doorway. She was wearing a summery dress and when her eyes landed on me, they grew wide.

'What the hell is going on? What was Clive—' My anger gave way when I noticed she'd been crying.

She dissolved into a puddle on the top step. I remained standing, my mind dog-paddling as it tried to make sense of what was happening.

'Did—did he hurt you?'

Adeline shook her head vehemently. 'Oh god no, nothing like that. He wanted to come over and discuss an opportunity with me. He offered me a job.'

'A job?'

'Yeah, doing some photography for the studio he works for. It would've been huge—'

My neck felt hot as all the images of Adeline and Clive rushed back to me, but instead of feeling guilty for how quickly I'd jumped to conclusions, my annoyance turned to Mum. If she hadn't put the idea in my head in the first place…

'—I said no, of course, but I can tell Clive's annoyed with me. It sounds like he really talked me up and now he'll have to go back and tell them I can't do it.'

I dropped onto the step beside her and put my hand on her knee. 'Well, he shouldn't have done that,' I said. 'You don't have to feel guilty for saying no. Remember there's no pressure on you to work. You can just concentrate on the girls and—'

Adeline jolted back and frowned at me. 'Wait. You think I'm upset because I let Clive down?'

'Yes?' I said, my voice uncertain. 'I thought you wanted to stop doing photography and just be able to concentrate on the girls?'

'But I love photography and it's a once-in-a-lifetime kind of job. I wanted to be able to take it!' She stood up and started pacing up and down the veranda behind me. 'Don't get me wrong, I love being a mum too, but I used to be so much more than that; it feels like all the things that made me who I am are gone and I don't know who I am anymore.'

I hadn't realised.

'If you want to take the job then you should.'

'I can't though, can I? Because I'm just going to keep having the same issues, again and again. Struggling with the girls. Falling behind on work. You don't get it, Tom.'

'I can help.'

Adeline ran her hands down her face, frustrated. 'But you don't! You just waltz off to work every morning and it's me who is left juggling everything. I've got to schedule my work around your job, the girls, the housework, the cooking.'

'I can take over the cooking to give you more time—'

'I don't want my work to be relegated to evenings or weekends or whatever crumb of time I can find. I love what I do; why does that make it less important?'

The first thing that drew me to Adeline was her determination to do what was right and what made her happy regardless of what anyone else thought, yet here I was, forcing her into the usual boxes. When I'd convinced her to stop her business, I'd thought I was being supportive and doing the right thing. When you love someone, you marry them, buy a house, have children, be a provider. Right? But that was never what Adeline wanted or needed from me.

A strong work ethic had been pushed onto me from a young age, but it had meant giving up play time in the afternoons, and not being able to go to friends' houses; dragging yourself away from the things you loved to do something you didn't. On some level, I'd learnt to equate work with a lack of enjoyment, and maybe I hadn't put the same value on her work because it hadn't looked like work to me.

Across the road, there was the sound of a screen door opening and Claire emerged from inside her house. She walked down the path and pushed her front gate open. When she looked up and saw Adeline, she gave a small, sheepish smile, laced with an apology, but as she came across the road and passed my car, something inside caught her attention. She stopped, looking at something in the backseat.

Suddenly Claire looked up towards us with panic in her eyes. 'Oh my God! Unlock the car!' She pulled at the door handle, over and over. It wouldn't open. 'The keys!'

I think I looked for the keys. I know I couldn't find them. A dark vignette was swallowing the world.

Adeline sprinted down the stairs, towards the car.

A high-pitched wail rang out through the street.

Like someone screaming.

Through the haze, I saw her grab a rock from a garden. Run back over to my car.

My knees wobbled and I folded onto the ground.

Nearby, the sound of glass.

Smashing.

ISO 64,000

THE SPEED LIMIT drops from eighty to sixty to forty, and up ahead
flashing amber lights come into view. The roadworks ahead serve
as a momentary distraction, and I'm glad for the pause in conversation. My eyes are stinging, and there's a lump in my throat—I'm
not sure I could talk even if I wanted to.

Afterwards, Adeline had taken Charlotte and left. She'd told
me not to contact her again, but I had no intention of trying. I
was a monster, a terrible father, and I deserved to rot in hell—the
anonymous notes in my letterbox, the opinion pieces in the media,
and the comments from strangers online all agreed. I didn't know
where they'd gone, and I didn't try to find out. Wherever they
were, I was confident it was better than with me.

Orange traffic cones blink passed as we crawl along the narrow
strip of road. Floodlights are dotted along the median strip, illuminating Lottie for a few seconds before plunging her into darkness
again.

Hearing Lottie speak about Adeline was pricking holes in the
delusions I'd clung to for sixteen years. I knew losing Elodie would
have devastated Adeline—how could it not?—but she'd always
been so resilient, capable of cutting off parts of her life that were

damaging and starting over. She wasn't to blame for what had happened, and I'd convinced myself that with Lottie to focus on, she'd be able to rebuild her life from the ashes. Yet she hasn't left her house in years, struggles to connect with her children and is back living with Gerard. He was possessive and controlling even before he had a genuine reason to be, and she'd run back to him to get away from me.

The lesser of two evils.

The traffic cones fade away, and a temporary sign marks the end of the nightworks, the road before us opening into inky blackness. There are no other cars to be seen, no houses close by, and the enveloping darkness feels suffocating, yet safe.

'She cares about you.' My voice is confident. Definitive. I sense Lottie turn in her seat to face me. 'But she's been through a lot. I guess eventually everyone gets to a point where they can't keep getting back up."

'I know she cares,' admits Lottie, 'but it's like something stops her being able to show it. I dunno, it's like she has a wall up.'

I think of Freya. 'You're probably right about the wall,' I say. 'And I know it might not feel like it, but I don't think it's there to hurt you. It's a defence mechanism. To protect.'

'To protect me or her?'

I don't need time to consider the answer. 'Both.'

Up ahead is a turn-off, and Lottie directs me to take it. I know this area; I was here just the other day with work. The suburb used to be rural, with rundown post-war houses on large blocks, but now most of the land has been sold off to developers who have squashed as many blocks into each development as they can. The new, the modern, has been spreading slowly, insidiously; grass slowly losing out to concrete.

'It's just down that street.'

The headlights sweep over a dead wallaby on the side of the road. A few metres further lies a mangled possum.

'There. On the left.'

A rusted letterbox materialises from the darkness—fifty-four stamped on the front—and I turn the car slowly down the driveway.

Lottie, I notice, has her eyes fixed on me. 'You and Mum,' she says. 'You weren't just friends, were you?'

I open my mouth. Close it. Don't know what to say.

'It's just, well, Dad used to sometimes imply he couldn't trust Mum, that she was disloyal in some way. I wasn't sure if he was just being paranoid or if maybe she'd had an affair.'

Where to begin? It may have started that way, but how can I explain to her the five years after that point. Still, one thing's become apparent to me. Mum was right. Lottie does have a right to know.

But I'm not the person to tell her.

'She wasn't just a friend,' I say finally. 'But I think you need to ask her about that.'

Lottie nods.

The headlights swing across the front of the house as I pull up. It's cluttered and overgrown, much like Mayfield.

'Thanks so much for driving me.' Lottie opens the car door. 'And for the chat.'

My heart is hammering in my chest as she steps out into the night.

'If you ever want some photos of Coral,' I yell out, 'I would love to take them for you. Free of charge, of course.'

Her head ducks back down and she smiles. 'That would be amazing. Do you have a business card or something?'

My car has everything in it, but it takes a minute of searching before I find one in the centre console, slightly bent.

I watch as Lottie walks towards the house. The door opens before she reaches it, and a figure of a woman appears in the door-way. I squint, desperately trying to see her face but the lights inside are on, her features hidden in shadow.

Nothing but a silhouette.

But even with the light working against me, I would recognise her anywhere. The hair piled on top of her head. The way she leans casually against the doorframe. The hand on the hip.

Adeline.

Photography is a time capsule.

I'd lost sight of that, somewhere along the way. When it had transitioned from a hobby into a job it became less about documenting moments and more about mechanics—the shutter speed, aperture and ISO. The aim no longer capturing things as they were but as you wanted them to be. Each image manipulated and curated until it was flawless.

But fake.

To highlight a strength, you can draw attention with lighting and leading lines.

If there's something you want hidden, you can simply erase it altogether.

But most of us don't use photography that way.

We use it to remember.

You see, our memories are flawed.

We all forget, yet we're prone to overestimating our own abilities. It makes it easy for us to judge the actions of others while making exceptions for ourselves. Their mistakes and misfortunes could never apply to us.

You wouldn't have an affair and break off your engagement.

You wouldn't drink two bottles of wine a night.

And you would certainly never ever forget about your baby in the back of a car on a hot summer's day.

We lie to each other, but the person we lie to most is ourselves. If you're truly honest with yourself, you have to admit it.

You forgot too.

ACKNOWLEDGEMENTS

This book was written on the lands of the Jaggera and Turrbal people. I acknowledge the Traditional Custodians of these lands and their continuing connection to knowledge and storytelling. I pay my sincerest respects to Elders past and present and I recognise that sovereignty was never ceded.

Firstly, I would like to thank the judges of the Dorothy Hewett Award: Tony Hughes-d'Aeth, Kate Pickard, Astrid Edwards and Thuy On for seeing something in Depth of Field, and The Copyright Agency for supporting the award. Thank you, thank you for your part in making my dreams come true.

To Kate Pickard, Lauren Pratt, and everyone at UWA Publishing. Thank you for believing in this book. I am forever grateful.

Kirstie Innes-Will for such considered editing. Sorry about the comma splices!

Brendan Fredericks for being the powerhouse behind the scenes. From the moment you said hello to my dog over Zoom, I knew you would be a great match. Sorry in advance (I don't know what for yet, but trust me, it's coming).

Mika Tabata for the gorgeous cover design. It's perfect!

I am so grateful to my fellow writers who have been so generous with their advice and encouragement when I was feeling lost in the process, particularly Siang Lu, and Brendan Ritchie, who are not only incredibly talented writers but also the most wonderful people. Also, a heartfelt thank you to Sarah Sasson, Graham Akhurst, and Sharlene Allsopp (superwoman!). Special mention to Lisa Kenway and the rest of the 2024 debut crew—being able to connect with you all has been lifesaving.

Anthony Campbell for the advice. I hope this is even better than a signed copy!

The teachers who made a difference: Dianne Bates, with whom I did my first ever writing course at the age of 13 and Anita Baker, who wrote in my year one book that I would one day become a writer.

David, for being one of the few people I trusted enough to read my early manuscript. Thank you for always being there.

Gar'ry Yeates, for your feedback—your opinion means a lot.

My wonderful friends. Jane and Emily, for a lifetime of friendship; we're still attached! Also, Rudra, Terry, Rachael and Joelle (although you are forever Lyra to me).

Luke (so many Lukes in my life, which one?). I'm grateful to be forever linked to such a calm and generous person. Also, Amy, who is equally so.

Uncle George for all your support, Aunty Skai for being one of the best cheerleaders, Angie for the chats about everything and anything and Jo for the advice. I'm lucky to have you all.

Mum, for always giving me your absolute and unwavering support to follow my dreams, regardless of how difficult or unlikely they appeared to be. Without a doubt, it was your encouragement over the years that helped me get to this point (finally!!!). Thank you for providing me the space to write and the freedom to follow whatever path I wanted. For taking me to workshops when I was a kid, tagging along to festivals, bribing me with rewards (which didn't work), listening to my annual breakdowns and continuing to believe in me year after year after year.

Danica, for being the very first fan of my stories. The little stapled-together books I wrote for you (Moppo the Hippo) were what ignited my love of writing. You've also been the one person over the years whose feedback I trusted above all others. Isadora and Chastity would be proud. And to Olivander and Mirabelle, I love you both.

My Penwing (Benedict Cumberbatch style), Liam, for your endless love and patience. Thank you for confiscating my phone, disconnecting my laptop from the internet (when I'm trying to write, of course—you aren't my kidnapper), asking the right questions at the right time, and understanding when I am off in my own world. You are my human dictionary, thesaurus, and Encyclopedia all in one, as well as my IT assistant, personal chef, and psychologist. I know being with a writer can be all kinds of frustrating, but I'm glad you've only ever provided me with encouragement.

Evie and Amelia, thank you for being the best bonus babies I could ask for. It'll be a while before you can read this book, but I am grateful for your enthusiasm for it regardless. Also, you can show your friends this!

Caitlin and Larissa. Capes, you are my own personal Coral. You've been with me my entire adult life and I can't imagine my world without you in it. And Bear, you completed me and made everything brighter. No doubt you both made the writing journey longer, but also, without you, it probably wouldn't have been possible. You have both given me a purpose in life, taught me so much and made me who I am. I'm grateful every day that I get to be your mum. I can't wait to be old ladies together.

I'm sorry to be the kind of person who includes my dogs, but I have to mention Tucker and Rafferty because they are my *actual* babies, and no one can tell me otherwise.

Finally, to Dad, Grandma and Aunty Inta. Despite my faith in science, there's still a part of me that chooses to believe you've been by my side.